### In the Land of Thay

"You are a slave and will die a slave. The decree is irreversible by our laws. And should you and another ever mate, any issue of yours will be a slave, as will their issue and their issue's issue until time's end. Slavery here in Thay is final."

Tazi blanched at the ramifications of the decree. It was most definitely not how she had expected the situation to resolve itself. For the moment, she was at a loss as to how to proceed. However, as a slave, that was not even a concern of hers any longer. She had lost all rights and others would decide what she could and could not do from then on. Tazi could not fathom the turn fate had taken. . . .

**From the mean streets of Faerûn.
From the edge of civilized society.
From the darkest shadows.**

# The Rogues

# THE
# CRIMSON
# GOLD

## VORONICA
## WHITNEY-ROBINSON

The Rogues

# THE CRIMSON GOLD

Cover art by Mark Zug
Map by Dennis Kauth
First Printing: December 2003
Library of Congress Catalog Card Number: 2003100848

9 8 7 6 5 4 3 2 1

US ISBN: 0-7869-3120-5
UK ISBN: 0-7869-3121-3
620-96453-001-EN

U.S., CANADA,
ASIA, PACIFIC, & LATIN AMERICA
Wizards of the Coast, Inc.
P.O. Box 707
Renton, WA 98057-0707
+1-800-324-6496

EUROPEAN HEADQUARTERS
Wizards of the Coast, Belgium
T Hofveld 6d
1702 Groot-Bijgaarden
Belgium
+322 467 3360

Visit our web site at www.wizards.com

For my father
Russell P. Whitney
1946-2002

*3rd Ches, 1373 DR*

Adnama Stoneblood slipped farther into the inky
darkness. He ran one callused hand along the
wall to his left and let his heavily corded arm
rest against the rockwork. He closed his eyes
and let his senses spread through the stone,
feeling every crevice and weakness. Nothing,
he thought to himself. He opened his eyes, replaced his gauntlet, and turned to another of
his senses. His darkvision revealed the sharp
turn the tunnel made directly ahead and he
once again mouthed a brief prayer of gratitude
to Deep Duerra for her gifts. Not many of his
kind thanked their gods that often, but Adnama realized how difficult this search was, and
he would not risk angering anyone or anything
at this point. The duergar knew, even though
he called the cavernous depths his home, that

he was a fish out of water here in this accursed place. And yet, he pushed forward.

He moved along soundlessly, even though he wore chainmail over his thin shirt and trousers, and gauntlets covered his hands and thick forearms. His family was well-known amongst the gray dwarves for their metal craft, and his sister, dead nearly two years now, had been renowned for her oils and rendered fats. She could make anyone's equipment, no matter what its age or condition, as silent as a breeze.

Lucky for Adnama, she'd grudgingly passed along her secrets to her brothers just before she died of the wounds she had received in a skirmish with a band of marauding drow. Adnama carried a small pot of the arcane grease in his sack, no matter where he traveled. Silence was his ally and only friend. He recognized his lot in life, though that did not mean he didn't want to change it. And that desire had brought him here.

Turning to the right, Adnama spied an opening in the tunnel. With his right hand, he freed the war axe he had slung along his back and moved up alongside the wall. Slowly sliding against it, Adnama peered into the opening. He almost could not believe his coal-colored eyes.

The chamber, like one other he had come across in his search, was lit with a diffuse light. Adnama couldn't see the source, but he suspected it was of sorcerous origin, considering where he was. While the chamber, really no more than a large cavity in the rock's natural wall, was devoid of anything resembling furniture, it was nonetheless frequented by something.

Adnama's keen eyes could detect the evidence of pick and hammer on the walls. The site had been worked recently and for obvious reasons. Every few feet, a clear light twinkled out like a star on a winter night. Adnama, certain that he was alone, re-slung his axe and moved closer to the clear, teardrop shaped glimmering objects.

"Kings' Tears," he whispered in awe.

He leaned one shoulder against the wall as he removed his gauntlet once again. He rubbed a grubby forefinger over one of the hard, smooth stones. The walls were littered with them. He turned and leaned back against that same wall, stroking his braided beard thoughtfully. Adnama realized that there were probably enough gems in this niche alone to keep him in wine and comfort several lifetimes over. In his mind's eye, he could see the envy on his brother's face while he dumped a sack full of the "lich weepings," as his people called them, on the tavern table. The thought made him smile, and he nearly unfastened his small chisel, caught up in the temptation. But he stopped himself and shook his head. Sadly, he caressed one of the tears before re-entering the main passageway.

The dwarf continued farther into the catacombs. Most of his explorations had proven uneventful, with the exception of the treasure trove he had just abandoned. He knew his luck could not last much longer, but he harbored a perverted hope that it might last long enough. Almost like a sign, the winding stretch of tunnel in front of him shimmered with a faint, green glow. He moved cautiously forward, wiping a bit of perspiration from his bald pate.

Ormu, he thought to himself. This deep, the tunnels had become quite steamy. He was mildly surprised he hadn't come across the fluorescent moss sooner. However, he would not look the gift horse in the mouth lest he find it rotten, as his father was fond of saying. Better to accept it without question or disappointment. The mild, green glow made his gray flesh take on a sickly hue, not that Adnama ever looked very healthy. Like all of his duergar kind, he looked wasted when compared to other dwarves, with the exception of his broad shoulders and wiry muscles. Adnama was momentarily shocked by his own complexion in the fungal radiance.

"And if we hadn't been abandoned all those years ago," he whined to himself, "perhaps we wouldn't have suffered so. Perhaps we would look as hale and hearty as the others. And I wouldn't have to be here."

Still, the glow made it somewhat easier to maneuver, and he was able to use his senses for other purposes. Adnama could make out that the tunnel widened perceptibly, and he reached for his axe once more. The spot was ideal for an ambush, and he craned his head as far back as he could, studying the ceiling. His sister had met her end when she was lured into a similar spot and attacked by a group of drow that had hidden themselves by levitating near the cavern ceiling. He was always mindful to look upward after that. But his concern was misplaced this time, for nothing hovered above. He didn't relax, though; he couldn't afford to.

Slowly going downward, Adnama's vision was slightly obscured by the increasingly dense steam hanging in the air. He could feel beads of sweat start to roll down between his shoulder blades, and he scratched at himself savagely. He was caught up in his own discomfort for a brief moment—a moment that was one second too long.

A volley of longspears whistled through the thick air. Adnama was caught off guard. One spear snapped on impact against his adamantine chainmail, and the other two bounced harmlessly off of the wall to his right. Adnama drew his stonereaver's war axe and scanned the passage from one side to the other, unwilling to give his attackers another opening. From the opposite side of the tunnel, he finally spotted two troglodytes melt away from the wall. Standing five and a half feet tall, they were not much bigger than Adnama. The upright, lizardlike creatures' ability to change the color of their skin had provided an excellent disguise, blending in against the stones. The random pockets of warmth emanating from the tunnels had also masked their own heat signatures from Adnama's vision, rendering them invisible to the duergar. No longer flush against the natural wall, though, the trogs' skin rapidly changed color to a dullish yellow. Adnama could even make out the single frill along their scalp that ended just behind the nape of their necks. Both were frayed, and the duergar suspected that these two troglodytes had not eaten well in quite a while. The scales along their bodies were also a dull white; another indications of poor health. Realizing they had lost the element of surprise, the two creatures charged forward.

Only one of the two had on any armor at all, ragtag as it was, and it was worn by the one who led the attack. It drew its own axe, a bit of hewn stone lashed haphazardly to a piece of wood, and swung it menacingly in the dwarf's direction. Adnama easily blocked the swing with the handle of his own axe and thrust the chisel-pointed pick opposite the blade back at the trog. The lizardlike creature fell back a bit and tripped up its fast-approaching companion. That proved to be its undoing. Adnama pressed his assault, slashing back and forth with his stonereaver axe. His next swing cut through the trog's makeshift breastplate, and once that bit of vulnerable flesh was unprotected and exposed, he drove the pick into the trog's heart. Blood oozed from the wound, and the creature fell back shrieking and clutching at its chest.

Adnama regarded the other trog. As it watched its partner die, the surviving creature began to secrete a foul-smelling musk. The odor filled the tunnel, and Adnama stumbled back from the stench, nearly overcome with nausea. He leaned against the side of the tunnel and spread his hands flat against the wall. Even through his intense queasiness, Adnama could feel the fault in the composition of the stones behind him. He resisted the urge to vomit and called out to the remaining trog.

"Come on," he taunted. "Don't just stand there staring at your dead friend! Come on then!"

The unarmed troglodyte hesitated for a moment.

Adnama could see it glance from him to another of the tunnels, possibly an escape route the dwarf wagered, and back to him again, torn by indecision. Adnama shouted once more.

"Come on, stink-meat! Let's see what makes you smell so rotten!"

The troglodyte grabbed his fallen comrade's remaining longspear and charged for the dwarf, mindless of all else. Adnama held his ground until the last possible moment. When the trog was upon him, he dived to the right and rolled a few feet away from where he had been standing. The trog was not able to stop its bull-rush attack, and it plowed directly into the wall. As Adnama had expected, the creature struck the focal point of the wall's fault, and the force of its collision caused that section of the wall to crumble. Several large chunks of stone crashed down on the hapless lizard and buried it from waist to head. Adnama heard the sick crunch of the trog's skull shattering under the weight of the boulders. In death, the creature released the last of its natural musk, and Adnama gagged on the odor. The dwarf drew himself up to his knees and leaned to the side to retch.

When he had rid his stomach of its meager contents, Adnama scrubbed at his mouth and stood up. He eyed the creature suspiciously as its legs still twitched spasmodically. Adnama knew it was dead but also knew that one could never be too careful. He walked warily over to the first one he had killed. Adnama rummaged through the sack it carried and discovered nothing useful. He shoved at the body in disappointment and regarded the creature's armor. Like an appraiser examining a work of art, he moved various pieces this way and that under his scrutiny, but let them fall to the ground. A moue of distaste crossed Adnama's lips, and he wiped his hands on his trousers as though they were fouled. He looked at both creatures and scratched at his head.

"Why did you stay," he wondered, "when it would have made more sense to run away? That's usually what your kind does, unless you hopelessly outnumber the enemy. What are you hiding here that is so important? You certainly don't have it on you."

Adnama moved toward the direction the two had appeared from and held up his axe as his vision revealed a crack in the tunnel. He was fairly sure that if there had been more troglodytes, they would have attacked already. But caution was his watchword. He realized that he was going to have to wedge himself in sideways, if he was going to pass through the opening, and leave himself somewhat vulnerable. But he was curious. Slightly smaller than the trogs, Adnama was still broader in the shoulders, and he had to force himself through sideways to squeeze through the fissure in the wall. He popped out the other side into a small, moist cavern.

Like the other niche, this one held a treasure as well. However, it was not a treasure that the duergar valued at all. In fact, it was a cache only another troglodyte would cherish. The dank grotto was littered with trog spawn.

Adnama was overcome with disgust at the clutch

of speckled eggs. He swung his axe from side to side and smashed most of them, heedless of the noise he created. The few he didn't crush with his axe he ground under his worn boots. He smiled at the sound of the developing trogs splintering and squishing under his heels.

"That's a few less stink-meats cluttering up the world," he said to himself with a small measure of satisfaction. Seeing that there was nothing left in the grotto to destroy, he squeezed back out into the main tunnel. He looked once more at the dead trogs. Satisfied that they would no longer trouble him, Adnama continued deeper into the catacombs.

The heat continued to climb the farther Adnama moved down. He listened more closely to the slight hiss of steam, wary of any sudden burst of moisture. He had been scalded only once as a child by a concentrated jet of steam, but he still wore the scar on his shoulder, a constant reminder of the cost of carelessness.

More than once he had to ignore the glints and gleams along the walls. He was certain he was passing rich veins of ore along the way, and the glitter tugged at his heart. Still, he continued on.

Coming to a split in the path, he paused for a brief moment to scan both passageways. To his sharp eyes, both corridors initially continued deeper. But Adnama wasn't sure for how long, and he didn't want to waste the time of backtracking if he chose one that eventually started to snake upward again. He picked up two stones of similar size and tossed one down the channel on his left. He listened closely to the sounds the rock made on its course. Then he duplicated the procedure with the path on the right. The second stone made a different sound. That sound meant the second tunnel curved upward after a few hundred feet. He smiled grimly and went left.

Along with the rise in temperature, the tunnel also began to narrow. Adnama came to one area where he was forced to his knees to clear the low overhang and eventually had to slide along his belly to pass through to a larger cavern. None of the close quarters disturbed him overly much—wherever there was rockwork, there was home for him. And he was counting on the fact that it was home to more than just him.

As he rose to his feet, he examined the cavern for traps. A cursory glance revealed very little as the cave was studded with multiple pools of lava, though each one was no larger than a few feet. They bubbled cheerfully, and Adnama carefully maneuvered around them, knowing full well his armor would not protect him from this liquid fire. He watched his footing as he stepped from one solid patch to another until he was nearly free of the lava field. Just as he was clearing the last pool, the ground he thought was solid cracked under his weight. He tumbled backward toward the puddle of molten earth. Adnama only had a moment to act.

Without conscious thought, he used the momentum of his fall to launch himself backward and tuck himself into a ball. His face brushed so close to the pool mid-flip that a few of the braids of his beard caught fire. Despite the close call, Adnama successfully cleared the magma and landed on the opposite side of the pool. Coming down full force, the dwarf breathed a sigh of relief when the ground beneath his feet held firm. He batted at the ends of his beard to smother the burning hair and made his way around the other side of the pool without incident.

The cavern narrowed to another tunnel, and Adnama entered without hesitation. He had to rely on his darkvision again as the area was now too warm for ormu to thrive in any significant amount any longer. The ratty cotton shirt he wore under his mail was completely drenched with perspiration and the dwarf was tempted to peel it off. He knew if he did, though, the chainmail he wore would chafe and eventually blister his skin. It was wiser to leave the sopping fabric on as a bit of padding. He paused for a moment and pulled out his water flask, wrinkling his nose at the scent of his own burnt hair. Adnama was careful to ration out his supplies and only drank enough water to moisten his mouth and parched throat before replacing the stopper. He stored the flask, but before he could move on, a faint rumbling froze him in his tracks. He leaned against a naturally formed archway and braced himself for the impending quake. The trembling was not, however, what he expected.

Not five feet in front of him, the ground erupted in a spray of rocks and gravel, and the force blew the dwarf off his feet. He landed hard, the breath momentarily knocked from him. He rolled to one side and watched as a blood-red dragon's head appeared from the newly formed crater. Adnama crawled backward like a crab, still unable to catch his breath, as the creature pulled itself completely free of its burrow and rose to full height.

Standing almost nine feet tall, the creature carried a shield the same color as its body. Adnama could see he had initially been mistaken in his assessment of the threat. While the creature had the head of a dragon, the rest of its body was mostly humanoid. And, in the glow from the lava pools behind him, the dwarf could see light winking and shimmering off the creature's gemstone surface.

"Golem," he wheezed and pushed himself up on one elbow.

The ruby golem, seeing that Adnama was unarmed, dropped its shield and plodded forward, wasting no time with the intruder. Adnama knew that the monster outweighed him by a few thousand pounds and could easily crush him into the ground. Still short of breath, the dwarf dived between the legs of the approaching beast—but the golem was faster.

The duergar screamed in pain as the monster caught him by one of his ankles. The golem's grip was so tight that Adnama feared that his bone might snap. He was dragged face first along the cave floor back between the construct's legs. Rocks tore at his face and scalp, but that was the least of Adnama's worries. The golem slammed him into the tunnel wall. It turned to one side, and Adnama could blearily see the creature was searching for something to bludgeon him with, as though it didn't want to sully its ruby fists on dwarf flesh. Adnama had one chance left.

With blood stinging his eyes, the dwarf groped for his leather sack. He knew he possessed no shield capable of defending himself against the golem's near-impervious body. The dwarf's only defense was an attack. He rummaged about frantically. Panic momentarily froze his heart when his fingers did not brush against what he was searching for. One maddening heartbeat later, however, Adnama's hand closed around it. As he pulled the small, fist-sized object from his pouch, the golem lifted up a boulder nearly as large as the dwarf.

As the creature towered over him, Adnama threw the thunderstone at the monster's chest and buried his head under his arms. The sound the weapon made when it struck the gem creature was nearly deafening, and the dwarf could feel the blast resonate within his own ribcage. Adnama winced as bits of the cavern ceiling rained down, and he momentarily wondered if his defiant act would bring the whole structure down around his ears. But the roof held, and everything eventually grew quiet around the dwarf. Blinking dust and debris and blood from his eyes, he finally cracked them open to peak at his attacker.

A mountain of maroon dust was heaped up in a great pile where the golem had stood. Adnama rose on wobbly legs and tried to calm his pounding heart. He knew he had narrowly escaped death. If he hadn't thought to pack a few thunderstones, he would have been ground to dust himself. Pulling a rag from his pouch, he wiped his eyes clear and daubed at the wound on his scalp that was still seeping blood. When he had collected himself somewhat, Adnama moved over to the pile of dark dust. Nestled in the center of the powder was a perfect ruby. Adnama let the bloodstained rag slip from his fingers and lifted the gem to inspect it.

Even in the poor light, he could see the gem was of the highest caliber. It was a shade of maroon so dark that it was nearly black. He hefted the gem in his hand and estimated that it weighed at least a pound or so and would fetch quite a few coins in the right market. Then his dark eyes spotted a mark on one side that he initially mistook for an inclusion. Moving closer to the nearest pool of lava for better light, his fear of the magma overcome by his greed, Adnama sucked in his breath with a whistle. Absently, he realized that sound meant he had cracked at least one of his remaining teeth. But that was of no matter at the moment. He could see the mark on the gem was actually a design etched on one of the ruby's facets. It was the image of two hands, one living and one skeletal, gripped together.

"Szass Tam," the dwarf breathed almost reverently. The signature of the most powerful of Thay's Red Wizards alone increased the value of the gem as well as the danger to the dwarf.

"It figures this one would belong to you," he continued, "but I never thought I would hold something of yours in my grip, even for a moment." Adnama passed the jewel back and forth between his hands as he contemplated what to do next.

I'm not here for this kind of treasure, his mind raced, but how can I pass this up, this prize within my reach?

He knew the risks of trying to smuggle something like this out of Thay. Yet, if he ultimately succeeded, his conscious argued with him, he would have no difficulty at all leaving with such a treasure. And it was a small trophy, compared to what he planned to accomplish. Without deliberately coming to a decision, Adnama slipped the heavy stone into his sack and moved from the glow of the lava fields deeper into the bowels of the catacombs. Adnama didn't notice the fell thing that slithered from the shadows and sniffed interestedly at the bloody rag he had discarded.

As Adnama dropped deeper into the catacombs, he noticed more and more pools of lava. He could still catch a whiff of his own burnt hair and moved more and more carefully around their growing numbers. The molten slag bubbled and burped as he continued, with increasing difficulty, to navigate between them. The smell of sulfur grew stronger and, while he held one hand sealed against his mouth and nose, the dwarf cursed himself for leaving behind his face rag.

Balanced precariously between two pools, he barely managed to steady himself as a small tremor rattled the cavern. Adnama grabbed for a thunderstone and stood poised to fling it at any attacker, but none appeared. After a moment, he replaced the powerful weapon when he realized that the tremor was not the herald of a creature's attack, but an actual quake, albeit a minor one.

"Gettin' jumpy," he chided himself in a feeble attempt at humor. But Adnama was vaguely disturbed by the growing number of lava pools and now the tectonic activity. The indications were pointing to a chance of trouble on a grander scale. He had seen enough signs like this back home to realize the entire country could be in danger. If some large-scale eruption took place, Adnama had no idea how he might accomplish his goal, let alone save himself. He shook his head and slid over to a relatively stable section of the cave to consider his options.

He was once again faced with a fork in his path. Both choices proved to be descending tunnels. Realizing that there was no easy method to tell which way to go, Adnama pulled off his left gauntlet and pushed up his grubby shirt sleeve past his elbow.

Along the top of his forearm, his gray skin was covered by a series of black lines and symbols, but the pattern was not just an innocuous design of vanity or even a rank of station. Adnama had tattooed a rough map on himself, and he consulted it now. But even before his eyes fell upon the markings, he somehow knew—or dreaded—that the answer would not be there. The information he had was incomplete before he had left the Orsraun Mountains, and now he was truly at a crossroads. So he trusted his instincts and made a choice. But before he could move on, he needed to do one last thing.

Planting himself as securely as possible against a wall, he reached around his neck and pulled at a leather thong fastened there. From under his mail and cotton shirt, Adnama pulled free an unworked piece of stone. He grasped the sending stone with his right hand and closed his eyes. He composed a mental image of his location and his decision in his mind's eye and sent that image off to the matching stone far from where he was. Satisfied he had left word of his location, Adnama replaced the stone under his armor and moved on.

The path sloped down at an even and gentle pace, and the dwarf was pleased that there were not nearly as many pools of magma here as there had been in the preceding chambers. The air even became marginally clearer the farther he went, and Adnama wondered if there might be some sort of vent or fissure that connected the depths ahead of him with the outside air above. He suspected it might be possible—even necessary if other, less inhuman creatures frequented these catacombs.

He could see that the walls were smoother here. This stone had been intentionally worked. A slow smile spread across his face. Ahead about fifty feet, the dwarf could make out the faint glimmering of light—not the chaotic shimmer of molten earth, but the familiar flicker of torchlight. He nearly broke into a run.

"By Deep Duerra," he whispered, "I've found them. I've found them."

At the bend in the tunnel, Adnama turned to the right with a look of absolute certainty fixed on his face. But as he rounded the corner, he slowed to a trot and covered only a few more feet before he stopped entirely, like a clockwork toy that had wound down its spring.

"It can't be," he choked out. "It's not possible...." his voice trailed away.

What little color Adnama possessed drained away immediately. A figure separated itself from the side of the catacomb, and the duergar recognized the bloody scrap in the thing's claws—the face rag he had abandoned earlier. The shadow held the cloth up to its face and drew in one long, almost loving breath as though the cotton had been scented by the finest of perfumes. Then it slowly slid the rag down over its mouth, all the while licking at it hungrily. Adnama turned and tried to flee, only to realize with a dawning dread that the shadowy masses surrounded him, and he was cut off from any avenue of escape. He turned in a helpless circle.

They were everywhere.

His mind could not wrap itself around what his vision had revealed to him, and it started to shut down. The dwarf could not have moved at that moment even if the ground itself had tried to shake him loose. Black spots crowded across his line of sight. He was vaguely aware that his knees were buckling out from under him, but he was powerless to stop his fall. He hit the ground with a dull thud. As the last of his consciousness faded, Adnama could see the black shadows peel themselves from the darkness and start to swarm him. For the first and only time in his life, Adnama fainted from pure terror.

⊙

The rumblings of the ground rose and fell in waves. However, it was not loud enough to disguise the wet, slurping sounds drifting up from one of the many channels in the catacombs. Nor did the noise last long enough to cover the screams or the angry growls.

As it turned out, there was not enough gray meat to go around.

# CHAPTER ONE

**15 Mirtul, 1373 DR**

Thazienne Uskevren controlled her breathing. Only the lightest, frosty wisps escaped her nostrils. She knew it would take sharp eyes for something to see her, but she knew any creature down in these caves with darkvision would be able to spot the heat of her breath like a beacon. So, she used the chunk of ice she was squatting behind as a shield of sorts and let it intercept her slight puffs. She waited, watched, and, as she quietly flexed and moved her gloved fingers, tried not to think of the cold.

The acquaintances she loosely referred to as her peers would be hard pressed to recognize her here. The twenty-four year old woman had traded in her sumptuous, Sembian gowns and jewels for more practical wear. Tazi, as her family and most trusted friends called her, was well over thirteen hundred miles from her comfortable rooms in Stormweather Towers. The daughter of a noble family of Selgaunt, arguably one of the most powerful families in the governing body of that commerce-driven city, should have been out of place in this frozen tomb—but she wasn't.

She sported well-tailored woolen pants tucked into short leather boots with sturdy, gripping soles and a shirt with a high collar that masked her nose and mouth for additional warmth. Over her coarse shirt, Tazi had a heavy, leather vest. Matching bandoliers crisscrossed her chest, with various and sundry bits of climbing gear and tools strapped tight. A sack, coil of rope, and one of her Sembian guardblades all hung from her wide belt. The only concession she refused to make to the bitter cold was that she sported no cap over her jet-black hair, which she had tied back. It wasn't an issue of vanity, though. Years ago, Tazi had proven she cared little enough about that when she cut her then-waist-length wavy hair to a style a bit more boyish. Tazi, who enjoyed any and every opportunity when she could be contrary, had done it for two reasons. The first was to irk her mother, who was always aware of their family's station and need for proper appearance. The cut was more suited to the styles of Cormyr at the time, a very gauche look anywhere in the fashion-conscious Sembia, and that act set her mother's blood boiling. The second reason was a bit more practical.

As a young girl, Tazi began to pilfer items from the family coffers and the servants' pantries. She normally returned the goods, simply enjoying the challenge of the theft. As she matured, Tazi did not outgrow her love of thievery. In fact, she turned to her peers as a source of challenge and entertainment, each job a little grander and more daring. She embraced it as another life and disguised herself accordingly. With the short hair and appropriate thieving leathers, Tazi did a more than fair job of concealing her identity and even her sex when she explored the night. But she loved these "wildings," as she liked to call them. Each success made her feel more alive and more in control of her own destiny, a security Tazi valued above all else. Mostly ignored at home except by a special few, she longed to feel safe in who she was. Her wildings provided that and more.

Her thieving ways eventually caught the attention of two unique men. Tazi, who tormented and tossed aside every eligible bachelor her mother sent before her, found that she could not ignore either of them. One, a mage-in-training close to her age, actually shared her adventures of the corrupt life. He appeared to enjoy thumbing his nose at his destined station as much as Tazi did hers. However, when one of her wildings went horribly awry, she discovered he had been a hired bodyguard on her father's payroll all along. Tazi was more devastated by that betrayal than by the fact that that same night she had to take her first life in an act of mercy. The sense of security that she had fought for in her own manner was horribly fractured.

She turned away from him and the other one, a family servant, no longer certain who to trust. The second man, several years her senior, had mentored and tutored the young Thazienne in the finer art of theft and had even given to her her first quality set of lock picks. But circumstances had taken Tazi from her home a year ago on a heartbreaking quest, and the situation had driven her closer to the mage while wedging her farther away from her mentor. It was only upon returning to her family estate that she discovered the man she always sensed was more than just a servant had given over his heart to her as well as his loyalty. But by then, a family tragedy changed everything for her. And here Tazi was.

She peered down from her frozen perch, and narrowed her sea-green eyes. The large vault in front of her glowed an icy blue. Tazi wasn't sure just where the light originated, whether it was from an external source or from within the icy blocks that formed the room itself. The chamber, larger than a cavern, was roughly three hundred feet across and at least half as high, with various tunnels that emptied into it. Between the tunnel openings was a section of frozen wall that ran in an unbroken line except for a few shelves that had obviously been hewn out of the ice. There was a series of waist-deep ruts that ran the length of the vault, and Tazi suspected ancient streams must have cut those ages ago. Stalactites sporadically hung from the ceiling, ranging in size from three to thirty feet in length and a few stalagmites jutted up from the vault floor. Tazi noted them carefully, as it would be easy to turn an ankle or worse around them.

She absently brushed a stray hair away from her

face and finally saw what she had been waiting for. About seventy-five feet away, Tazi caught a glimpse of what looked like a humanoid figure, pale skinned in the blue light and of average build, nearly nude and devoid of any hair at all. She squinted for a better look at the lean and lanky man, but there wasn't enough light for more details than that. She could see, however, that he was filling a recessed ledge with an armful of something that glinted dully in the weak light, and he had some type of weapon dangling from his waist. Tazi dropped a little lower and began to mark the time. She frowned slightly when she realized how stiff her legs had become while crouching there, and she berated herself for her carelessness. While she counted off silently, she began to tense and relax the large muscles in her thighs and calves, readying herself.

When the first figure had left and another one similarly burdened replaced him, Tazi knew approximately how many minutes she had. She passed her hands over her gear. After taking a quick inventory of supplies, she freed her coil of rope and knotted it around the frozen stalagmite to her right. She let the other end of the rope drop to the vault floor and snapped a clip from her bandolier onto it. She threaded the rope behind her waist, grabbing the tied-off side with her left hand and the free end with her right. She tugged once to test the knot and, satisfied that it was secure enough, she launched herself over the ledge.

Tazi dropped down in an arc that curved back to the ice wall. She braced her legs for the impact and launched herself back out as soon as she made contact. As she pushed away, she let another ten feet of rope play out before she touched the wall again. Tazi rappelled down the icy face in less than a minute before her feet touched the bottom. She unclipped herself from the rope and moved silently toward the cache set in the wall.

Tazi glanced once in the direction where the figures had disappeared to verify she was alone. The diffuse light in the large cavern didn't accommodate much of a view, so she had to satisfy herself that she had their timing down. Tazi hurried over to the recessed ledge and the pile of rocks that twinkled in the sick light. She gave the wall a cursory glance for traps, but couldn't discover a single one. She suspected there wouldn't be any considering how haphazardly the two humanoid creatures had dumped their loads, but Tazi always checked.

She moved up to the natural-rock shelf and slowly pulled down her muffler in awe. Lumped in a pile was what appeared to be a mound of gold. But this was no ordinary metal. Even in the half-light, Tazi could see that the odd-shaped pieces had a red cast to them and also emitted a faint, crimson glow of their own. She used her teeth to pull off one of her gloves and tucked it into her belt. She picked up a piece in her bare hand and smiled a little at the slight tingle she felt from the ore. It should have been freezing to the touch, but a gentle heat radiated from it. Tazi tossed the chunk in the air a few times and judged its weight. Finally, she pulled a small dagger from her left boot and tried to knick the gold, to no avail. Satisfied, she smiled and filled the sack at her hip with a few pounds of the stuff. Caught up in her success, Tazi didn't notice the pale figure that emerged from the tunnel to her left.

But he saw her.

Fastening her pouch shut, Tazi nearly dropped the whole sack as a high pitched whine echoed throughout the frozen chamber. She slipped her glove back on while she whirled in a circle to discover the source of the noise. She eventually spotted the pale creature, whose cache she was robbing, near the entrance to the tunnel off to her left. Tazi realized his cry was one of alarm. She didn't know how many of the creatures she might face and had no intention of waiting around to find out. With a lopsided grin plastered to her face, she made a mad dash back to her rope, over a hundred feet away.

Tazi didn't bother to look back and see if any were gaining on her; she knew they would be eventually. The series of icy hedges were all that lay between her and her rope. Tazi didn't miss a beat. Placing both hands on the waist-high barrier, she swung her legs together as one over the side, easily clearing the hurdle. She cleared the second swinging her legs the other direction like a pendulum, but felt something grip her left ankle at the third hurdle. Tazi let the subterranean dweller spin her around by her foot. As soon as she was facing his direction, she braced her hands on the ice hedge, now behind her, and brought her right leg around in a powerful sweep. She heard the crack as she made contact with the thing's jaw. Caught unaware, the thing was knocked backward off his feet by the momentum of her blow. Glancing past the fallen creature, she could see he was no longer alone. At least four or five more of his kind ran from the far tunnel in her direction. Tazi wasted no more time and sprinted the remaining distance to the rope.

Casting safety to the wind, Tazi leaped the last few feet for the line and started to shimmy up the coil, now stiff with the cold. With lightening speed, she moved hand over hand and pistoned her legs all the way to the ledge of her original perch. She grabbed the stalagmite and swung herself up, only then affording herself a glance at her pursuers. The first one she had kicked was receiving a helping hand from the reinforcements, while one of the others had just grabbed Tazi's rope. She watched, momentarily amazed at his strength as he began to pull himself up using just his arms, but snapped herself from her reverie. Tazi drew the same dagger that she had used to test her treasure's hardness and hastily cut her rope free of the stalagmite. As the length of cord whistled away, Tazi leaned forward to see the creature tumble back to the frozen floor, not much worse for wear. She shot him a mock salute and turned to flee, realizing she had probably only bought herself a few minutes at best.

With her legs pumping away, Tazi ran through the passage, all the while reversing the turns she took to get to her vantage point. She had hesitated to use any kind of glow stones or other markers along her path for fear of drawing unwanted attention. Still, some attention was unavoidable, no matter how cautious one was.

As she took a corner while looking over her shoulder,

Tazi nearly struck her head on a low ceiling. She did bump into something soft and velvety that exploded into a flurry of wings and screeches. Tazi had crashed into a nest of ice bats. Larger and covered by thicker fur than ordinary bats, they had razor-sharp claws to better grip and pierce the slick, cold surfaces of their frozen depths. Tazi drew her guardblade and cut a swath through the swarming eruption of beating wings and raking talons. She skewered a few, but mostly nicked a wing here and there until the majority fled into one of the many crevices in the passageway. She sheathed her weapon and continued along what she hoped was the right direction.

The tunnel narrowed a bit, and Tazi paused for just a moment to lean forward with a hand against her side and the other braced against her thigh. Running in the cold had taken a toll on her, and every breath burned like a shaft of fire cutting through her chest. Her ragged breathing, however, masked the sound of gentle slithering directly above her until it was too late. Just as Tazi started to straighten herself, a thick coil, four feet long, dropped down in front of her. It wrapped itself around her neck with lightening quickness and yanked Tazi a few feet off the ground, nearly snapping her neck. She grabbed at the red- and black-stripped, scaly loops in an attempt to free herself or, at the very least, take some of the pressure off her throat. Her legs kicked futilely at the air, in a dizzy parody of a jig. As Tazi felt herself raised toward the broken and uneven ceiling, a withered face lowered itself into her view.

It looked like a female human head, with greasy, black locks and a forked tongue that flicked in and out between its cracked lips. Tazi could make out that the rest of the monster tapered down to the banded snake body that held her like a noose. Even in the extreme chill air, Tazi could smell the foul odor of decaying meat on it. She also thought she could make out a pile of half gnawed bones on a rock shelf behind the naga's snug warren.

"What have we here?" the thing hissed at Tazi slowly. "Something more to eat?" it questioned.

Tazi could feel herself start to lose consciousness, yet she was nearly mesmerized by the glowing intensity of the being's intelligent stare. Against her will, Tazi could feel her eyes droop and her arms grow heavy and leaden. The naga moved its face closer and tentatively let its tongue trail down Tazi's smooth cheek. The leathery touch galvanized Tazi into action.

Her eyes flew open, and she grabbed tighter at the coils, desperate to relieve the strain on her windpipe. She flailed her legs about even more frantically.

"I like it when they fight," the naga chuckled in a lispy way. "It makes the meat that much sweeter."

"Not today," Tazi gasped out, and she could hear the naga's throaty chuckle over the pounding blood in her own ears. While she pulled at the naga's body, Tazi swung her right heel around until it struck the tunnel wall at just the right angle. The impact caused the mechanism in Tazi's climbing boot to release the two inch pick located in the toe. It was meant for giving the owner a better hold when scaling an icy crevasse.

But it had other uses as well.

Tazi let go of the naga's coils and grabbed its greasy head. The naga was momentarily startled by its victim's aggressive move and didn't immediately resist. Tazi wasted no time in pushing the naga's face as far away from her own as she could.

Tazi swung her boot straight up and caught the naga where she guessed the thing's throat was. A hot spray of blood shot out from the jagged wound, and Tazi could hear the sizzle as it spattered on the frozen floor. She suspected the naga's blood was acidic, judging by the sound it made, and slashed once more across the beast's throat, uncertain how long her boot's tough hide would protect her from its burn. The coils slackened around her neck enough for Tazi to slip free of the deadly grasp. Tazi, sure the thing was dying, wasted no time in continuing her flight.

Moving a little slower, she rubbed at her neck and tried to collect her thoughts. Her tangle with the naga had left her somewhat disorientated. Tazi glanced around, looking for a familiar sign as she reviewed a mental list of landmarks in her head. The wide passageway she had escaped into looked like most of the others she had run through. Weakly lit by the blue glow of the ice, this one had more visible rock and fewer frozen columns. As she moved forward, Tazi hoped that the change in landscape was an indication she was moving closer to the exit of the subterranean catacombs. Whines directly behind her made Tazi turn suddenly. Four of the pale humanoids rushed around the corner and forced Tazi's hand.

"Well," Tazi nearly laughed, "I guess that makes this an easy choice." With that, she ran up the path she had been contemplating, no longer having any other options.

As she snaked back and forth around several sharp turns, Tazi wasn't sure her choice was the same path she had descended by. Cornering to the left, her feet skated across a wet surface, and she came dangerously close to losing her footing. As Tazi spun around unwillingly, she could see that there was more exposed rock and less ice in this portion of the passageway. She also realized the overall light was growing brighter. She looked at the width of the tunnel with a critical eye and yanked a fist-sized metal object off one of her bandoliers. As the pale men came into view, Tazi threw the metal thing to one side of the tunnel. The springwall, a single-use item created by some industrious gnomes, sprung open upon impact. The tightly coiled mesh expanded to a barricade ten feet wide by ten feet high and attached itself to both sides of the walls. Two of her pursuers could not stop in time and became hopelessly entangled in the trap. The other two managed to jump around their squirming companions and continue the chase.

Tazi continued her dash to the surface, legs pumping furiously. She knew she was at least heading toward some kind of opening as the air was not quite so frigid and there were the beginnings of small clumps of moss and other vegetation appearing sporadically in the rocky tunnels. As she rounded another gentle bend in her flight, Tazi could see that a patch of fungus completely ringed the tunnel. Tazi quickly rummaged in her sack and pulled out a small flask. Ripping the stopper free with her mouth, she doused the pale fungus and tossed the empty container aside. She flipped a pocket open on her vest and removed a small wire mechanism that resembled a clasp of sorts, then she snapped the device over the moldy growth a few times.

"Come on," she urged the tool impatiently.

Finally, there was a shower of sparks sufficient to ignite the combustible oil Tazi had soaked the plant life with. The flames erupted and shot across the trail she had made until that whole section of the passageway was a ring of fire. The two creatures that hadn't been tripped up by Tazi's snare rounded the corner but threw up their hands at the blaze. One shrieked piteously and turned away, but Tazi could tell through the smoke and the fire that the other one was looking for a way to pass. The smile faded from Tazi's face and she continued her escape.

Spotting a familiar archway in the rocks, Tazi knew she was almost free of the icy passageways. She could see a patch of sky up ahead that was colored yellow by the first rays of dawn. Her smile faded as a cry rose up once more behind her. Tazi turned to see that the fire had not stopped the last creature. She reluctantly drew her sword.

A beam of the rising sun shot through the tunnel, bouncing madly across several patches of melting ice, illuminating the entire section in a maze of golden light. Tazi backed up slightly and got her only good look at the creature she had stolen from.

Taller than she was, the man had flesh so pale that it was albino and completely devoid of hair. Leanly muscled, he wore almost no clothing and carried only a single weapon. Tazi marveled at how tough his skin must have been, to insulate him from the intense cold without the aid of coverings. He returned Tazi's scrutiny with nearly white eyes and tilted his head just a little. She raised her sword a little higher and adjusted her stance farther into the encroaching sunlight.

"Please," she finally said. "I don't want to do this."

The creature looked at her once more and turned to disappear back into the cold darkness. Tazi was not sure if it was her entreaty or simply the creature's natural aversion to light that made him back down. She suspected she would never know, and that was just fine with her. She slowly backed away, only sheathing her sword after she had completely exited the tunnel.

When Tazi turned around, she squinted against the daylight and raised an arm to shield her eyes from the glare. The entire, snowcapped mountains were softly glowing a warm yellow-pink from the first rays of the sun. Satisfied she was no longer being followed, Tazi rummaged around under a cairn of rocks near the entrance and shook loose a full-length cloak. Made of patches of white, beige and pale blue fur, it provided the perfect camouflage against the snowfield. She slipped it around her shoulders, grateful for its additional warmth. Now that her eyes had adjusted somewhat from her time in the gloom, Tazi glanced once more at the sight in front of her.

"I can see now why he called them the Sunrise Mountains," she said to no one in particular. Watching her footing as she began her descent down the mountainside, she added with a chuckle, "But I will have to let that guide I hired know that the Buried Ones are a little more than just a child's bedtime story."

The skeletal figure bowed over the dark wood table. Its glossy surface was covered with a variety of bottles and flasks. Some of them glowed in the dim light of the chamber, while others bubbled without any overt sign of heat. A long millipede rippled its way, unnoticed, across the arcane collection of items on the table. A collection of odd, furry creatures scuttled around the necromancer's feet. Though the lich could have replaced the simple desk with a larger, more ornately carved one if he desired, he was partial to the antique. It was one of the many artifacts that had belonged to his mentor and last teacher. They had all become his property, an inheritance of sorts, when the lich murdered him many years ago. Even his mentor's body remained as a twisted legacy, roaming about as one of the many zombie guards protecting the keep. Szass Tam hated waste of any kind and never let a good body rot unused.

For the last few days, the lich had been driven. For hours at a time, he had floated throughout his immense library, scanning the thousands of texts and scrolls the Zulkir of Necromancy had spent the last two centuries collecting. Szass Tam, so absorbed in his studies, had been barely aware of his servants scuttling in and out to replace the candles he was forever burning. Unlike most lichs, Szass Tam could move about in broad daylight, but he preferred not to. In fact, he shrouded his keep's few windows in sumptuous, black velvet drapes, blotting out all natural daylight. And though he could easily have lit his entire residence with various enchantments and glow spells, the lich had a fondness for the simplicity of candles. The keep was filled with them, even though many members of his vast, undead armies were fearful of fire. Szass Tam enjoyed their dread with a perverse humor. However, he could not tolerate wax spatters anywhere and his servants were well aware of the consequences if they didn't clean them properly or failed to refresh the hundreds of pillars throughout the keep on a daily basis. They were constantly busy with the chore.

In his searches, the lich had pulled out a variety of obscure tomes and manuscripts. He had spread them about in an unusually disorganized fashion, too concerned with adding notations to a well-worn folio that was now lying at the center of his table to care about the books. With bony fingers that resembled nothing so much as birds' talons, Szass Tam traced the runes and words he had inscribed over the last few months and murmured softly. His paper thin skin was lined with wrinkles of concentration, and his graying wisps of hair were slightly askew, oddly framing his balding pate. When he was alone, the necromancer cared little for his outward, physical appearance, but didn't indulge in the habit of wearing the clothes he had died in as so many of his kind did. He normally sported a simple linen tunic and the rich, maroon robes that marked his station as a Red Wizard. For anyone other than a Red Wizard, it meant death to wear such a garment. In fact, most Thayans were so fearful of the punishment, the majority never sported the color in their wardrobe at all, whether they were slave or master.

He squeezed his eyes shut and rocked back and forth on his heels as though struggling with some unseen force. He repeated a phrase over and over, forcing his will to dominate that invisible entity. His scrawny fingers clutched the ends of his folio, and he crushed the edges of the parchments, caught up in the battle of wills. Finally, he threw back his head and nearly screamed out the words a last time. The air was sucked out of the room in a thunderous whoosh, extinguishing every candle in his library. Szass Tam lowered his head in the absolute darkness and remained that way for several moments. Eventually, he lifted his head wearily and made a slow pass of his hands, and the library was once again illuminated by a hundred points of light.

The Red Wizard moved slowly over to a luxurious, oversized chair, covered in the hide of an animal long-since extinct in Faerûn. He carefully lowered his thin skeletal frame into the comforting cushions, a ghost of a smile playing about his thin, parched lips. A small table to his left held a heavy-cut crystal decanter of garnet wine, but he did not avail himself of any refreshment. The lich no longer needed food or water, or even sleep for that matter, but he preferred to surround himself with the trappings of the living and only the finest would suit his tastes. He steepled his fingers in front of his face and leaned his skullish forehead against the bony latticework they formed. He had succeeded, but Szass Tam was far too intelligent and practical to fool himself into believing his spell was anything more than a temporary measure. He knew he would have to discover a permanent solution, but he secretly harbored a growing feeling of certainty that there might not be one. He wondered once more if this would haunt him for all his undead years.

The Red Wizard slowly raised his head, and his form shimmered and coalesced into something else. Suddenly, his arms and legs filled out, and his tunic no longer had the appearance of being a few sizes too big. His spine stretched out, and his chair sagged under the additional weight. Szass Tam's face grew fuller, and his cheeks took on a color that was almost healthy. His jet-black eyes burned brightly and his hair darkened and thickened, creeping back up to cover the top of his skull once more.

"Come," he called out in a deep, melodic voice, though there had been no knock on the thick chamber door yet.

Slowly, almost hesitantly, that entrance swung open. A human woman, no older than twenty or so, peeked in.

"What is it, child?" the lich purred solicitously.

But beneath that pleasant demeanor, an undercurrent of impatience rippled. It was not lost on the young servant.

She quickly entered the room, and Szass Tam could see she would need a little prodding to get her to speak. He sighed imperceptibly and once again thought back to his former chambermaid, Charmaine. He found especially at times like this that he missed the thin, middle-aged woman who had served him faithfully for over thirty years. She was poised and polite, qualities the lich appreciated and even valued, to an extent. Charmaine had worked tirelessly over the years in his largest keep here, situated between Eltabbar and Amruthar, and asked for no monetary payment other than food and shelter. She had made it clear to the Red Wizard that she longed for immortality; it was a desire he understood all too well, and he had admired her directness. He promised her after four decades of services he would have one of his vampire generals bestow that "gift" on her, and she could serve him forever. But a misunderstanding occurred a few months ago.

A new vampire in Szass Tam's service had been attracted to her, not knowing her important station amongst the thirty or so living servants that worked within the keep. He approached her one night, and Charmaine mistakenly thought he had been sent by Szass Tam. She believed her moment of reward had come. She willing gave herself to the young vampire, and he, caught up in his own bloodlust, drained her dry and murdered her. When Szass Tam discovered his favorite servant had been killed, he incinerated the vampire with little more than a single thought. He debated long and hard about raising Charmaine as a zombie, hating to lose such a good servant. But he knew she had always detested his legions of ghouls and zombies, only acting with the utmost civility around them because she knew the lich hated impropriety. And so he decided instead to let her be in peace as her final payment, though it caused him a great inconvenience. As he watched Charmaine's replacement nervously fidget with a small, draped bundle in her arms, he sighed again.

"Is everything ready for my guests, Neera? Bedchambers freshened, clean linens?" he prodded the red-haired girl. "You know I would hate for them to be lacking any comfort, don't you?" With that last question, he eyed her meaningfully. Szass Tam knew full well that her left arm was still healing from the burn he had inflicted there not too long ago when Neera had neglected a few pieces of cutlery at a place setting for one of his "special" dinner gatherings.

"Yes, m-my lord," she answered meekly.

"And the meeting hall?" he nudged her along, tired of the game already.

Perhaps sensing her master's growing impatience, she stood a little straighter and replied more confidently, "Everything has been made ready. You won't find anything lacking, I assure you." Szass Tam smiled a bit and thought to himself that the woman might have promise after all.

"Is that all then?" he asked her, looking pointedly at her bundle.

"No, my lord," she replied. "I have word from one of your patrols." He simply stared at her, no longer willing to cue her any more this evening.

"One of the ghoul brigades returned from the lower depths of the Citadel," Neera explained, her voice growing stronger. "They described seeing increasing collections of magma, and one even reported a river of lava flowing through a former passageway, now impassable."

The lich lowered his head and nodded to himself. It was as he expected, though the news did not please him.

"And," she added, "they found this." She held out the wrapped bundle, uncertain if she should approach the Red Wizard.

Szass Tam drew himself up to his full, however false, height and approached the chambermaid. He could see her tremble at his approach, and that pleased him.

"Let's see what they discovered." He took the bundle from her unresisting arms. He smiled charmingly at her. Even though she feared him, she could not stop the stain of red on her cheeks. "You may go for now," he dismissed her. She dropped her eyes and curtsied briefly before slipping out of the library.

Szass Tam carried the carefully wrapped bundle over to his desk. He laid it to one side and prudently replaced the pages of his folio and stored it in a special location of his library. He made a mental note to himself that he would need to bring it with him for the gathering a tenday hence and deposit it in a very guarded location.

Considering the company he was drawing together, the lich was grimly aware that it would not do to have the collection end up in any one of their hands.

Having satisfied himself that the pages were secure for the moment, he turned his attention to the cloth-covered package. Szass Tam unwrapped the parcel and tilted his head. Lying in the center of the cloak were several bones, picked clean of all flesh. He lifted one up toward a candelabrum and sighted down the length of it like a carpenter with a level.

"Dwarven," he whispered and caught a whiff of the remains. "Duergar," he deduced.

Caught up in his ponderings of the rare discovery, Szass Tam relaxed his appearance spell and reverted back to the thin skeletal body he truly possessed. His red robe pooled at his feet like a puddle of blood as he shrunk a few inches. He ran a thin claw along the leg, pausing to finger a few deep gouges in the bone. As he absently rubbed the marks, the lich grew thoughtful. In his two hundred years of experience, he had never seen bite marks quite like these.

"This will require some investigating," he murmured to himself. After a moment more of silence, however, his thin, cruel lips parted in a grin.

"But what a delightful addition to my collection," he added, always able to put leftovers to good use. Still smiling, he covered the bones and prepared for his next move.

# CHAPTER TWO

The dream was always the same. Naglatha found herself on a windswept plain with fertile farming lands as far as the eye could see in every direction. The air was charged with an electric energy that was palpable. Not far from her, atop a slight knoll, stood a small but powerful enclave of men clothed in crimson cloaks. She recognized their leader, Ythazz Buvaar, by his fiery eyes and vigorous manner. She moved closer to the group of men to hear him better.

"The time has come," she heard him shout, "to shake off the chains of the pharaohs. Their days are over."

Naglatha moved a strand of her midnight-black hair away from her eyes and mingled with the group of red-robed men. None of them saw her, and she was free to step about and study them all without changing the events of the vision. Naglatha could see some were moved by the words of the man who would be the first leader of the Red Wizards. Before this time, they were simply a group of renegade spellcasters that hid themselves from the watching eyes of the god-kings of Mulhorand. Their numbers were scattered throughout the kingdom, but a core group of the sect, that called themselves by the title of Red Wizards, demanded freedom from the theocracy of the old empire. They wanted the right to study and learn about every form of magic that existed in Faerûn and discover that which did not. And the god-kings would not give them their freedom willingly.

Concentrated mostly in the northern provinces, these men did not have the backward, inbred worship for the pharaohs that most of their society possessed. And Ythazz Buvaar had stepped forward from that consortium. He foresaw a kingdom without the pharohs, where anyone could attain the same position of power as the god-kings, but through magic instead of worship. He rallied the others to his vision. They had caught his enthusiasm enough to raise an army and sack the capital city of Delhumide. But now, the rulers of Mulhorand had sent an army to crush the rebellion, and Ythazz Buvaar had gathered the most powerful wizards here on the hills above Thazalhar to stop them. Naglatha could feel her heart quicken its tempo in expectation of what she knew was to follow. She could have recited the words herself, she knew them so well.

"Now is the time," Ythazz Buvaar told the others.

"Now is when we show those god-kings just how powerful our magic is and why it is like the sea. Whether they choose to believe in it or not," he said with a slight smile, "they have entered the water. And they are about to get wet."

Naglatha watched as the select men joined hands, almost as if in prayer. She longed to enter the circle herself, but she was never able to do that. Each time she had tried in the past, the dream simply faded away. So now she made herself content by studying the proceedings as they unfolded. But it chaffed her to sit along the sides and not be a part of the glory of the birth of Thay, even though the events occurred four and a half centuries ago and these men had long since turned to dust, their time come and gone.

Ythazz Buvaar led the chants. Most of the words were lost on Naglatha, though she always woke with them ringing in her ears, and they haunted her waking thoughts. The spells were lost to time as well, though she never gave up hope that she would one day rediscover them. She worked tirelessly in her search, and no price was ever too great to pay for even the slightest scrap of information. She approached all her tasks with the greatest of zeal, and her ruthlessness set her apart from many of the other Red Wizards. She had garnered a reputation as an individual who would do anything to further their cause, no matter the cost. But, in her heart, she wished they were more like the men of her recurring dreams; men who seized glory without hesitation.

Ythazz Buvaar raised his head to the sky and said,

"We call you, Lord of the Hidden Layers. We beseech you for aid, and we bind you to us. We call you by your true name. Come, Eltab, for we have great need!"

The wind died down and fell silent. The very air seemed alive with energy. At first, there was the sound of distant thunder. Eventually, though, the men gathered there realized that the sound was the ground that rumbled beneath their feet. Naglatha could feel the vibrations deep within her own chest, and her breath became rapid. A great tearing sound was heard, and the land split wide beneath the spell-casters' feet, throwing some to the rich soil. However, Ythazz Buvaar and Naglatha held their ground.

With a hiss of steam and eldritch smoke, a figure slowly rose to the surface. Standing almost fifteen feet tall, the demon-king Eltab stood before the group of stunned wizards. His body was completely covered with black and red plates, like some unholy armor. While he was vaguely human in shape, his hands ended in fearsome claws, and his head was that of some great muzzled beast. Multiple horns sprouted from his head, and he flexed monstrous, insect wings that spanned almost twenty feet. Naglatha held her breath in awe, and she watched the dark lord regard the gathered men with his malevolent, red-slitted yellow eyes.

Many miles to the north, a similar rending took place in the land, and a river was born that would, for years to come, bear the name of the abyssal demon these men had summoned.

"Who has called me forth?" the tanar'ri lord

demanded in an ancient voice that chilled Naglatha to her very core.

Most of the Red Wizards cowered or were paralyzed by the creature's frightful gaze, but Naglatha saw with a mixture of envy and admiration that Ythazz Buvaar stepped forward.

"We have done so, lord," he spoke with only the hint of a quiver in his voice. "We have freed you by word and deed, and we have great need of you." He bowed when he finished.

Eltab stood there and flexed his wings in thought. "And what would you ask of me?" he finally demanded.

"We ask you for the blood of our enemies," Ythazz Buvaar explained. "We ask that these plains run red and the land is drenched with it like an unstoppable tide." Naglatha could see the demon was intrigued and even relaxed his frightful stare for a moment.

"And what would you give me," the tanar'ri asked slyly, "if I grant you this favor?"

"We will give you your due and our worship," Ythazz Buvaar promised. "Lead us in this, and we will follow you for all our days to come. We will guide you to the descendents of the Rashemaar usurper, Yvengi, and there you may take your just revenge." Ythazz Buvaar watched the demon closely after the last offering.

"Yvengi!" the demon king cried, and the ground shook again. Naglatha watched as he crouched lower and held his hands out as though he were strangling someone. "Yesss," he hissed, clutching at the air, "I would grind his descendents to dust for their ancestor's crimes against me. If not for him, I would not have been trapped. If not for him..."

Naglatha swelled with pride at the way Ythazz Buvaar manipulated the demon-king and the way he stood his ground as the others trembled in the shadows. This was a man who could control the country and rule the way kings should. This was the way of power, she thought, the way of a true Red Wizard of Thay.

"We will take you to his line," Ythazz Buvaar continued, and Naglatha could see the shrewd gleam in his dark eyes, even though the tanar'ri lord could not. "We will give them to you and more."

"Yes," the demon said, "you will give him to me and more. Much more than that." The demon-king turned, and for one moment, locked eyes with Naglatha. She was startled, for in all the times she relived the dream, that had never happened before. She stood transfixed, uncertain what to do next. However, the tanar'ri lord turned away and was flanked by the frightened and awestruck Red Wizards. And he led them into war.

When Naglatha turned around, the battle was over, and the Red Wizards were victorious. She lifted the hem of her robe and picked her way carefully over the many Mulhorandi corpses that littered the plains, bodies stacked like cordwood. The scene was what Ythazz Buvaar had asked for: blood covered the earth like a crimson sea. And, atop the same knoll, the victorious wizards gathered once more, but not in the company of the demon-king.

"Victory is ours," he told the surviving spellcasters. "And this land is now ours. We will become more powerful than those religious fools to the south. We shall be the power to be reckoned with." Naglatha was rapt with force of his words.

"And what of the demon," a wizard named Jorgmacdon asked, "now that we have won?"

"We called him forth, and now we will send him back," Ythazz Buvaar answered defiantly.

Naglatha lowered her head in sorrow, though, because she knew that was not to be. Her mind raced over the details of how more than a few of those wizards lost their lives in their attempts to return the demon-king to the Abyss. Baus Ilmere, the youngest among them, was sliced neatly in half by Eltab's rending claws with almost surgical precision. He was one of the luckier ones. Even Ythazz Buvaar did not escape completely unscathed. They learned at a high cost that once called, the beast could not be easily dismissed by them or anyone else, for that matter.

When she raised her head next, she was standing in the capitol of the newly created Thay. The leaders of the rebellion had chosen to name their country in honor of Thayd, who led the first uprising against Mulhorand two thousand years ago and prophesized the empire's eventual fall. Mulhorand refused to admit defeat and continued to include Thay in their maps as a part of their empire, but it was in name only to them and ridiculed by the rest of Faerûn. The Red Wizards had won their freedom. Many of the men from the Battle of Thazalhar stood united within the newly walled city as Jorgmacdon, now the first Zulkir of the School of Conjuration, strained to place the final glyph that would seal the abyssal lord beneath the city, which would forever bear his name: Eltabbar. Tremors shook the buildings, and the demon's cries of fury echoed throughout the streets.

"This is not the end," Eltab raged. "This I promise you!"

But as Jorgmacdon and the others weaved their spells, those cries grew weaker and weaker. None were able to divine a way to return him to his Abyssal Plane, but the Red Wizards were able to bind him for many years to come beneath the city's canals and waterways, whose very purpose was to be his prison.

"It is done," the exhausted zulkir proclaimed though there were still the faintest rumblings beneath their sandals. "We are free of him," he told the other Red Wizards. "And now we can build our own empire."

Naglatha smiled warmly, and her black eyes glowed at the thought of the dynamic future the country had and the possibilities that were open to these powerful men who were not afraid to wield that might. Caught up in the ecstasy, she moaned softly in her sleep.

"Mistress," a worried voice called out, "is anything amiss?"

Naglatha resisted the pull of the sound of her bodyguard. She hated the thought of awakening to find she was in a land of commerce now, populated by traders and merchants. Eventually, however, she could no longer refuse the worried queries. She opened her eyes gradually, adjusting to the light. Naglatha raised herself slightly, and the silken sheets slid down to rest on her thighs. She propped herself up by her elbows and shook her head gently, her waist-length hair falling away from her smooth face. Naglatha blinked the grains of sleep from her eyes and turned slowly toward the door of her room.

"Come," she said in answer to the insistent knocking on the heavy oak door.

A tall man, nearly six and a half feet in height, strode forcefully into the room. He moved quickly for one who carried slightly more weight on his frame than he should, and immediately surveyed the chamber. He was completely bald and had on fairly expensive servant's garb. He sported elaborate jewelry and that, coupled with his girth and clean-shaven body, created the impression that he was a eunuch from Mulhorand. It suited Naglatha to have people believe that of her servant and not recognize him as a bodyguard and a Thayan Knight.

Naglatha could see her other bodyguard, similarly outfitted, kept his station in the doorway, however, and did not enter the room. Milos Longreach had served his mistress for many years, and he knew better than to enter into her presence unless the danger was real, or if she beckoned him. Naglatha smiled at his wisdom and knew she could trust his ability to wield his massive scimitar if truly needed. She turned her attention to the other and sighed in resignation.

Heraclos the Quick was a relatively recent addition to Naglatha's stable. The previous "eunuch," who had served her well and longer than Milos, had met an untimely accident a few years back, and Naglatha had been forced to find a replacement. Heraclos had come somewhat recommended with the caveat that he needed breaking. Naglatha accepted his service, sure she could master him quickly. Unfortunately for both of them, Heraclos bore more than a few scars from her efforts at training.

"What brings you into my chamber," she demanded, "unbidden and unwashed?"

Heraclos slowly approached her bed and lowered himself to one knee. "Mistress," he offered, "I feared for your safety."

Naglatha made a show of investigating the ornate and obviously empty room before she turned her gaze back to the guard. "Explain yourself," she ordered.

With the color slowly rising to his cheeks, Heraclos said, "My lady, in my few years of service, I have never known you to fall asleep at mid-day. And so soundly, too," he added. "I know you must be weary. We made the journey back here from Selgaunt in record time, but still, when you did not answer the first of my knocks, I wondered what had happened." He lowered his head after that and awaited his mistress's punishment. He did not have to wait long.

Naglatha pulled back her bed sheets, swung her legs to the floor and withdrew a long, thin rapier she had secreted next to her. While still seated on the bed, she placed the tip of the sword under her servant's chin and raised his face with it until she caught his eye.

"You will never," she said vehemently, "enter this chamber unless you have just cause to suspect my immediate peril." The rapier made a thin hiss in the air as she sliced Heraclos up his left cheek. "Do you understand?" she questioned him in a deadly whisper.

A second hiss and blood flowed down his right cheek as well.

"Yes, Mistress," he answered submissively.

"Good," she smiled at him. "Now go and clean up. And," she added, "do not return until I summon you."

"Yes, my lady," he replied and left the chamber swiftly.

Naglatha sighed and reached over to the end of the bed, where she had carelessly tossed her robe before she had lain down for her brief nap. She slipped the rich garment over her and savored the feel of the scarlet material against her bare shoulders. Only in private did she don the clothing that marked her true station as a Red Wizard. Most of her time was spent in clandestine service of her fellow wizards, and her identity had to remain a secret. That was one of the reasons she had not shaved her head in true Thayan fashion, nor sported any visible tattoos as did many for ornamentation and protection. The other reason she did not cut her hair was because Naglatha reveled in its heavy weight and ebony color. Her hair was so black that it actually glinted blue in the right light. She was proud of her mane.

She put her arms in the air and let her head fall back, stretching the muscles along her neck and spine like a cat. When she straightened, she moved over to the heavy drapes and threw them open. Bright sunlight streamed through. Naglatha was loathe to admit to her servant that he was right: she normally didn't sleep while the sun still rode high in the sky. Then again, she had never had to return so quickly from Sembia to Thay before. She padded barefoot over to the large desk she had requested from the innkeeper to review her plans.

On one of the two chairs by the desk was a small bag. Naglatha began to empty the contents onto the writing table. As she rifled through her own belongings, she mused once again how she hated travel. Working out of Sembia and Thay was not bothersome in and of itself, only moving between the two cities and staying at inns along the way was. She longed for the comforts of her own homes, not the impersonal possessions of someone else, no matter how expensive they might be.

Naglatha removed a folded black robe. Like her red one, this cloak was also decadently soft and sumptuous. A matching mask with a strange, red insignia followed. She placed both items carefully on one of the chairs. She regarded the pile and, after a second thought, passed her hand over the collection. The robe and mask disappeared from sight, cloaked in an illusion that made them look like part of the chair. Naglatha pulled out a bundle of letters, neatly tied up. She dropped the empty satchel to the floor and sat down on that chair, untying the missives and spreading them out carefully on the wooden desk.

Most unusual was the correspondence at the top. The insignia on it was that of two clasped hands, one human and one skeletal: the mark of the Zulkir of

Necromancy, Szass Tam. Naglatha traced the design with one hand and propped up her head with the other. It was this message that had caused her to pack her belongings and make the mad dash back to Thay. A few Red Wizards knew of the presence of a secret, recruiting agent in Selgaunt by the name of The Black Flame. However, the Zulkir of Necromancy and the former chief of foreign activities, Alzegund the Trader, were the only two who knew Naglatha's true identity and understood the nature of her business there. With Alzegund dead nine years now, Szass Tam was the only one who could find her wherever she was in Selgaunt.

She read the note over again, still somewhat in shock. Szass Tam had called a meeting in the Thaymount region. What was nearly unheard of was that he had invited all the tharchions and zulkirs who were available to attend the impromptu assembly. The numbers were startling, and the fact that the lich would ask all these Red Wizards to abandon their seats of power, no matter for how short a time, was historic. There was no way Naglatha could refuse, just as she knew no one else would either, regardless of the temporary cost and the outward protests they made.

Just what are you planning, old lich, she wondered, and why?

Shaking her head, Naglatha replaced the note on the desk and sifted through the others. Some were letters sent directly to her, and some were notes that had been intercepted or stolen outright by her extensive network of spies and thieves. She had taken on the mantle of chief of foreign activities very seriously and with an aggressiveness never shown by her predecessor, Alzegund the Trader. Perhaps that was why, she often supposed, that no one looked too closely into the causes of his deadly "accident" and her sudden opportunity for advancement. Everyone, herself most of all, was pleased at the change.

She opened a small, worn register that contained the names of the Thayans who held positions of note within the borders of Thay. Naglatha had made a careful tally of each person's rank, and beside their name was one of three marks. The symbols, whose code was known only to her, signified whether that particular tharchion or zulkir was loyal, disloyal, or undecided in regards to Szass Tam. A few remained guardedly neutral and were, therefore, questionable to Naglatha. She suspected some of them would only too gladly go over to the most powerful side of the moment if the scales were tipped.

One communiqué that stood out amongst the many was a brief note from Tharchion Azhir Kren of Gauros to Tharchion Homen Odesseiron in Surthay. Naglatha unconsciously shook her head in amazement when she thought of Homen Odesseiron. She had never in her life known of anyone who had willing stepped down from the rank of Red Wizard, but he had—and he had survived. He made little secret that he preferred to spend his time maintaining and drilling a sizeable army of his own rather than maintain his spells and magics. Many knew of his hatred of Rashemen, but the tharchion did not reach his advanced age by chance. He was careful to always openly support Szass Tam's policy of trade over war and did nothing to draw the lich's attention or ire upon himself. But a few knew full well that Homen Odesseiron did not believe in the path of commerce the Zulkir of Necromancy was leading Thay down. And no one knew this better than Tharchion Azhir Kren.

Situated in the forbidding and desolate pine forest wilderness and ruined towers of Gauros, Azhir Kren was restless for battle. As an accomplished general, she looked for any excuse, short of manufacturing one, to lead Szass Tam's formidable troops against Rashemen. And Naglatha knew she was nearing the point where a fabricated slight against her was not out of the question. Both she and Homen Odesseiron felt as though they had been denied the prosperity that Szass Tam's plan had brought to many of the other Red Wizards and leaders. The letter Naglatha held in her hands was full of anger and dissatisfaction. Both tharchions felt they were no longer as powerful as they had been when Thay was more aggressive in its conquests, and both felt that an invasion was the only way they could restore their power bases. Both believed open conquest was for the overall good of Thay as well.

Naglatha ran her finger down her columns. Though it appeared that there were more friends than foes of Szass Tam on parchment, scraps of information had trickled down to Naglatha that indicated more than a few of the lich's allies might be swayed or were already on the fence. Even amongst his supporters, there was dissension. Word had come to Naglatha that Tharchion Invarri Metran of Delhumide was fearful of a Rashemen invasion. And Naglatha knew full well what fear could drive one to do. Then there was Tharchion Dimon of Tyraturos. Loyal to Szass Tam, he had become disillusioned with his faith and had recently embraced the Black Lord.

If he could lose his faith, Naglatha pondered, how hard would it be for him to lose his allegiance?

It was also no secret that there had been a falling out between the lich and Zulkir Mythrell'aa. She declared her neutrality, but Naglatha suspected she would be secretly pleased to be an instrument of the necromancer's downfall if a plan looked like it could succeed. And Tharchion Dmitra Flass was so enamored with herself and her husband that she rarely concerned herself with anything that happened outside the walls of the city that once imprisoned the demon-king Eltab.

When it comes right down to it, she mused to herself, Szass Tam was walking a fine line. How much would it really require now to knock him down?

Naglatha piled the parchments together and rubbed her eyes tiredly. She was more exhausted than she cared to acknowledge. But even though her body failed her at the moment, her mind was racing. It had been many years since Naglatha had dreamed of the birth of Thay. With all that she had been planning lately, she took the dream as a sign of things to come. She threw back her aching shoulders and shrugged off her fatigue. Now was the time for action as events aligned themselves. As a member of both the School of Illusion and Divination, Naglatha took her dreams very seriously, as they often contained portents of future events.

She was never more certain of that than she was at this moment.

Masking her stolen communiqués much in the same manner she had the disguise of The Black Flame, Naglatha moved from the desk over to the more conventional wardrobe. Opening it, she regarded the huge selection of her clothes, all neatly arranged by type and style. Each garment had been carefully straightened after her long journey. Like her hair, this was another of the Red Wizard's vanities. In fact, she wouldn't even let her two servants attend to her wardrobe, save to carry her trunks into the room. Naglatha wanted no one to touch the things closest to her body. After a moment's consideration, she pulled out a fresh tunic and pants, made from the finest spun linen and as light as a feather. While the weather of Selgaunt had still been a trifle blustery and cool, it all changed predictably when she had crossed back over into Thay. One of the reasons the country remained so fertile and kept the local granaries fat and close to bursting was the machinations of the Red Wizards. Working in tandem was the biggest problem Naglatha could see them suffer from, but they had united long enough to spin a delicate web of spells that let the mild rains fall during the night, and kept the days warm but not uncomfortable. Perfect conditions for farming and pleasant for most day-to-day activities, she mused.

Neighboring Thesk paid for Thay's comfort with tempestuous turns in their own weather, but this did not concern the Red Wizards overly much; Thesk's climate was not their problem.

Naglatha dressed carefully, keeping her colors bland and her jewelry to a bare minimum. She could not shake the feeling that something important was going to occur today, and she did not want to call attention to herself. She wanted to blend in and observe, as she was so good at doing in Selgaunt.

When she was properly attired and coiffed, a process that took nearly an hour, Naglatha called for her two bodyguards. Silently, the men entered, and she could tell immediately that they had bathed and changed their garments per her orders. They knew better than to ignore her demands. But she preferred not to acknowledge that.

"I thought I made myself quite clear earlier," she cast a pointed glare at Heraclos, "that I wanted you to be clean." He looked down at his thin cotton trousers, tunic and robe for any stain or smudges and—finding neither that nor a garment askew—then looked back at her.

Naglatha enjoyed playing with him. She sauntered over and was even more pleased when he took a slight step back at her approach. She raised her hand to his cheeks and traced the path of his newest injury. She pulled her finger back and held it in front of his face. The pad of her index finger was red, and a single ruby drop dangled there. Naglatha brought it to her lips and licked her finger clean.

"Please do better next time," she warned him with a wicked smile.

"Yes, mistress," he replied and lowered his eyes.

"Now then," she addressed them both, eager to leave. "We cannot spend all day lounging about. Have you scouted out the locations I told you to?"

"Yes, lady," Milos replied. "A few of the taverns have changed hands since we were last here. I don't think the Weeping Slave will have what you are searching for as its clientele have run decidedly downhill," he added. He turned to Heraclos, and Naglatha could see that Milos was giving him a chance to gain back some favor in his mistress's eyes. Naglatha was always surprised with Milos' desire to grant second chances. She was certain that quality would be the end of him one day, and she dreaded having to break in yet another replacement.

"He is correct, Madame," Heraclos added, sounding eager to redeem himself. "That place caters to the lowest sort, mostly drunks and cripples, and they would be of no use. I think you would be well advised to check both Laeril's Arms and The Black Unicorn."

"Really?" she drawled. "And why is that?"

"It seems that Tharchion Nymia Focar has raised the price of her little venture, and it's attracting sturdier, more adventurous types into Thay," he finished, seemingly pleased to have that bit of information to give her.

Naglatha was silent for a moment. She was well aware that the tharchions from here, Surthay, Gauros and Thazalhar had believed that there might exist a secret passage—buried somewhere in the nearby mountains—that led to the Endless Wastes beyond. Most thought it was only a foolish dream; not even a legend. Obviously, if such a passage did exist, trade might be diverted from the Golden Way, and whoever held that information would be powerful indeed. But Naglatha thought they had abandoned the search. If Nymia Focar was offering another reward, then she must have discovered a new piece of information. The woman loved the clink of coins and hated to part with them unless absolutely necessary or unless there was a sure thing. Naglatha decided this would bear watching, but also felt that the influx of outsiders here in Pyrados was most fortuitous. One more bit of information that Naglatha took as a favorable sign.

"Well then," she told her servants, "I'm suddenly very thirsty. Let's be on our way."

As she motioned to the eunuchs and followed them out, Naglatha felt her pulse quicken.

Today is the day, she thought to herself, more certain than ever.

# CHAPTER THREE

*Later That Afternoon*

Tazi sipped at her ale. As was her habit, she had managed to secure a table toward the back of the tavern. The strategy afforded her two things: a certain amount of privacy and the ability to observe almost everyone else in the room. It was something she picked up from the man she could only think of as her mentor; there was no other word to describe him adequately. She had learned many lessons in her life and most had come at a cost. However, Tazi valued all of them. For only having lived twenty-four years, she had already paid a high price for her life.

Located on the outskirts of Pyrados, the tavern catered mostly to outsiders like her. Tazi, who had secured a room upstairs after her return from the Sunrise Mountains, had spent little time in Thay proper and was now eager to return home. When she arrived in the country, she only lingered in the city long enough to obtain the appropriate permits for her foray into the mountains. Tazi hadn't wanted to pay, but she had received information from a reliable source that her trip would go that much smoother if she played by the rules. She had grudgingly handed over a fee that was practically thievery in itself for the authorization. But Tazi had passed through the garrison stationed in the foothills of the Sunrise Mountains with little trouble once she showed them her officially endorsed traveling permit.

"Coin always smoothes the way," her father had liked to say. Sometimes he had been right.

Since returning, Tazi had packed away her woolen mountaineering clothes for more familiar ones. Upon entering Pyrados, the mild temperatures made her other attire heavy, itchy and unnecessary. She now sported snug black pants with a matching vest, and boots laced up to her calves—all made from the finest leathers. Her hair hung loose, brushing her shoulders. She left her arms bare but wore short gloves and an armband that had her favorite lock pick secreted inside. From a wealthy family, Tazi only dressed like this in the seediest quarters around Selgaunt. Where she found herself now fit that bill adequately. Surreptitiously peering over the rim of her mug, Tazi scanned the room and its patrons.

Laeril's Arms, as the tavern was named, had a motley crew of customers. Though Tazi had studied only the bare necessities of Thay's customs and history, she definitely got the sense that Thayans didn't tolerate foreigners very much or for very long. The Tharchion of Pyrados, to Tazi's good fortune, didn't hold the same prejudices. Or if she did, Tazi surmised, gold helped her look past them, and that went for the store owners as well. Tazi had nearly screamed at the price she was quoted at a local shop to replace the coil of rope she had been forced to abandon on her most recent escapade. Coming from a city of trade, she was used to bartering, but that was not an option here. The shopkeepers knew they were the only game in town and happily fleeced everyone who needed to purchase supplies. She had paid the fee, hating to be without her usual equipment, but had muttered some choice oaths while she handed over the coin. The sallow-faced shop keeper simply smiled and took her gold. He had obviously heard worse.

To her left, two women were deep in discussion. By the light of the fat candle in the center of the table, Tazi saw that one was completely bald with an extensive range of tattoos along her skull and shoulders. The other, who had a thick crop of black hair, appeared to be much shorter than her companion, though it was hard to tell for certain while they were both seated. The one with the dark hair was dressed nearly as fine as the first, but Tazi could see that the bald woman regarded the other with a touch of disdain. Between them stood a young man and, judging by his slight build and stature, Tazi suspected that he had some elven blood in him. While most folk of Selgaunt despised elves, Tazi had always had a soft spot for them. Her father did too, as it turned out. A few months past, she had been shocked to discover she had a half sister who had elven blood in her veins. Life continued to throw surprises at her, but, as Tazi took another swig of her ale, most were less and less pleasant lately.

The bald woman finally tossed a small sack onto the table, toward the black-haired woman. Payment, Tazi deduced. It was only then that she noticed the elf had on a collar and a fine leash. The black-haired woman smiled to her customer and turned to the young man. She yanked so hard on his tether that she brought the elf crashing to his knees. Then she handed the leash over to the bald woman. Tazi watched, sickened, as the bald woman placed her foot upon his back and forced him to prostrate himself on the filthy tavern floor. The gaunt, bald woman regarded the other, and the two women exchanged a hearty laugh. Tazi pursed her lips and turned away. Her knuckles turned white as she clenched her mug fiercely.

Slavery, she thought with great disgust.

Closer to the bar, a group comprised mostly of humans had commandeered a large oak table. Piled on top were various supplies. Tazi could see some mountaineering equipment in addition to spelunking gear laid out. A young woman with thick, golden braids and an upturned nose was arguing heatedly with a young man about the correct way to use one of their lantern helmets. Tazi had to lower her face to keep from laughing out loud because the girl had it on backward. But Tazi could see the young man was too enamored with her to point out her mistake. And she could overhear another talking about just needing one or two more things before they left for the Sunrise Mountains.

You'd better add a pack animal to your shopping list, she thought to herself, because there is no way you four are going to be able to carry all that on your own. You'll learn, though. Tazi shook her head and wondered how anyone survived to adulthood, watching them. And she also wondered, sadly, when she had gotten so old.

The fourth member of their team was leaning against the bar, Tazi noted, talking to the same old woman Tazi had before her foray into the mountains. Obviously, the old woman spent her days here, selling the same bits of information over and over again. At least, mused Tazi, the information had been mostly useful, so perhaps the intrepid band had a small chance of success. She shifted her gaze away, however, when the man who had been pumping the old woman for directions looked her way.

A light haze drifted up as the few, regular patrons lit pipes and started in on their serious drinking. The smoke started to blur her view, and Tazi found herself thinking of the inn in Selgaunt where she kept a secret room. The owners of the Kit had treated her like a daughter, and Tazi realized she missed the place. Caught up in a flash of homesickness, she turned her gaze toward the far corner of the bar and almost gasped out loud. Standing in the shadows of the support timbers was a tall man dressed entirely in black. Taller than most humans, he appeared almost awkward in his movements, as though he was a touch uncomfortable with his long body. And in the fading daylight, Tazi could see he was completely bald. She unconsciously raised a hand to her open mouth.

How could he be here, she thought in wonder, of all places?

Starting to rise and grinning in spite of herself, Tazi saw that he was getting ready to leave. He paid the barkeep and turned toward the door. His actions afforded Tazi with a full view of his face. Like the woman who had purchased the slave, this man bore an elaborate design on his forehead. It was not the face Tazi expected and half-hoped to see. She sank back down into her chair, unaware that she had even started to stand. Not him, she thought. Not Cale...

Several months ago, her mentor had taken his leave of the Uskevren family. Circumstances had really left him no choice. Tazi had found that she didn't know how she felt about it all. She had recently grown closer to Steorf, the mage-in-training she had traveled to Calimport with, and thought very little of Cale while she had been gone. On her return home, all hell had broken loose. And, in those ashes, she had discovered that Cale had loved her all along. Tazi was torn as her emotions raged. She rejected his initial confession of love as something selfish, but she found that when it came time for his departure, she couldn't leave it that way between them. She knew, and she suspected Cale did too, that there would always be something unspoken between them. It was only when he was gone that Tazi discovered what she had been truly angry about: wasted time and wasted chances. Caught up in her daydream, she didn't notice that the Thayan she had been staring at did not appear to appreciate her attentions.

A squat barmaid with a dusky complexion and black hair moved over to Tazi's table with a rag. She wiped down the small table and checked on the level of Tazi's drink. Seeing that Tazi needed a refill, the barmaid reached over and plucked the mug from her unresisting fingers.

"Want another?"

When Tazi didn't answer immediately, the woman followed her gaze to the Thayan who was still lingering at the bar. He was starting to glower back at Tazi, but she was a thousand leagues away. The barmaid shook her head and leaned closer, as if she was taking an order.

"Listen, dearie," she spoke in a conspiratorial whisper, "you don't want to be doin' that."

"What?" Tazi finally asked, partially breaking off her daydream.

"You can't just stare at them of Mulan blood. You're beneath their station, and you don't want to make them angry at you."

"Why not?" Tazi asked in a half-interested tone.

"Because," the woman told her, "if they decide they don't like you or something you did, it's off to the magistrate you go. And you're done for."

"Thanks for the suggestion," Tazi replied. "But why bother yourself over me?" Tazi was leery of advice she hadn't solicited or paid for.

The flat-chested barmaid sighed. "Because you seem like an all right sort. You've paid your bills and haven't smashed the place up as so many of your kind do. And I think you're the sort that if you're not careful, you fall into trouble. In fact," she said, scrutinizing Tazi carefully, "you look like the kind that trouble just plain follows. And I'd prefer that it follows you somewhere else and not in my father's place. Another round?"

Tazi nodded numbly, the words "father's place" ringing in her ears, as the barmaid walked away. She slipped back into the past—to the day she left her father's place to come here. Tazi's gear had also been spread out on her bed, much like the youngsters' at the inn, as she conducted a last inventory. Counting off crampons, Tazi was startled at Steorf's unannounced entrance.

"Where are you going?" he had demanded.

"To do what I have to," Tazi had replied in a clipped tone. Her hackles had risen immediately at his intrusion. Just because she and the blond-haired mage had grown closer did not mean that they shared a bed, regardless of what others thought. And Tazi had not given him free run of her private rooms.

"You're going to follow him, aren't you?" he accused her. Tazi noticed that Steorf avoided using Cale's name whenever possible.

"No, I'm not," she answered more softly when she realized he was acting out of jealously.

"Then why won't you let me come with you?" he asked, calming himself down as well.

"Because this is something I have to do for myself," she had told him honestly. "Please understand that. Besides," she had joked in an effort to lighten the somber mood, "you have studies to complete."

"They don't matter anymore," he had said darkly. Tazi had frowned at his words a little. Since they had returned from Calimport, she had noticed he was quieter than he had ever been. And there were times she felt certain he was hiding something from her. She had resolved then that when she returned from Thay, she was going to find out what was going on. But she had to come to Thay before all else.

"Well, that may be, but I have to go alone. It's the only way to make it right," was all she had offered him by way of an explanation. She recalled how his steel-gray eyes had softened at her entreaty.

"I'm not sure exactly what you mean," he had replied, "but I think I understand. Would you do me one favor, though?"

She had moved to stand next to his large frame and had looked up into his eyes. "If I can, I will," she had promised.

"Wear this and think of me." Before Tazi could say or do anything, Steorf had fastened a thin, silver chain around her neck. Tazi craned her head down to get a better look at the unexpected gift.

Dangling on the end of the delicate necklace was a shard of an amethyst gem. The stone was all that Tazi had left to remind her of her fateful journey to Calimport and of the friend she had sacrificed there for a greater good.

"How did you get this?" she had wondered in amazement. "I've kept it locked up ever since we returned."

For the first time since entering her rooms, Steorf looked slightly pleased. "You're not the only accomplished thief," he reminded her, "or have you forgotten some of my other skills?"

Tazi had smiled up at him. "It's lovely," she whispered. "But it looks so fragile. Maybe I should leave it here."

Steorf placed his large hand over the stone and against Tazi's throat. "Don't worry," he had assured her, "I've seen to it that the chain won't fail." He ran his finger along the edge of the silver. "It's much like you. It looks delicate, but it is as strong as forged steel."

Smiling, Tazi played with the chain unconsciously as she sat at her table, unaware of the fetching picture she presented. The young man who had been gathering information nodded to the old barfly and approached Tazi's table.

"Successful?" he inquired as he sat down opposite Tazi.

"Excuse me?" Tazi demanded, perturbed that her daydream had been interrupted and that he dared to sit down uninvited.

The young man was undaunted by her sharp tone.

"You have the look of a cat that's swallowed the song bird," he told her.

Even through her irritation, Tazi could see the young man was pleased with his turn of a phrase.

"I do, do I?"

"Well," he added and brushed some of his auburn hair away from his face. Tazi could see he had a scar along one cheek. "As I understand it, you've just returned from the Sunrise Mountains."

"And how do you know that?" Tazi asked, playing with him a bit and knowing full well the crone had sold her out.

"My informants are well connected," he replied sagely.

"Your informants are everybody's informants for enough coin," Tazi shot back at him. She noted he had the good sense to look somewhat abashed.

"Never mind that," he tried to change his tack. "My name is Gaed Attimthree, and I have an offer to make you." He studied her earnestly with his hazel eyes.

"And what might that be?" Tazi asked, enjoying the game in spite of herself. She leaned forward expectantly. The young man became flustered under her scrutiny.

"My friends and I," he motioned half-heartedly in the direction of the mountain of gear, "are getting ready to travel the road you've just returned from. You may have heard of Tharchion Nymia Focar's generous offer for the path through the mountains to the Endless Wastes. My companions and I are certain we can find it, and we would gladly share a portion of the reward with you."

"Then why do you need me? You'd only have to cut the pot more?"

"As you can see, my friends and I are well supplied. We don't like to take any chances, and I would be a fool to pass up the opportunity to have someone with me who was as experienced as you obviously are."

Tazi smirked at his lame attempt at flattery. "It's obvious that you are well prepared," she answered and suppressed a chuckle at his ineptness, "with the finest supplies that coin can buy. You don't need to buy me."

"I didn't mean..." he trailed off helplessly.

"No offence taken," she told him, "but I'm not interested."

"I understand," he finally replied. "Since this is our last night before we leave, perhaps I could buy you another drink and you might share some of your travels with me. Any detail would be helpful." And Tazi noticed a shift in his look.

"I'm fine. Besides, these days I travel alone, and I prefer it that way," she told him and motioned her mug toward her mouth. She hoped her tone would indicate that as far as she was concerned, the interview was over. But the hazel-eyed man just leaned in.

"If it's too crowded here," he said softly, "we could go up to my rooms. I could give you my undivided attention." He tilted his head.

Tazi sat straighter and replied more forcefully, "I don't think so." The young man obviously fancied himself a ladies' man.

"No?" he asked.

Tazi smiled sweetly and let her hand fall to her boot. Just as the would-be suitor leaned in even closer to her, Tazi brought back her hand with lightning speed. When her fist reappeared, she had a knife in it.

Balancing the point of her razor-sharp dagger on her index finger, Tazi bounced the mean weapon from one finger to the next, all the while staring at the young adventurer.

His face paled so suddenly that Tazi could see a smattering of freckles across his nose stand out in sharp contrast. Whether it was her easy proficiency with the small blade or the hard glint in her eye, he finally got the message.

"I understand," he said as he hastily rose to feet. "No means no." And as he scurried back over to his friends, Tazi laughed.

She leaned her chair back against the wall and slid her blade back in place. As she continued to sip her ale, she glanced around the room. Judging by the furtive looks that met hers and the quickly downcast eyes, Tazi was certain she had made her point. She was sure that no one else would trouble her this evening. However, Tazi didn't notice the pair of coal-black eyes that remained steady and gleamed with interest.

Naglatha was finally impressed. For the last hour, she and her two bodyguards had been observing the inn's customers. They had stopped at The Black Unicorn first, but Naglatha had been disappointed beyond words by the dismal selection of potential candidates. She had verbally abused both of her Thayan Knights for their ineptitude in reconnaissance. By the time they reached Laeril's Arms, she was certain she was not the only one who had a vested interest in success; the servants now knew they would pay a steep price if there was no better luck at this tavern.

Located at a table against the wall opposite from Tazi, Naglatha had initially only caught glimpses of the woman during her survey of the tavern. She first noticed Tazi's black hair. She would never admit it, but Naglatha was a vain creature, and when she met or observed another woman, she always looked to her hair first. It stemmed from the fact that most Thayan women of Mulan heritage were bald or artificially devoid of hair. Only slaves were not allowed to cut their tresses. Even the Thayans of Rashemi extraction cropped their locks as close to their scalp as possible to separate themselves from the enormous slave population. So, Naglatha's interest was piqued when she saw another woman with long, black hair that was clean and healthy like hers. Of course, she thought, it's not as long as mine.

The other aspect that initially intrigued Naglatha was that the woman sat by herself. And she didn't sit like someone waiting for another person to join her; she sat alone but not lonely. Naglatha had made herself a mental note—the woman bore watching. But, in the course of her perusals, not many of the other patrons appeared very promising. They all looked too young and too inexperienced. Eventually, she had turned her attention back toward the black-haired girl, who appeared to be a bit younger than she was, just in time to see her handiness with the tiny dagger.

"Subtle, discreet, and she gets her message across

with minimal effort or show," she whispered approvingly to Milos Longreach. Naglatha tried to get a better look at the woman, shifting her head from one side to the other, endeavoring to see past the regulars seated in front of her.

After a few more moments, the customers finished their drinks and left, affording Naglatha with her first, unrestricted view of the young woman. Naglatha nearly gasped out loud. What she discovered was totally unexpected. She *knew* the woman. Though Naglatha was no mathematician, she was aware that the chances of that were almost astronomical. She couldn't stop her thoughts traveling back to earlier in the day and her dream of Thay's creation.

"To have had that dream," she murmured, "and to discover her here, with all the ramifications that this discovery heralds, is not possible. Unless this is exactly how it is supposed to happen."

"Mistress?" Milos questioned. Naglatha was not normally given to randomly speaking aloud, so she forgave him his impropriety.

"It is nothing," she assured him, and she beckoned to her younger bodyguard.

"Heraclos," she said softly, "I need your assistance."

"Anything," he replied properly, "and everything at your wish." The instructions that followed were inaudible to everyone else but Heraclos. She spoke so softly, she was sure even Milos was not able to hear her words. Heraclos nodded quickly, and Naglatha knew he would do his best to fulfill them. Naglatha repositioned herself in her chair, arms folded, and smiled wickedly. What was about to happen next was critical.

Her bodyguard made his way across the large, poorly lit room and stopped a few feet short of Tazi's small table. Naglatha placed one finger against her lower lip and watched the scene unfold with growing excitement. She could see Heraclos motion to the empty seat opposite Tazi and say something. The woman declined to let him join, as Naglatha knew she would. After all, she had made it clear to all those around her that she was unavailable. Then Heraclos leaned in closer, placing his hand under Tazi's chin, and Naglatha leaned forward in her chair out of anticipation. Heraclos tilted Tazi's head up slightly. His face was only a few inches from the woman's ear, and Naglatha had a good notion of the offer he was making. In fact, she had suggested a few descriptives she knew were guaranteed to provoke any woman, whether they were barmaid or noble. In the ruddy glow of the candle on her table, Tazi's face twisted in anger. Naglatha had to hold back a laugh. It was perfect.

Tazi reacted as if on cue. As soon as Heraclos propositioned Tazi, Naglatha watched her hand drop to her boot once more. Faster than anyone could follow, Tazi had the blade unsheathed and under Heraclos's chin with deadly precision. Naglatha saw, from her vantage point, that Tazi had even drawn blood. That was the signal she had given Heraclos to move forward.

"You dare strike me?" Heraclos demanded indignantly.

Before the first drop of his blood hit Tazi's grimy

table, Heraclos had shrugged off his expensive cloak and revealed a large scimitar sheathed at his waist. He drew it with deadly precision. Naglatha saw that he wasted no time. With incredible force, he brought the sword screaming down at Tazi, splitting the oak table right down the center. At the same time, Tazi pushed away from the splintered table, crashing with her chair to the floor. She used her momentum to summersault backward and away from Heraclos's imminent threat. When she rose to her feat, Tazi had one of her Sembian guardblades withdrawn.

Heraclos pivoted and swung his blade with both hands. Tazi parried the blow. At the sound of crashing steel, the other patrons had stopped their activities and turned to watch the excitement. Naglatha was quite sure that it was not the first time a brawl of this nature had erupted here. In fact, her own table leg looked as though it had only been recently repaired. She suspected the break had nothing to do with the heavy food they served at the tavern.

Heraclos easily outweighed her by over a hundred pounds, and Naglatha was curious to see how Tazi handled herself against a larger opponent who had the advantage of surprise on his side. Her bodyguard did not give Tazi a moment to catch her breath. While Naglatha knew he lacked the finesse and overall skill that Milos possessed with the scimitar, he never tired in his assaults. Each of her two servants had his strengths, and they were learning to work together over time. Naglatha considered sending the older bodyguard into the fray as well, but she knew they didn't have much time. Fights as destructive as this one was shaping up to be invariably brought the attention of the local enforcers. Naglatha could see some of the tavern's clients leaving already, some afraid to be around when the reinforcements arrived.

A cowardly lot, Naglatha reflected disgustedly, and not a single one of you raise your hand to help the girl. Naglatha even thought she saw the auburn-haired man that Tazi had so eloquently rejected smile at her misfortune as he gathered his companions and gear and hastily retreated up the wide staircase that led to the rooms above. Fools, she thought.

Tazi matched each of Heraclos's blows, but Naglatha could see that her bodyguard was forcing Tazi back. The two knocked over tables and chairs in their deadly ballet, but Tazi never cried out once for aid. Naglatha suspected the girl wouldn't as, technically, she had started the fracas. You take care of your own problems, don't you? Naglatha deduced. Good.

Heraclos forced Tazi toward the stairs with a series of blows that grew in intensity. It was clearly visible to Naglatha that her candidate was tiring. She appeared so fatigued that she was unaware of her surroundings and tripped on the wide stairs behind her. Tazi fell back onto the staircase and lost her sword. Heraclos raised his scimitar high overhead and swung the huge blade whistling down. Naglatha momentarily thought she might have to interview another candidate until Tazi hugged herself and rolled quickly to her right. The force of Heraclos's swing was so strong, his blade became momentarily embedded in the stairs.

Tazi used the opportunity, as she lay stretched out on the steps, to kick savagely at his knee. The blow was enough to topple Heraclos, and it gave Tazi the chance to bolt up and rush past him. By the time he had recovered his feet and his blade, Tazi had retrieved hers as well and the duel continued.

With all the patrons gone, they had the run of the bar. Naglatha watched as Tazi, who must have found her second wind, danced around Heraclos. She jumped onto chairs and swung around support timbers, making good use of whatever shields she could find to block his powerful arm. Resourceful, Naglatha said to herself, and she was more certain than ever that this woman was the one she needed.

Heraclos's color rose in his face, and Naglatha suspected it was not just because of the physical exertion of the swordfight. He was becoming enraged at the girl who spun around him and was still standing despite his best efforts. What expertise he had mastered was evidently lost under his growing anger. Naglatha saw that his attacks were becoming more bullish. He was relying on his strength alone, a shortcoming Naglatha had pointed out to him on more than one occasion.

His pendulous swings forced Tazi to back peddle toward Naglatha and her other bodyguard. Naglatha nodded to Milos, and they made an expedient retreat behind the bar. Heraclos continued to push Tazi back to the now-abandoned table in the corner. She rolled backward along the length of the table and landed on the floor in front of Naglatha's empty chair. Heraclos leaped onto the tabletop and stomped his way to the end where Tazi was crouching. Naglatha saw the woman look around and suddenly smile a lopsided grin. She kicked out at the mended leg, which gave way at once. As the table listed to one corner, Heraclos lost his balance. He dropped his scimitar as his arms pinwheeled about in a frantic attempt to keep his footing. It was no use, and he crashed back full length onto the table. He was dazed and breathless. Tazi did not waste the chance.

She braced her left hand against the cockeyed table and placed the tip of her blade up under his chin with the other. Breathing hard, Tazi cocked back her sword arm but then stopped. Naglatha was prepared to lose the bodyguard as an unfortunate business expense; however, she was surprised at her candidate's lack of action at that point. Naglatha could see hesitation cross Tazi's features, and she deduced that killing did not come easy to the raven-tressed woman. It was something to note.

Before Tazi was forced to make a decision, a small garrison of the tharchion's guards burst into the tavern. The five well-equipped men rushed over to Tazi and Heraclos. Two of them seized Tazi, each grabbing one arm and pulled her away from the prostrate servant. Naglatha smiled at Tazi's shock as they yanked her roughly to the bar. She argued with them and struggled. Naglatha was certain that if they had arrived earlier, Tazi would have put up a better fight, but she was clearly winded now. They slammed her against the bar and pinned her there while their comrades helped Heraclos to his feet. Naglatha's other bodyguard used the commotion to retrieve and secret Heraclos's fallen scimitar.

"I was defending myself," Tazi sputtered to her captors. Naglatha smirked at her distress. "He left me no choice."

"Shut yer mouth," one of the guards snarled back at her.

"I have a right," she demanded. "Ask that woman over there," Tazi demanded and nodded in Naglatha's direction. "She saw the whole thing."

Naglatha slowly walked over to the captain of the tharchion's garrison, who was standing a few feet in front of Tazi. The other two guards had walked Heraclos back over to Milos, and they remained stationed there. Naglatha could see Tazi's face brighten as she turned to look first to the guard on her right and the one on her left with a certain amount of smug satisfaction. It was obvious she was certain Naglatha's testimony would absolve her of blame. As she looked toward the Red Wizard incognito, Naglatha returned her smile warmly.

"Milady," the captain addressed her, "what has transpired here?"

Naglatha looked at Tazi and watched the captive woman stand straighter in expectation. She turned to the captain and replied, "I am glad that you and your men arrived when you did. This was an extremely unfortunate situation and entirely my fault." She paused and regarded Tazi once more. She could see the younger woman's confidence grow.

"I had been warned about the types that frequent

establishments like these, but I was certain I would not have trouble since I was accompanied by my servants. As you can see," Naglatha paused and pointed to Heraclos and Milos, "my eunuchs are hardly a match for anyone, unarmed and so obviously out-of-shape as they are."

"What?" Tazi shouted, and the guard who had warned her to be silent struck her in the mouth.

"Milady," the captain responded, "I am only sorry we could not have arrived before your property was damaged. We will see to it that this ruffian is properly punished." Then he tipped his head deferentially to Naglatha and turned in militaristic fashion toward his men.

"Take her," he ordered. The men restraining Tazi started to drag her toward the main door. She pulled at her captors as they hauled her away, and she twisted her torso to look back at Naglatha.

"That's not how it happened," she shouted at the Red Wizard.

As they yanked her out the doorway, Naglatha waved farewell sweetly to the furious woman.

"Just perfect," she whispered.

# CHAPTER FOUR

**T**azi stood in the center of a small chamber with her arms bound behind her at the wrists and a guard flanking her on each side. Her lip, where the guard had struck her at the tavern, had finally stopped bleeding. Only a thin trail of dried blood remained between the corner of her mouth and her chin. She looked calm, but Tazi was seething inside. She had been standing roughly in the same spot for over an hour and hadn't been allowed to move or speak during that time.

The room she had been taken to was in one of the inner studies of Pyrados's magistrate's office. It was dark and somber, devoid of any windows. Along three of the four walls were floor to ceiling bookcases in a rich, ebony wood. A few sconces dotted the walls and cast odd shadows along the tomes and floor. It reminded Tazi of one of her father's rooms, crammed full and somewhat stuffy. Each shelf was bursting with scrolls and manuscripts, but Tazi doubted that Thay could actually possess that many laws and bylaws. She wondered if, along with the black wood, the shelves of books were meant to intimidate the less intelligent of those dragged before the 'court.' Tazi refused to be such a victim.

She stood facing a large desk, almost like a podium, made of the same wood as the bookcases. It was set on a raised section of the floor, similar to a dais, so when the magistrate sat behind it, he always looked down on whoever was brought before him. All she could see of the official who was perched back there was his bald, wrinkled head with its single tattoo and his cloaked shoulders. The Thayan sat bent over some documents that he was ostensibly reading through, accounts of various transgressions, Tazi imagined. She had tried to crane her neck once to get a better look and was cuffed for it. She kicked at the guard who did it and was struck again. She had settled down over the last hour, realizing that struggling at this moment was not in her best interests.

Her weapons, including her boot dagger and even her lock pick, rested on a small table to her left. Her worn, leather sack containing the crimson gold was also amongst her things, and she occasionally cast a longing eye toward them. But one of the guards caught the direction of her gaze and moved closer to Tazi. She knew she had little chance of retrieving her weapons quickly and decided it wasn't worth the risk for now. Not for the first time since she was taken into custody, Tazi berated herself for not paying closer attention to the Rashemi barmaid back at Laeril's Arms.

She tried to warn me, Tazi thought morosely, about how things worked here. I should have listened more closely. I should have had a plan just in case. The magistrate's artificial cough snapped her back to her present situation.

"I have given this matter a great deal of thought and consideration," the older man began as he opened a large ledger and made a show of selecting a quill.

About an hour's worth, Tazi mused to herself. And never once talked to me.

"It is fairly clear that a terrible crime was committed," he continued, unaware of Tazi's internal monologue, "and reparations must be made. In addition, suitable punishment must be meted out. It is the law, after all." He began to scratch some words onto the parchment pages.

Unbidden, Tazi responded, "I agree with you. I was assaulted."

The old man looked up. It was plain to see he did not appreciate what he viewed as an interruption and continued speaking. "Because you, young woman, did visit damage upon the property of a high-ranking Thayan citizen, all your goods and possessions are now forfeit."

"What?" Tazi shouted. She made a step toward the desk, and the guards pulled her back. "You can't just take my things."

"They will go to the woman whose goods you damaged as her compensation," he explained. "Furthermore, injuring the property of a citizen is the same as injuring the citizen herself, and that is a grave offense in these lands. Because of that," he paused dramatically and looked Tazi straight in the eye, "it is the decree of this court—"

"How can you call this a court?" Tazi demanded. "I never heard the details of my 'crime,' never heard the woman I supposedly injured tell her side of it, and I never got to tell my accounting." She shrugged out of her captors' grasp and moved right over to the desk and stared up at the official defiantly. "Just what kind of court is this? Please explain that."

The two armed men each grabbed a shoulder, but did little else to Tazi other than to pull her back to her original spot. She suspected they were simply saving up their anger for later and didn't even want to contemplate that. Blackly, she saw only one way out and she detested playing that game. But she recognized she was running out of any other options.

"As I was saying," the official continued as though there had been no outburst, "it is the decision of this court to commit you to eternal service to Thayan country and people."

"Slavery?" Tazi sputtered. "I don't think so!"

"You may now have an opportunity to say your last words for the record before you cease to exist as a person," the magistrate magnanimously allowed and held his pen poised over his ledger.

Tazi bit back on the first thing that came to mind,

knowing that it would be a mistake to say. She reigned in her temper and pulled out her trump card, though she hated to have to resort to it.

"How much?" she asked simply. "How much will it take?"

"Excuse me?" the magistrate questioned her, genuinely shocked.

"I have coin," she told him.

"That pittance over there?" he asked and pointed to the pile of Tazi's effects on the small table. "Perhaps I spoke too quickly for you to understand. That now belongs to the Thayan citizen you assaulted. It is no longer yours to bargain with."

"No," Tazi sighed. "I have access to a near limitless amount of funds. I am Thazienne Uskevren of Selgaunt. My family will gladly pay whatever price you can dream up to free me. Name it, and it's yours."

"You *were* Thazienne Uskevren," the old man corrected her. "Now you are the property of Thay."

"No," Tazi said and struggled against the men who restrained her. "I am not! My family will find me," she warned him, "and there will be hell to pay! Trust me on that!"

"Let me explain something to you: you have broken Thayan law. You have been tried and found guilty. You have now been punished and no longer exist as a person in your own right. Do you understand?"

"They will find me," she warned him.

"Even if they could, which I seriously doubt," the magistrate wheezed, "there is nothing for them to do. You are a slave, and slavery in Thay means in perpetuity."

Tazi cocked her head at the pronouncement.

"You are a slave and will die a slave. The decree is irreversible by our laws. And should you and another ever mate, any issue of yours will be a slave, as will their issue and their issue's issue until time's end. Slavery here in Thay is final."

Tazi blanched at the ramifications of the decree. It was most definitely not how she had expected the situation to resolve itself. For the moment, she was at a loss as to how to proceed. However, as a slave, that was not even a concern of hers any longer. She had lost all rights and others would decide what she could and could not do from then on. Tazi could not fathom the turn fate had taken.

"You may remove her now and take her to the pens," he ordered. The guards began to tug her from the magistrate's study. Tazi tried to dig in her heals and slow them down. "I'm not done yet," she shouted over her shoulder.

The magistrate closed his ledger and shot her a deadly look. "I am finished here," he told her. "And so are you, Thazienne Uskevren."

The two guards dragged Tazi out into the cool, evening air. The distant roll of thunder echoed, and Tazi half-consciously realized that the nightly rains were about to commence. The Thayan sentries took her through to a rather large building annexed to the magistrate's offices. To Tazi, it looked like nothing so much as a grandiose stable. After the initial shock of her sentence, Tazi was numb. Now, her mind was thawing, and she began to study her surroundings very carefully.

Two other men stood guard in front of a pair of large double doors. One of her escorts approached them, and he and they exchanged a word. Tazi supposed it was a password of sorts, but she suspected that as the two easily recognized each other, the safeguard was merely a formality. The two doormen slid the long beam aside that secured the doors across the center and swung them in for Tazi and her party. She was shoved into the black maw, and the first thing that struck Tazi was the smell. It was beyond nauseating. As her hands were still bound behind her back, she couldn't block her nose, but she stopped in her tracks and turned her head aside, her face twisted in disgust. The guard who struck her earlier, obviously used to the smell of human waste and sickness, laughed as he shoved her harder.

"Sorry to offend yer sensibilities, 'milady,' " he mocked. He and his cohort exchanged a raucous laugh.

As they pushed her through the building which had been a stable for centaurs some years past, Tazi was horrified at what she saw. The whole structure was two hundred feet long and one hundred fifty feet wide. There were rows and rows of former stalls. These stalls had been converted into pens of steel and wood. The metal bars were woven so that each cluster of folk could see the other captives, and there were a few openings in each cage to allow small articles to be passed in and out by the guards and the occupants within. But the pens were placed just far enough apart so that the slaves could not reach their neighbors. Nevertheless, Tazi could see that some tried.

The first pen she passed held four men inside and one small girl. All of them were nearly naked and Tazi was shocked by how thin the girl was. Every one of her ribs was clearly visible under skin that looked like it had been stretched too tight. She was whimpering slightly, but none of the adult men raised a hand or offered a word in comfort. They were sitting about with dull, listless eyes.

In the pen adjacent to theirs, which held two women, that was not the same case. One of the prisoners, with matted hair that might have been the same color as the little girl's, strained her thin arm through the cage and called out a name. Tazi winced when she saw the festering wounds on the woman's arm. She had rubbed it raw trying to comfort what Tazi guessed must have been her daughter. One of the guards stationed intermittently along the aisle leaned across and hit the woman with a short staff.

Tazi's escorts pushed her along the poorly lit aisle. Only a few torches were blazing, scattered sporadically through the stable. Underneath the smell of vomit and waste, she could also detect the odor of damp decay. She rightly suspected that these stables were never even given the most basic maintenance, not even mucking. Anger and disgust filled her up and pushed aside any fear she might have felt, however fleeting. Now, in a red haze, Tazi was searching for any way out. If she had still possessed her lock pick, the cage itself would have been simple enough. Though a heavy length of chain and a large padlock sealed off the cage door, the locks were old and rusty. Tazi recognized the style and knew they presented no challenge, but she was empty handed. She suspected her best time to flee would be when the guards actually unlocked the pen.

However the deeper she went into the stable, the more difficult she found it to scheme. The conditions only worsened. Just like the first set of pens, obvious families were kept apart. The better to demoralize them, Tazi thought. And each prisoner was nearly nude, their emaciated bodies covered by varying degrees of sores. It was a rag-tag collection as well. Not only were there humans imprisoned, but halflings and other creatures Tazi could not easily recognize, partly because of the poor lighting and partly because of their filth. Only one or two looked up as she was marched past. Tazi was overwhelmed by their unresponsive, sunken eyes. Her jaw was beginning to ache because she had it clenched so tight. The buying and selling of living creatures was something she could never reconcile herself with, and these images were beyond haunting. As she neared the end of the aisle, her captors stopped her and spun her to face one of the pens.

"Yer new home," sneered the guard

Tazi was only able to see one other occupant. All she could make out was a small, dark shape in the far corner of the ten-foot-by-ten-foot cage. Before she could do or say anything, one of the guards spun her around again and slammed her back against the cage door. It was the one who had hit her earlier. He pushed her so hard into the door that her hands were bruised against the cage bars. His sweaty face was only a few inches from hers. And there was no mistaking the leer on it.

"Well, 'milady,' " he said, "as you may have noticed, you're a bit overdressed for your accommodations."

"Am I?"

"I've been waiting for this since we took you from the tavern," he sneered. "All right then, uniform of the day," he ordered.

With callused hands, the lecherous guard grabbed the top of Tazi's laced vest and started to tear it open. Tazi wasted no time. She grabbed a hold of the metal crossbar with her bound hands and braced herself. Then she brought up her left knee straight between his legs. The guard released his grip and staggered back, cupping himself and cursing. Still gripping the bar for support, Tazi swung her right leg around full force and caught the pain-blinded guard solidly on his chin. He fell to the floor, semi-conscious. She released her hold on the bars and started to run, but the other escort, still laughing about his friend's condition, lost no time catching Tazi from behind.

He wrapped his arms around her in a powerful bear hug. She slammed her head back into his forehead and brought her right boot down on his foot, crushing at least one of his toes in the process. He loosened his hold, and Tazi slipped free. By this time, though, some of the other guards had arrived, and Tazi, bound and unarmed, was outnumbered. As the reinforcements started to unlock her pen, the first guard had recovered enough to charge at her with a murderous gleam in his eye.

Two of the others stopped him.

"Let it go," one of them said to the enraged guard. "She'll get hers soon enough. Remember?" he finished, and Tazi wondered at the last, cryptic remark. The injured guard shrugged his way out of his comrades' restraining grip.

"All right," he muttered. He stared at Tazi once more and seemed mollified at the thought of her "getting" hers. His foul humor was almost restored by the time he helped his partner up.

"Let's get a drink," Tazi heard him tell the other, and they sauntered off.

The remaining guard swung open the cage door and pushed Tazi inside. With her hands still bound behind her, she lost her balance and fell to the dirt floor. As she struggled to turn around, she heard the ominous snap of the lock's closure.

"Damn."

Tazi squirmed around on her backside to get a better look at her cellmate. The dark figure remained in the corner of the cage and. Judging by its size, Tazi suspected it was another child. She was certain he or she must have been terrified.

"It's all right," she said soothingly. "I'm not going to hurt you. I was only hurting those men so that we could get away."

Thinking that her words had made the child feel

safe, Tazi watched as the small shape separated itself from the shadowy corner and moved slowly a few feet into the dim light. She gasped in surprise at her error: her roommate was not a child at all, but a dwarf.

Tazi initially thought the dwarf must have been a prisoner for a long time. His coloring looked terribly off. She assumed it was a male because it had a ratty beard, but she wasn't sure. Tazi remembered Cale had once told her that some of the females sported them as well. He was very gaunt compared to the few dwarves she had met in her life.

"They've gone for now," she told him. She moved her bound arms a little and said, "Could you help me untie my hands?"

The dwarf squatted down and turned his back to her. Tazi was taken aback because she had initially thought he was scared and that was the reason why he was unable to help her. Now, as she got a better look at him, she changed her mind. His coloring, she realized, was not off. It was naturally gray. And even though he was not as stocky as the other dwarves she knew, Tazi could see his arms were wiry and muscled. He wasn't wasted; that was his natural state. Tazi searched her memory and came up with a name: duergar. He wouldn't help her, if what she had heard about the creatures was even partially true.

She shrugged and moved to her knees. Tazi stretched her arms down as far as possible and sat back, fitting her backside between the circle of her tied arms. She straightened her legs in the air and formed a **V** with her body. She passed her bound hands under the length of her legs and over her feet so that they were in front. The leather thong that tied them together had a piece that dangled somewhat. Grabbing it with her teeth, she started the process of pulling it apart.

Between mouthfuls of leather, she grumbled at the dwarf, "This would go much faster with a little bit of help, you know." The only response she got was best described as a snort.

Once her hands were free, she resisted the urge to throw the line away in anger. Instead, she tucked it in her waistband, thinking to herself that she never knew when it might come in handy. Tazi massaged her wrists, and winced at the raw spots. As she circled her arms around in an effort to restore the circulation, she regarded her cellmate once more.

He wore a tight, long-sleeved tunic and pants, though they were both ragged. Tazi wondered how he had managed to keep his attire. Everyone else she had seen was nude. Then she realized she had kept her own clothes, so perhaps he had put up a good fight as well. Like most dwarves, he had hair around the side of his head but was bald on top. His beard was short and hung in little, matted braids. The brief glance he had given her revealed he had the blackest eyes. Tazi tried once more to make conversation.

"How long have you been here?" she asked.

Silence.

Tazi decided to give up for the moment. She settled her back against one of the cage walls and started to watch the guards, learning their patterns.

After an hour, Tazi straightened as a guard approached, carrying something at waist height. On closer inspection, it turned out to be a tray. He stopped at her cell and placed the tray on the ground near one of the small, deliberate openings between the bars.

"Back away," he ordered Tazi and the duergar. When they obliged, the sentinel slipped two bowls into the cell, picked up his tray and continued to make his way down the aisle. Tazi watched as he repeated the same steps at each pen.

The dwarf snatched one of the bowls and moved to the far corner of the pen. By the sound of the slurps, Tazi guessed the stuff was edible. She picked up the remaining bowl and sniffed it. It would never win any cooking awards, but it smelled all right. She sipped it experimentally and realized the broth was little more than lukewarm water. Tazi began to understand why the others were so emaciated. Not sure when the next serving might arrive, Tazi gulped hers down. The guard returned to collect the dishes, and they doused the torches as they passed.

The dwarf continued to ignore her, and she pillowed her head on her arms and lay down for a few hours of sleep. After that, she would figure out what to do next.

Tazi awoke suddenly. Lying on her side, she pushed herself upright and leaned on one arm. Blinking sleep from her eyes, she looked around. For one moment, she was disoriented. She didn't know if it was day or night. Only a distant torch flickered, providing little illumination. As soon as Tazi spotted the bars though, she remembered everything.

A shuffling sound drew her attention to the door of her cage—the same sound that had roused her. Tazi jumped to a squatting position and placed both her hands on the ground in front of her. From outside the pen, she recognized the murmur of the lecherous guard's voice. He was chuckling softly about something with his cohort. Tazi heard them grapple with something decidedly metallic and realized they were fumbling with the lock to her prison. Then there was the telltale *snick* as the lock disengaged.

Come to finish me off, she wondered silently, or perhaps take up where you left off on my vest? Tazi decided to remain silent; better to let them think she was asleep and give her the advantage, however brief. Her breathing quickened, and she tensed. She recognized that their amorous advances might yet prove her means of escape.

Come on then, boys, she thought. Come on.

The heavy shuffling continued, and Tazi found herself squinting, straining to see what was going on. The noise didn't sound like the men moving about. She turned to see if the dwarf was awake as well, but she couldn't tell in the darkness. Tazi cursed to herself and planned on working alone. A strange gurgle puzzled her, and she didn't know what to make of the sound other than knowing it was in her pen. In a burst of light, the mystery was solved.

The guards relit most of the gutted torches. By their flames, Tazi had her answer. Lumbering just inside the pen was a creature almost eight feet tall. It was covered in short, gray-green fur, mottled in a few places. The body was generally humanoid, but its hands ended in claws. It had a yellowish mane and the head was hyenalike blended with something else. Instead of a canine snout, the creature's nose resembled a pig's snout. The creature was much beefier than any gnoll she'd ever come across—obviously well fed. She deduced that the animal was someone's creation, a wizard's experiment or even his pet. It was covered in rags and makeshift bits of armor. A sword dangled from its belt, but Tazi knew that weapon was not what made the gnoll dangerous. What made it truly lethal was the fact that someone, the guards more than likely, had taken a smoldering stick and put out its eyes.

There were other wounds, but none as severe as the ones to its face. It clawed at them piteously. She inched back and turned to check on the dwarf once again. In the torchlight, she could see that the duergar was very aware of their predicament. Even with an ally, they were both still unarmed. Backing toward the dwarf, she faced the monster holding her breath.

For one moment, no one moved.

The lecherous guard let out a sudden whoop, and his friend moved around the cage near Tazi and the dwarf. He rammed his longstaff in toward the gnoll and jabbed it in an open wound at its side. The now-enraged beast moved toward Tazi, flailing its claws.

The other guards surrounded the cage, calling and

shouting. Tazi thought they were trying to anger the beast until she heard numbers—they were calling out bets, wagering on how quickly she and the dwarf would die. As the gnoll lumbered closer, Tazi tossed aside all other thoughts and focused on the threat before her.

Another jab incited the beast further. It charged Tazi and the dwarf. They split up and each ran to a different side of the cage. The gnoll smashed into the bars and howled. The guards stabbed at it further, only this time the gnoll stayed in place and swung its long arms around him, trying to strike its tormentors. Tazi and the dwarf met up on the other side of the pen.

"If you can maneuver behind it and get low," Tazi whispered to him, "I think I could knock it over. A good crash into the metal bars, and we might be able to knock it senseless." The dwarf just ignored her.

The sentries stopped their torture of the gnoll, and it turned toward Tazi like the beast was regaining its bearings somewhat. It stood tall and raised its odd snout in the air. It snuffled from one side and the other.

It won't take long to sniff us out in this little pen, she thought.

The beast began to shamble in Tazi's direction. With each hesitant step, the gnoll swung one of its massive arms out in a wide arc. Tazi could hear his claws whistle through the air. She looked to the dwarf in hopes that he might attempt her plan and move up behind the beast, but he was trying to climb the cage and get above the creature's reach. But the guards decided that was not allowed, and several of them used their staffs to smash at the dwarf's hands until he fell. Tazi felt the cage bars behind her and realized she had no where else to go.

"Don't be shy, 'milady,' " she heard from behind. And she felt the sharp jab of a staff in her back as the lecherous guard forced her closer to the gnoll.

Tazi whipped around and grabbed the staff before the startled guard could retract it. Pulling it about two feet in, Tazi leveraged the weapon against a bar and pulled it toward herself as hard as she could. The wooden stick snapped and she was left with a small club. She turned back in time to duck as the gnoll nearly took off her head. Trapped in the corner, Tazi had nowhere to run. The gnoll smelled her and yanked her to her feet. The beast's claws tore into the flesh of her upper arms. The gnoll raised her high overhead, nearly smashing her skull against the pen's ceiling. Tazi gripped the club with both hands and swung it full force against the beast's head. The weapon made a solid crack as it struck the gnoll's jaw. It screamed in a mad frenzy and tossed Tazi across the cell, unknowingly at the dwarf.

The dwarf didn't even attempt to break Tazi's fall, but hurried out of the way. The gnoll had caught his scent by this time and made a move for the duergar. But the dwarf nimbly dropped low and rolled beneath its legs, pausing only long enough to deliver a devastating punch to the beast's groin. The dwarf clambered away, and the gnoll continued to swing its massive arms, desperate to claw either of its opponents.

Tazi regained her footing and slipped past the monster, but the gnoll turned and sprang into the air after her. They both tumbled to the ground. The gnoll flipped Tazi onto her back and pinned her with its massive bulk. Tazi looked up into the horrendous visage of the beast, with its blood and pus-matted fur and snapping jaws a few inches from her face. She only had one chance. Just as the beast reared back its head, opening its mouth wide to rip out her throat, Tazi freed her hands enough to use the wooden shaft again. When the beast descended on her, she wedged the club between its yellowed teeth, barely keeping its head above hers. Tazi twisted her head to one side and called to the dwarf.

"Get over here," she screamed. But the duergar remained impassive.

Realizing she was on her own, Tazi kneed the beast where the dwarf had already inflicted some damage. The gnoll loosened its grip, and she drew both her knees up to her chest, kicking out at the gnoll. The beast was knocked flat onto his back, though Tazi lost her club in the process. She scrambled to her feet.

Since the gnoll landed close to the dwarf, he tried to climb up and around the beast again. This time the guards were ready for his acrobatic trick. The moment he grabbed the bars, several sentries pinned each of his arms. While they held him, one of the other guards prodded the gnoll—who had regained its footing—in the duergar's direction.

"Let me free, you bastards," the dwarf screamed, but they held him fast. The gnoll was practically on top of him when Tazi suddenly remembered the length of leather cord in her waistband. Pulling it free, she wound each end around her fists a few times. She tugged on the length between her hands once and launched herself onto the gnoll's back.

With her arms crossed at the elbows, Tazi looped the thong around the beast's head and wrapped her legs tightly around its waist. She pulled her arms apart, the tether hard against the gnoll's throat. It bucked and spun around, desperate to shake Tazi loose as she crushed its windpipe. In desperation, the gnoll ran itself backward into the cage bars in an attempt to smash her, but Tazi held tight despite the pain. Eventually, the beast sagged to its knees and collapsed face first.

Tazi rose to one knee, breathing ragged, and pulled on her makeshift garrote until she was sure the creature was dead. The cheering from the guards faded into silence, and they released their hold on the dwarf.

"That's one you owe me," Tazi said breathlessly, when the duergar moved over to inspect the dead gnoll. He said nothing.

From a corner of the stable, Heraclos stepped into the light. He looked no worse for wear from his skirmish with Tazi, sporting a fresh cloak and no obvious signs of injury. Tazi was both surprised to see him and not so. Since her mock trial, she suspected something. Events had seemed contrived, and she knew someone was manipulating her. The bodyguard's appearance at this moment merely confirmed her suspicions. All that had just transpired was a show for his benefit. Tazi wasn't certain if it had been for his amusement or something more, but she was sure he had arranged it.

"Take that thing out of there," he ordered the guards, pointing at the very dead gnoll. They obeyed him instantly, even the lecherous one. So much for him just being a servant, she thought.

Two of the guards forced Tazi and the duergar against the far side of the cage with their staffs. Tazi was still breathing hard, as was the dwarf, and she realized they didn't have the energy to escape. Four others entered and each grabbed one of the gnoll's limbs. Between them, they were able to haul its dead-weight out of the cell and down the aisle, though Tazi heard more than a few curses drift back to her. She glanced past the sentry with the longstaff to watch the Thayan bodyguard.

"That is to be all for tonight," he instructed the guard who had mentioned Tazi would 'get hers' earlier in the evening. She was positive some coins changed hands.

"Let them be," he added, and Tazi saw the guard nod in acquiescence. The bodyguard turned with a flourish of his cloak and strode down the aisle toward the exit. Tazi noted he never spared a single glance toward any of the other pens' occupants. The remaining guards looked at Tazi with a more appraising eye and whispered amongst themselves. Finally, they filed away as well and extinguished the torches as they passed by them for the second time that night.

"If it is night," Tazi muttered. "No way to tell in here."

Utterly exhausted, Tazi lay down in one of the corners of the pen. She was too tired to even try to talk any further with the dwarf or make certain he wasn't injured, though she was confident he had managed to escape serious hurt; he seemed skilled at looking out for himself and himself alone. There would be time enough tomorrow, she mused. She also felt confident enough that they would be left undisturbed for the rest of the shift, and she planned to make the most of it. The last sight Tazi saw before her heavy lids closed was the duergar watching her coldly. Then, for a few hours, she saw no more.

# CHAPTER FIVE

Tazi unwillingly opened her eyes, unable to ignore the incessant shaking that disturbed her troubled dreams. She discovered the duergar was hunched over her, shoving her shoulder roughly.

"What is it?" Tazi demanded, squinting from her exhaustion. "Have we got more company?"

Her morose companion simply shook his head and pointed down to one of the distant cages. Tazi followed the length of his arm and saw the guards had returned. They moved methodically from pen to pen, rousing all the occupants and forcing them to stand in the aisle. The prisoners scuttled and scurried as best they could to obey the guards' demands. In one pen, however, a woman mewled like a sick cat and could not rise. She waved a weak arm in their direction. The guards exchanged a quick word, and the one closest to her ran her through with his sword. Tazi turned away, digging her nails so deeply into her clenched fists that she drew blood. She felt the dwarf grip her shoulder.

"No," was all he said cryptically.

Before Tazi could say anything else, three guards arrived at their pen and opened the lock.

"Get going," a man Tazi didn't recognize ordered.

Must be the next shift, she thought to herself.

"And no tricks," he warned her. Obviously, they had heard of the previous night's event.

Tazi slowly rose to her feet. It wasn't the first time she had slept on hard ground, but she still ached from her battle with the gnoll. The dwarf, sprang nimbly to his feet. Of course, he didn't expend nearly the same amount of energy that I did, Tazi reflected. Why would he be sore at all?

Silently, Tazi and the duergar marched along and joined up with the rest of the slow moving prisoners. While none of the other slaves were restrained, the guard who had spoken to Tazi bound her hands in front of her. Two guards led the procession, and three surrounded Tazi and her former cellmate as they brought up the rear. Along the way out, Tazi saw that the woman wasn't the only slave not to leave her pen alive. As they passed the first pen, Tazi caught sight of the little girl. She lay in a skeletal heap in the corner, finally overcome by starvation. Tazi stopped so suddenly, the guard trailing her drew his sword.

"Move it," he snarled. Tazi turned around savagely

and looked as though she would've ripped the guard's throat out herself, bound hands or not. But before she could make a foolish mistake, the dwarf shoved her along himself.

Once outside, most of the slaves covered their eyes, wincing at the daylight. Tazi found herself blinking a bit at the morning sun, but she didn't mind. The ground was still damp from the morning dew and the rains from the night before. A slight steam rose up from where the sun started to warm the earth. But all Tazi noticed for the moment was how sweet the air tasted. She drew in several deep drafts and felt her head clear. She noticed the dwarf did the same. While they were prodded along, Tazi was now better able to observe their route. The guards were herding them away from the magistrate's building.

Because of the size and ill-health of the group, they couldn't move all that fast. She had time to mentally note much of their surroundings. The guards used less force and no outward signs of brutality to coerce the slaves since they had left the foulness of the stables. They led the group past a series of small shops that were still boarded over from the night before, though a few of the shopkeepers had started to arrive. They stood and watched the slaves march past, and Tazi was able to recognize the appraising look in their eyes.

They turned left off of a narrow street. The way suddenly widened up, and Tazi found herself standing in an open market square. There were no carts or stalls as far as she could see, though the square was ringed by low buildings. The square itself was devoid of structures except for a raised stage and a podium in the center that was positioned toward the front of the platform. And along one side was a small table and chair.

Two men entered the square from one of the surrounding buildings and stepped up onto the stage. One of the men had a book tucked under one arm, and he seated himself at the table. The other moved over to the podium and waited. Tazi had a sneaking suspicion what the place was all about.

"Auction block," the dwarf said gruffly, confirming Tazi's worst doubts.

"There has to be a way out of this," she whispered back to him.

"Not here," he answered back.

Two of their guards gave them stern looks but did nothing else. Can't damage the merchandise in front of the buyers, Tazi deduced. All they did was direct the group of thirty slaves over to the side of the stage opposite the man at the table. He had set up a strong box next to his book and didn't bother to look at any of the slaves. Just the coin man, Tazi decided. The other one, however, jumped down and gave them all a cursory glance, pausing to stare a little harder at Tazi and, to a lesser extent, the duergar. He nodded curtly at the lead guard and resumed his position on the stage. The lead spoke a short command to another, who quickly trotted back to where they had entered. He disappeared around the corner.

When he returned, he led a different kind of procession.

Treading behind him were fifteen or so well-dressed folk. Most were tall and sallow. Tazi remembered that the barmaid from Laeril's Arms had mentioned something about the people of Mulan blood, and she figured it ran strong in the veins of this group. Tazi cursed herself again for not paying closer attention to the barmaid's words and for not learning more about Thay before she had crossed its borders.

I was in such a rush once I knew what I had to do. That's a mistake I won't make again, assuming, of course, that I ever get out of here, she mused.

The prospective buyers were all well-dressed, sporting fine linen tunics and cloaks. Almost every one of them was bald with more of the elaborate tattoos like the ones Tazi had seen in the tavern. She wondered if the marks were strictly decorative or if there was another use for them, such as familial affiliations or a symbol of rank in their society. Tazi was surprised to see that even a centaur roamed about in the midst of the humans. He had blond hair and a sleek coat that matched. Judging by his well-muscled physique, Tazi surmised that he was no stranger to hard labor. She suspected that he, unlike the others, was not looking for a house servant, but someone to work a stable or a farm. She was certain that she, and quite possibly the dwarf, would go to him as they were, without argument, the strongest of the lot.

Tazi loathed the thought of what was to come next. A few years ago, before she and her mother had come to a more gentle understanding, Lady Shamur Uskevren would parade her daughter around in front of her cronies and prospective beaus each chance she got. Tazi hated every moment of it because she felt as though she was just a commodity. Little did she know that she would end up exactly that: a piece of meat for others to barter for. Already Tazi could feel the eyes passing over her body, measuring her and weighing her value. She gritted her teeth and stood straighter.

I will find a way out of this, she promised herself. Or I will die trying.

The guards were moving some of the slaves onto the stage. As the first, scrawny man stepped up, the Thayan behind the podium motioned for the lead guard to approach. The two conferred, and Tazi got the distinct impression that the announcer was extremely critical of the "merchandise." The guard shrugged his shoulders at the announcer's obvious displeasure. They exchanged a few more words before the guard nodded in agreement. He went back down the steps, collected another man and a woman and returned with them onto the stage. The auctioneer seemed satisfied.

"And what do I hear for this fine group?" he asked of the crowd in a deep voice that belied his slight frame. "Do I hear one hundred? One hundred anyone?"

Tazi turned and glimpsed the merchants murmur amongst themselves. Most wore disappointed looks or ones of distaste.

When no one bid, the auctioneer continued.

"Ninety, then. Ninety and the high bidder will get himself some fine brood stock here." He pointed at the woman's thin pelvis and added, "Good hips for children. Free labor." The auctioneer eventually settled for thirty gold pieces. Tazi shook her head in sorrow, unable to understand how life could go so cheaply. She looked over at the duergar once, but he gave no outward show of any feelings. She wasn't sure how to read his stony visage.

The guards moved the majority of the slaves in groups of two or three. It appeared the auctioneer felt that was the only way the sorry batch would sell, and the guards accommodated his wishes. It was also clear to Tazi that he was saving the duergar and her for last. The prospective owners milled about the square, pointing and chuckling at many of the slaves. Whenever a lot was sold, there was a polite smattering of applause as the "winner" went on stage to pay the man seated at the table with the strong box. They handed over their coins and, in return, received a notice of ownership and a human being. Tazi felt the blood rise to her face.

"Excited?" a guard whispered hotly in her ear. "I imagine you'll bring in more than enough to make up for these wretches."

Tazi turned around and spit in the guard's face. He raised his hand to strike her, but Tazi stood her ground. One of his comrades moved to stop him. But the guard remembered himself at the last moment and scrubbed at his face instead.

"Enjoy it while you can," he warned her, "because your new master is going to beat the fire right out of you, one way or another. I guarantee you that."

The slighted guard's comrade grabbed Tazi's

bound wrists and started to drag her to the stage. She pulled herself free of his grasp and looked around. With nearly a half dozen, armed guards, the men on the auction block and the square of citizens, Tazi knew she realistically didn't stand a chance of escape here. But, she was certain, the time would come when someone would slip up and let their watch down. She would just have to wait for it.

While she struggled with the guard, the duergar squirmed his way over to them. "We're together," he told the guard in a gravelly voice, pointing at Tazi. "Where she goes, I go. So sell us together."

Tazi regarded him with surprise and pleasure. She smiled at him warmly, but was met, once again, with his stony countenance. She thought for a fleeting moment his cold look was for the crowds, but Tazi saw no warmth in his flint gray eyes. She was somewhat puzzled that he had actually tried to pair himself off with her.

Perhaps he feels he owes me for last night, she wondered. Or maybe, after last night, he thinks that there is something special in store for me and he wants a cut.

Tazi didn't have time to contemplate more. One guard pulled the dwarf aside, and another prodded Tazi onto the stage. She walked of her own accord over to where she had seen the other slaves stand. Even though her hair was tousled, her vest torn, and her shoulders gashed from the battle with the gnoll, Tazi was a sight to behold. She scanned the crowd as though she was the one in control, and more than one merchant glanced away from her hard, sea-green eyes. But, for as many that looked down, twice that reviewed her honey-colored skin with greedy gleams in their eyes. The announcer rubbed his hands together, and Tazi noticed he had finally smiled.

"All right then," he began, "do I hear—"

"One hundred," offered the centaur.

"One hundred gold pieces from the four-legged gentleman. Do I hear one hundred fifty?"

A fat woman with sunken eyes cried, "One hundred fifty!"

"Two hundred," replied the centaur.

"Now it's getting interesting," interrupted the auctioneer. "Do I have two hundred fifty?"

Tazi watched the crowd expectantly, wondering what her price would finally be. A field hand for the muscular horse-man or a maid to be kicked around by a spoiled woman who thinks life has passed her by?

Caught up in her daydreaming, Tazi didn't really notice that the woman with sunken eyes had driven her price up to three hundred seventy five. The auctioneer made his second call and was beginning his third and final challenge when a voice from the far corner of the square called out.

"One thousand and I will match any other offer."

The buyers turned their heads and even Tazi scrutinized the rear of the throng to see who her new owner was. The younger bodyguard from the tavern stepped forward, clothed in his rich tunic, pants, and cloak. Tazi suspected he would make an appearance, so she wasn't truly stunned.

"Sold!" shouted the pleased auctioneer.

Heraclos climbed onto the stage and approached the treasurer. Tazi watched as he pulled out a heavy sack and started to count out his coins. She chewed on her lip while he did that, her mind working away. As it stood, she was alone. Other than the few informants she had paid before her journey into the Sunrise Mountains, no one knew she was here. While she hated to ask for help, let alone admit that she needed it, Tazi was in a tough enough situation to entertain the idea she just might need someone. She turned toward the dwarf and reassessed her opinion of him. It was true she didn't know him or trust him much, but there had been a few moments where she wondered about his loyalty.

If he wants to escape as badly as I do, then at least he'll be committed to helping a common goal, she thought. Right up until he sells me out for himself. I just hope I'll be ready when he does.

Tazi let the guards press her over to her new owner. He was still counting out the coins, and Tazi realized that if he was willing to pay what was clearly an exorbitant amount for her, he, or his employer, valued her. But did he value her enough to meet one of her demands?

"I know you came here for me," she whispered to her new owner. He paused in his counting to look at her. The treasurer was plainly irritated with the interruption to their transaction.

"Is that so?" Heraclos asked her pleasantly.

"I want something from you," Tazi continued, "and it is within your means. Give it to me."

Heraclos smiled and replied, "You are in a rather precarious position to make demands of me."

Tazi moved in closer and whispered so only he could hear, "You know I can make things difficult. Give me this one thing, and I'll make it easy on you."

"What is it?"

"I want the dwarf to come with me. He's my partner, and I won't leave him behind," she finished and looked at him firmly.

The bodyguard looked at the duergar and the set of Tazi's chin. Tazi was counting on her belief that whoever wanted her, wanted her quickly and not too damaged. She guessed she had been tested for her strength and, having passed the test last night, would not be taxed until she was forced to do whatever it was she had been chosen for. She hoped the bodyguard feared his master enough to concede.

"Fine," he answered. Heraclos returned to the treasurer and said, "Throw the dwarf into the bargain as well."

"But that will be extra," the treasurer insisted.

"Throw him in as a gift for the great price you received for her," he indicated Tazi, not beyond some haggling.

The treasurer was about to protest until he saw the tattoos on Heraclos's right forearm. He blanched and dropped his eyes.

"Yes. Yes, of course," he agreed and hastily scribbled out a second writ of ownership. Heraclos collected the documents and gallantly swept his arm out, indicating that Tazi should proceed him. They stopped at the gathering of guards, and Tazi watched as Heraclos spoke to the one in charge. He showed him the paperwork and the dwarf was released into his custody.

As Tazi and the two others exited the square, she turned once to see the auctioneer in a heated argument with the treasurer. When the treasurer pointed to what must have been a name in the record book, Tazi saw the auctioneer grow quiet, and all the color drained from his face.

Just what am I getting dragged into? Tazi wondered.

A few hours later, Tazi stood once again and felt as though she was still being scrutinized. When her entourage had arrived at a rather luxurious inn, the bodyguard led Tazi and the dwarf to a simple, clean room. He released Tazi's wrists and made a point of checking the room's door. Tazi noticed the chamber had no windows, and she was certain that was no accident. Aside from a bed, table and chairs, the only other items in the chamber were a screen and a steaming tub of water.

"Please make certain that you clean yourself. I will re-enter the room with my associate in fifteen minutes to collect you," he told Tazi pointedly.

"I see you were expecting me," she told Heraclos with a nod to the warm water.

"Fifteen minutes," was all he replied.

Nearly an hour later, a much-cleaner Tazi was still standing, and she wondered who was watching her, or if this was simply her new owner's way of reinforcing the fact that everything was on his timetable now. A few feet on either side of her stood a bodyguard. Tazi had briefly "met" Milos, the older servant, when she had tested the door to her room. He had peered menacingly at her from the cramped hallway, and she had slammed the door in his face. Now he and Heraclos stood passively and bided their time. The only reaction Tazi evoked in them was when she tried to move. Either one or both would draw their scimitars and motion warningly to her with them. Though they rarely spoke, they communicated their message quite clearly. Tazi contented herself to exploring the room with her keen eyes alone.

While her room had been pleasant, if austere, this room was sumptuous and extravagant. Tazi noticed the sheen of silk sheets on the bed, the embroidered cushions on the settee, and the large, carved desk. All were quality items. In front of the wardrobe were several trunks, most likely full of clothes. Her host spared no expense for his needs. Even the servants were well dressed and sported weapons of fine craftsmanship. A lesser blade would have broken under the assault she gave the night at the tavern. Coin did not appear to be an object. Tazi's mind started to turn.

With all these belongings, my host doesn't like to travel lightly and appreciates his comforts. Probably a touch vain, judging by the obvious opulence.

Scattered on the desk were a few letters and

missives. Tazi suspected that her host was fairly well-educated. Not all of the wealthy class or the nobility could read, but Tazi suspected this person could. Desks themselves were not standard furniture in many rooms, because so few folk could use them. Her host would have requested it or was enough of a regular that the innkeeper knew to have it ready. Another piece in her puzzle as Tazi tried to read her owner and discover what he wanted from her. And all the while she was inventorying the room, Tazi was also searching for an avenue of escape. The room seemed ordinary enough, and that made Tazi suspicious immediately.

Too easy, she thought. There has to be more than what meets the eye here. With a soft thud, the door shut behind Tazi. It startled her because she hadn't heard it open. As she turned, Tazi saw both bodyguards bow deeply. She refused to do the same, and the men didn't force her to comply. She got a good look at her owner.

Much like the auctioneer did to her this morning, Tazi gave Naglatha a brief, cursory glance and attempted to sum her up. The woman appeared to be close to her in age, though a touch older. There were no wrinkles on her smooth face to belie her years; it was her black eyes that betrayed her. They seemed older to Tazi, perhaps older than someone twice her own age, with a dark wisdom in them. Tazi also noted the woman was about her height and build, though it was a little difficult to tell with the somewhat concealing clothes she wore. The woman wore a sleeveless, belted tunic that hung to mid-calf. It was split on both sides to allow easy movement. Under that, she sported a pair of lightweight trousers and delicate sandals. She had several rings on her thin hands, and she even had a ring on one of her toes.

But the most striking feature the woman possessed, with the exception of her obsidian eyes, was her rich hair. In a land where Tazi had seen most everyone crop their tresses or completely remove them, the woman standing before her had a thick, black mane. She wore it loose, with a simple band over the center of her head that kept some of the locks out of her eyes. She looked confident, very sure of herself. As Tazi studied her, she was also struck by a sense of familiarity.

I've seen this woman before, she thought and wracked her memories trying to place her. When Tazi finally looked back at her, she could see the other woman smiling at her when Tazi would have expected her to have been appalled and offended at the brazenness of her new slave. She walked past Tazi over to the small table nearby and further surprised her new possession.

"Please," she said in a low, pleasant voice, "have a seat." And she pulled a chair out for Tazi. Bemused, Tazi moved over and sat down. The woman picked up a decanter and gracefully filled two goblets with wine. She offered one to Tazi.

"I'm sure you're very parched. Have some. Not the best year, but it was the finest this establishment had to offer."

Dumbfounded, Tazi accepted the glass but hesitated to drink. Her owner smiled again at her and raised her goblet in a quick toast before drinking a few sips. Now fairly certain the wine had not been tampered with, Tazi followed suit. The woman nodded to Tazi as if acknowledging the importance of the little ritual. She set her glass back down and drew a chair for herself. Once she was seated, she placed her delicate arms on the table and loosely laced her fingers together.

"Now that you've had an opportunity to refresh yourself," she began, noting Tazi's clean appearance, "let's waste no more time."

"All right," Tazi replied.

"You can't possible imagine my surprise when I saw you in that tavern two nights ago," she explained.

"No, I can't," Tazi answered honestly. She was more puzzled now because she knew this woman and couldn't place her.

"I mean," she offered, "Thay is so very far from Selgaunt. You've traveled a great distance. Doesn't seem like you, really."

"And what would seem like me?" Tazi said, trying to bait her, incredulous that the woman thought she knew her at all.

Naglatha smiled and stretched her arm to stroke Tazi's shoulder-length hair. Tazi flinched slightly at her cold touch, but held her place. She glanced over to where the bodyguards stood. They were staring at the wall as though they were fixtures. But Tazi believed they would strike without hesitation if they thought their mistress was in jeopardy or if Tazi made any sudden moves. So she bore the woman's distasteful touch without saying a word.

"Shorter tresses for one," she astounded Tazi with her knowledge of her former look. "Perhaps a style a bit more boyish and more suited to your favorite activities?"

"Perhaps," a startled Tazi offered.

"I've been following you for years, actually," Naglatha admitted. "And I have been most impressed with what I saw. I mean, for someone of your relatively few years."

"What impressed you the most?" Tazi asked, convinced the woman and she must have attended one of her mother's many, opulent soirees. "Was it my charming wit or my keen sense of fashion that meant the most to you?" She saw the woman was not troubled by her bantering manner.

"Most definitely it was your keen taste in clothing. Perfect for those late night rendezvous with your young-mage-in-training, jumping from rooftop to rooftop." She smiled more fully at the confusion on Tazi's face.

"Many were the times I considered approaching you in my capacity as a recruiter for the Red Wizards," she told Tazi. "But, I hesitated because I worried about your ability, or lack thereof, to commit to a cause. Actually, I doubted your ability to commit to anything, and that would have been no good to me. But I kept my eye on you.

"Then I heard one day that the little girl had flown from her parent's castle to parts unknown. And when you finally returned home, the great Old Owl, Thamalon Uskevren, had died." Tazi blinked hard at the mention of her father's name. "How things have changed for you, little Tazi," she finished, using Thazienne's special nick name, and allowed her words to sink in.

In a flash of revelation, Tazi realized that she did know this woman from Selgaunt. She had seen her shop along Larwaken Lane more than once. It had been filled with oddities and curios from the South, Tazi remembered. The pieces had been relatively overpriced and gaudy, as Tazi recollected, but the woman's shop had always had a lot of traffic. Now she realized, after the woman's admission, that the business had not entirely dealt with the buying and selling of rarities. She knew something of the Red Wizards.

As she scrutinized her owner's face, Tazi had another recollection. She had barged into her father's study in typical spoiled fashion to demand something of him years back. What it was she had wanted, Tazi could no longer recall and that loss saddened her momentarily. But she remembered that her father had a beautiful, black-haired woman sitting opposite him at his beloved chess table. Tazi had backed away nervously, thinking that perhaps she had interrupted one of his many dalliances. He later told her that the woman was a business acquaintance, but Tazi never pursued the subject with him, preferring not to know the sordid details of his life. Now she realized that same woman was seated opposite her now. Recognition washed over her features.

"Naglatha," she breathed, finally placing her name.

"We are well met, Thazienne Uskevren," she acknowledged in return, and Tazi could see she was pleased with Tazi's memory. She rose from the table and padded over to the carved desk. Tazi watched as she passed her hand over an empty spot on the desk, and a sack appeared suddenly. Tazi shivered, realizing she was the unwilling company of a wizard. She wondered more and more just what it was that she was going to have to do for this woman.

Naglatha came back to the table and Tazi knew she was enjoying the little game. She stood next to Tazi and unceremoniously dumped her worn sack onto the table with a dull, heavy thud. She then resumed her seat and, with bended elbows, rested her chin on her hands.

"Enough of the cat and mouse," she brusquely informed Tazi. "I can see on your face that you realize I want something from you; that much is obvious. I have been looking for the right person for some time now, and fate has conspired to cross our paths. You are that person. Of that I am most certain now.

"This is an important task that is not without risk," she continued, and Tazi crossed her arms expectantly.

"Nevertheless, as the risk is great, the reward is commensurate to it."

"Well, I would certainly hope so," Tazi quipped. "But what could you possibly have to offer me that would be of the slightest interest?"

"Simply put, I can give you your freedom," Naglatha offered.

"I can take that for myself," Tazi said with deadly seriousness. Naglatha chose to ignore the tone of her voice.

"No... no, you can't. And I know the magistrate explained that portion of Thayan law to you most carefully," she responded in a motherly tone of rebuke.

"Then you have no offer to make," Tazi rebutted.

"Oh, but I most assuredly do," she promised. "I have means at my disposal, too complicated to explain right now, to accomplish the impossible task. Let me just put it this way," she told Tazi and leaned back in her chair, "I have the means to 'erase' your name from the ledgers. To, in fact, strike out the entire incident as though it never happened. No crime, no record, no punishment. You will be completely free under Thayan law.

"And," she motioned to the worn sack in front of Tazi, "you can even take your crimson gold with you. Though, I have to admit, it has some interesting properties I am not completely familiar with. Even still, it is yours once more."

Tazi's eyes flickered to the sack for a moment before returning to meet Naglatha's penetrating stare.

"Now," she told Tazi, "you may be thinking as you sit there so comfortably, that you don't need this offer. You may believe that you will find a way to escape on your own." She paused to lean forward a touch. "You may be right. You are a resourceful woman, and I actually have no doubt you could escape. If you couldn't accomplish that simple feat, you'd be no good to me."

"Since you know I will," Tazi promised her, "why bother with the pretense of this offer?"

Naglatha smiled and slowly rose to her feet. She moved gracefully around the table to stand behind Tazi. Tazi could feel Naglatha place her hands on her shoulders with a strong grip and lean down toward her right ear.

"For the simple fact that if you betray me, Thazienne Uskevren, or run away, or even refuse me, you will pay most dearly. You forget, I know where it is that you call home. Don't doubt the extent of my reach. I can always find your family." She released Tazi's shoulders and walked around the table to stand opposite her.

"You have lost one parent, and I know how heart-breaking that can be. Would you care to try for two?"

Tazi lost control of her restraint at the veiled threat to her mother and jumped to her feet, knocking over the small table as she did so. Everything tumbled to the floor with a clatter. Amidst the shinning shards of the now-broken goblets, the red gold spilled out like glowing coals. Before Tazi could make another move, Naglatha's bodyguards grabbed her. She didn't struggle, though Milos twisted her arms behind her back and held her while Heraclos moved to flank Naglatha. Tazi knew this was not the place.

"I can see I've struck a nerve," Naglatha said in a voice that Tazi realized was only mock apology. "My intent was only to stress a point, no more than that. I am generous by nature, so I will give you the entire night to think on what I've said. With a good night's rest, I'm very certain you will come to the right decision. You may rejoin your mysterious companion now."

Without waiting for a response from Tazi, Naglatha waved her hand to Milos, and their interview was over. As Milos led her from the chamber, Tazi could hear Naglatha ordering Heraclos.

"Clean this clutter up before I cut my feet on something," she snapped at the remaining guard in a much harsher tone than she had reserved for Tazi.

"Yes, milady," Tazi heard Heraclos acquiesce.

While she marched down the hallway to her room, Tazi's mind raced, trying to weigh her options. Either she did this woman's bidding or let her family face some nameless threat. With a dread certainty, she came to the conclusion that she really had no choice at all.

# CHAPTER SIX

*22 and 23 Mirtul, 1373 DR*

Tazi sat in shocked silence. She let her hands rest on her knees, and she looked at the nearby wall with a blank expression on her face. Her mind, though, was far from blank, as she turned over the recent events in her head. Her brain was like a dog worrying a bone; she kept playing the words over again and again, trying to make sense of them, looking at them from every angle. Tazi wasn't even aware of the close scrutiny her sullen companion gave her.

"What is it?" demanded the duergar. It was first time he had had spoken to her since they had been taken from the auction square. Tazi barely heard him.

"Hmm…" she vaguely replied.

"What do they want?" he asked her again.

The dwarf was standing only a few feet from

her. She suspected he had also taken advantage of the bath water as even his gray skin looked less grimy. Tazi also detected the faintest whiff of the sandalwood soap. Nothing could be done for his dirty pants and tunic, though the drab colors of the material muted the stains. She looked closely at him, taking his measure, and she weighed her options carefully. She decided to risk a chance and take the duergar into her confidence.

"What's your name?" she asked him. Tazi could see he was surprised by her question.

"Why?" he countered.

"Because I'd like to call you something besides 'dwarf,'" she snapped. "And because it looks like we're stuck in this together, that's why."

"Justikar Stoneblood," he eventually told her, and Tazi thought fleetingly that he might be lying.

"Good," she replied. "I'm Tazi."

He looked at her. "I know. You announce yourself everywhere we go. How could I miss it?" he quipped and finally demanded, "Now what is it?" Tazi motioned for him to draw up a chair, but Justikar shook his head in refusal, signaling he preferred to stand.

"Have it your way," she said. "I've met our new owner. It turns out that this woman is someone who has ties to my homeland. In a roundabout sort of way, I know her. Or, to be more precise, I knew of her." Tazi paused to see Justikar's reaction. He barely batted an eye. "She has been posing as a curio merchant in my city, but she is much more than that. She alluded to the fact that she works for the Red Wizards as some kind of recruiter." Tazi saw that the duergar was unmoved at the mention of Naglatha's employers.

"As you've already guessed, I'm sure, she wants me to acquire something for her. But, I don't know what it is. Naglatha's given me the night to consider my options. If I accept, she has promised to repay me by granting me my freedom and returning my gold to me."

"And if you refuse?" Justikar asked with a grim expression.

"My continued servitude was implied," Tazi explained. She hesitated to say anything else, but the dwarf's unmoved expression prompted her to tell him more. "And harm to my family was more than implied." Tazi watched the dwarf's face to see if her words had had any effect on him.

"That's it?" he asked brusquely.

"Yes," Tazi said, "whatever 'it' is."

"So you're going to do it then, aren't you?" he questioned, and Tazi could hear the undisguised disgust in his voice. Until he had asked the question, she had not fully realized she had already made up her mind.

"Yes, I am. There really was no choice."

The dwarf snorted at her answer. "And folk say my people are greedy. Humph...People should look to their own houses for cleaning before they look to others." With that, he turned abruptly from her and walked toward one of the small cots against the wall. But, before Tazi could say anything in response, the dwarf turned again and marched back to her.

"Are you a coward?" he demanded in his gravelly

voice. "Is that it? Are you afraid to try and take back your own freedom?" Tazi was shocked silent at Justikar's suddenly impassioned accusations. He put his fists on his hips and moved in closer. "Or is it greed, human? Is that crimson gold that glows so red too beautiful to resist? You'd sell out for a few lumps of metal?" he finished. When Tazi didn't immediately answer him, he continued on his tirade.

"It's true," he admitted grudgingly, "I owe you." The words seemed to stick in his throat. "And I hate debts." He slammed his fist on the table where the tub of water rested. Soapy suds splashed onto the floor with the force of his blow. He faced Tazi again with a severe look fixed on his face. "I especially hate debts to humans." She was amazed how filthy he made the last word sound.

"Aye, there is a debt between us," he growled. "But debt or not, I am not going to stick this out with you. Whatever is between you and this woman is between the two of you. I'll have no part in it. And that's final." His face was so close to Tazi's that she could count the number of earrings that studded his left ear. After counting four of them, Tazi exploded.

"How dare you?" she shouted. "Don't stand there and think to tell me who I am. You don't know a thing about me, little man." She rose to her feet slowly in an attempt to tower over the dwarf, and she could see he bridled at her last remark.

"Have I asked anything of you?" she demanded, and now it was she who stood defiant with her hands on her hips. "Have I?" she said down to him.

Justikar simply glowered back at her defiantly.

"There's the door," she continued and pointed to it. "If you see a chance to flee, then I suggest you take it. I wish you the best, but I won't go with you. I have to stay here." Tazi took a deep breath and tried to control her anger.

"My family means everything to me. You can believe that or not; that's your choice. But it doesn't change the fact that it is the truth. I wouldn't do anything to knowingly jeopardize their safety." She paused and walked away a few feet before turning to look at the dwarf.

He crossed his arms over his chest and simply kept his expression skeptical.

"I've seen something that makes me think Naglatha is more than just a recruiter for the Red Wizards," she continued more calmly. "I think she is one of them. And this woman has ties to my family. I can't risk it. Their safety means everything to me. I would walk through fire for them, and so I have to stay regardless. Even if I was to escape tonight, there is no way I could return to my home before she could have someone or *something* there. And I couldn't protect them. Maybe this way I can."

Justikar snorted at her explanation but regarded her briefly. "I understand a bit about family," was all he eventually said. Like the veracity of his name, Tazi didn't know whether to believe him or not.

She went over to one of the two cots against the wall and sank down wearily. "I meant it, you know," she told the dwarf. "If you see an opening, take it. I can't help you, but I promise I won't do anything to slow you down. That's the best I can offer." And she smiled ruefully. "But I'm staying." Without waiting for a reply, Tazi stretched out on the cot and closed her eyes.

Justikar hardly breathed as he sat cross-legged with his back to the wall on the small cot. The dwarf had held the same position for the last few hours as he strained to hear the sounds around him. The most obvious one that nearly drowned out the others was the soft snoring of the human who shared his incarceration. He shook his head slightly and was disgusted by how soundly the black-haired human slept. Not ten minutes after she had closed her eyes, her breathing had grown heavy. And now, the woman was making enough noise to rouse the dead. Humans!

He waited a bit longer, just to be certain she was not trying to deceive him, before he made his next move. When he was sure she was asleep, he uncrossed his legs and let them silently dangle over the side of his bed. He braced his hands on the wall behind him and slowly pushed against it. When his feet touched the floor, he firmly but cautiously raised his body off of the cot with excruciating care, fearful of any old or rusted bedsprings that might signal an alarm even though the furnishings seemed new and well made.

As soon as he was upright, Justikar stood motionless. With his eyes closed, he willed the blood in his veins to flow more freely through the various limbs that had stiffened up as he had kept his silent vigil waiting for the woman to doze off. He bit his lip in discomfort as the daggers and needles tingling within his muscles told him in no uncertain terms that he had restored his circulation.

Opening his eyes, he took a deep, silent breath. The duergar regarded his roommate for a moment longer. She continued to slumber undisturbed, and he wondered about her briefly and if he should do anything. If she wasn't being duplicitous about her family and her obligation to their safety, then she wouldn't leave and there was no point in rousing her. If she had lied and was in it for her treasure, or was simply inept, that was even more reason to let her bluster away and give him some cover. The fact that he owed her a debt gnawed at him, but he shrugged his shoulders. He owed someone else a larger one, and he could live with his discomfort at welshing on a human. He was a pragmatic dwarf, after all, and had his priorities.

When he was resolved to desert Tazi, the duergar moved stealthily across the comfortable room to stand near the only door in the chamber. He rubbed his thumbs against his fingers like one readying himself to tackle a difficult lock. Glancing back a final time at Tazi, the dwarf shrugged his shoulders again and abandoned her to her fate. He turned back toward the door and delicately placed both of his hands to the right of it, along the wall. And he closed his eyes once more.

It was simple enough for Justikar to clear his mind

even in his present situation. After years of conditioning in the Underdark where he felt little confusion and suffered from few distractions, he had almost no difficulty slipping into a light, meditative trance. Much in the same way that he could let his senses slip along rock or stone to search out their inherent weaknesses and faults, the duergar could also, to a limited extent, let his mind slip along the boundaries of other minds. Years of subjugation to illithids had left Justikar's people with certain abilities that came in very handy from time to time against others with weaker minds. He found the bodyguards easily enough.

Cautiously at first, Justikar moved along the edge of their awareness, testing to see if their wizard master had shielded their minds or laid down any wards. He couldn't feel anything other than their random thoughts, no matter how he probed them. He unconsciously shifted his hands' positions and turned his focus toward the younger man.

The bodyguard's mind was full of chatter, which surprised Justikar because he had carried himself with so much outward silence. Obviously, his master had trained his body well enough, but she couldn't stop the noise inside his head. He would be a simple enough matter, the dwarf decided. He planted the straightforward, but effective, idea in the bodyguard's head that his bladder was full. It was so full, in fact that it was close to bursting. With every passing moment, that discomfort grew. Justikar allowed himself a small smile when he actually heard Heraclos shift his weight from one foot to the other.

"What's the matter?" the dwarf heard Milos ask his companion on the other side of the wall.

"I think I drank too much at my meal break," Heraclos explained lamely, and Justikar heard him shift his weight again.

"Just go," Milos sighed. "I can't have you doing a jig next to me all night. Don't take too long, or Naglatha will have your hide," he cautioned as the younger man made a hasty retreat.

One down, Justikar thought. Now for the other one.

The dwarf shifted his stance somewhat and repositioned his hands. The remaining bodyguard was much different from the first. He was more centered and had few wandering thoughts. More disciplined than his younger companion, he would not give in to a basic bodily suggestion. The duergar was going to have to do something more challenging to distract Milos. Justikar had to strike at what he valued most.

*Milos, I need you.*

*Naglatha?* Milos questioned.

*Milos!*

Justikar was sweating profusely. It was difficult for him to directly speak with another's mind. And he could sense Milos' hesitation to desert his post even at the apparent request of his mistress. He had nearly abandoned his hope of escape until he heard the deliberate, heavy footfalls trailing away from his door. Now was his one chance.

The dwarf cautiously opened the door so as not to awaken the sleeping woman. A cursory glance up and down the hallway revealed that the duergar was momentarily alone. He slipped out into the dimly lit hallway and shut the door silently behind himself. He knew that he had a few moments at best. The dwarf couldn't chance an encounter on the stairs with either of the Thayans, so he ducked into the next room down from his and hoped that because it was unlocked, it meant that no one was renting it. No sooner did he close the door than he heard one of the bodyguards return. Justikar was too tired to try and mentally check which one. After another moment, the first bodyguard was joined by the second.

"Where did you go?" he heard Heraclos ask his companion.

"None of your concern," snapped Milos.

In the darkness of the empty room, Justikar leaned his head against the door and stifled a chuckle. He could only imagine what kind of reprimand Milos had received when he disturbed his sleeping mistress. Fools in love, he mused delightedly, always have a weak spot.

The duergar moved quickly over to the window and threw open the sash. From the view of a garden, he could tell that room faced the back of the inn. In the blink of an eye, he dropped over the side and shimmied his way expertly down the vine-covered wall. He jumped the last few feet, melted into the nighttime shadows and was gone.

"Where is he?" Heraclos shouted at Tazi. He did not display any of the restraint he had shown her the day before. Dressed in the same style of clothing as yesterday, he had roused Tazi from a troubled sleep and yanked her to her feet by fistfuls of her leather vest.

"I asked you a question," he demanded, still shaking her.

"Again?" Tazi mumbled. "Can't a body get any sleep in this country?" She could see the bodyguard had very little use for her sarcasm this morning.

"Where did your little tunnel rat disappear to?" he screamed.

Tazi looked past his shoulder to Justikar's vacant cot. It was neat and empty, as though he had never lain there. Milos flipped the flimsy bed onto its side with his scimitar and scowled. Sometime during the night, it appeared the duergar had managed to slip out of the room past Naglatha's bodyguards after all. Good trick, Tazi thought. Our room has no windows and only one door. And, presumably, these two were on guard. She smiled broadly and remained silent.

Heraclos released her abruptly. Tazi suspected he was going to pay for the duergar's escape and didn't want to risk increasing Naglatha's wrath by damaging Tazi as well. He scowled at her and motioned toward the door.

"Naglatha has requested your presence in her chamber. Move," he ordered, and Tazi could see he was struggling against the urge to take out his frustration at losing the dwarf on her. He shoved her toward the door when she didn't move fast enough to suit him.

"Tsk," Tazi clicked her tongue at him and brushed some imaginary mark off her shoulder. "It wouldn't do for Naglatha to see any new bruise on me, now would it?"

Heraclos was in her face in one stride. "Trust me," he whispered through clenched teeth, "I can give you some bruises where she would never find them. Don't push me." Tazi decided not to. She was escorted to Naglatha's room without incident. Only Heraclos accompanied her. She figured Milos would try to track Justikar down. Though he had been less than an ideal companion, Tazi hoped that the dwarf would be successful if for no other reason than she hated the idea of slavery. Luck to you, she said in silent prayer. May the wind be with you and the devils off your heels.

Heraclos pulled Tazi to a halt in front of the door to Naglatha's chamber. He composed himself and raised his hand to knock on the oak door. But, as soon as he raised his fist, a woman's voice bid them to enter. Tazi could see that Heraclos was not surprised by the omniscient invitation, and that just added to Tazi's belief that Naglatha was not just a recruiter on the Red Wizards' payroll with some minor, arcane abilities.

Heraclos opened the door and ushered Tazi inside. As soon as she crossed the threshold, the door slammed shut in Heraclos' face. Tazi jumped slightly at the crash. From the opposite side of the door, Heraclos twisted the doorknob once and, when it didn't give, he released it. Tazi assumed he would stand guard on the other side or, if Naglatha was a wizard of no small ability, he might join Milos in searching for Justikar knowing she could protect herself in this instance. Either way, it wasn't Tazi's concern. She turned to Naglatha.

Once again, the woman was impeccably groomed in fine linens and perfectly coiffed. Her room had been cleaned and Tazi could see that most of Naglatha's personal property had been collected and packed up. Only a few items remained scattered about. Tazi assumed Naglatha wanted to move out within the next day at the latest.

"Yes," Naglatha answered Tazi's unasked question, "we are preparing to leave soon whether we find your industrious companion or not." She smiled at Tazi's surprised look. "Of course I know he's flown the coop. But he's not the only one who has flown away," she added mysteriously. "And, since I see you are still here," she paused to stare hard at Tazi, "can I safely assume you accept?" And Naglatha held out her hand questioningly.

"Yes," Tazi said through gritted teeth. "How could I possibly refuse?"

Naglatha laughed deeply, "Exactly. We both know that you couldn't. Now, please eat," she invited and stood aside to reveal her small table that was now laden with a veritable feast. There were plates of meat, cheeses and fruit piled high. A wrapped bundle steamed slightly, and Tazi could smell the fresh-baked bread from where she stood. There was also a small pot of tea. Try as she might, Tazi could not keep her stomach from growling insistently at the smell of all the food. She could see Naglatha waiting for her to make a move. Considering how she had not even heard the duergar leave the room, Tazi knew she was low on reserves and she needed to maintain her strength. She remembered something Cale had told her years ago in his room at Stormweather Towers.

"Only a fool refuses out of pride what he desperately needs," he had said.

Without hesitation, Tazi pulled out a chair and seated herself. As she grabbed an empty plate and began to fill it with a large selection of the rich food, she invited Naglatha to join her.

"Aren't you having any?" she inquired.

"I've already broken my fast," Naglatha explained. "However, if you need me to prove that the food is safe—"

"No need," Tazi informed her. "Since I seem to be so important to you, I know my safety is assured until I disappoint you."

"You are clever, aren't you?" she complimented Tazi.

"You'd be surprised," Tazi said between mouthfuls.

"I certainly hope so."

While Tazi ate as much as she could without becoming ill, Naglatha returned to her desk, and Tazi could see she was finishing some correspondence. By the time Tazi was sopping up the last juices from the meat with a piece of bread, Naglatha finished her letter and sealed it. She placed the missive in a small satchel near her desk and removed Tazi's worn sack from the same bag. As Tazi wiped her fingers clean on a crisp linen cloth, Naglatha stood beside her and dropped the sack abruptly into her lap.

"I must admit to some curiosity, Tazi," Naglatha admitted. "Could you explain something to me?"

"Perhaps," was all that Tazi replied.

"I am a bit puzzled that you would travel alone all these miles to Thay for that," she said and motioned to the sack in Tazi's lap. "As I said before, the metal does possess some unusual properties, and I would love to study it a bit more if only there were time. Even still, what makes it so special to you?"

"I needed to replace something from a long time ago," Tazi replied slowly.

"Then why not simply pay someone to fetch it for you? You and your family certainly have the funds and the connections to accomplish that."

"It's something I owed my father," Tazi snapped and grew silent. She could see the wizard was intrigued by her clipped answers but appeared to let the matter drop.

Justikar ran silently through the woods.

Under cover of darkness, the gray dwarf had found it a simple enough task to slip past the few taverns and inns that were still open and make his way into the nearby woods. There, under the canopy of the trees, the duergar had moved like a part of the forest. His darkvision guided him as he leaped over thick tree roots and dodged low hanging obstacles. He could run great speeds in full armor carrying large loads, so, unarmed and wearing just a tunic and pants, he moved like lightning. He only stopped once, when a rock caught his attention.

A boulder must have tumbled down from a hill and fractured against the other stones nearby. One of the pieces was roughly the size of his hand and had a sharp enough edge to make it a useful hand axe. He stuffed it carefully in his leather belt and kept moving. Like all gray dwarves, Justikar could sense his depth when he was underground. But he and his family also had the facility to sense direction. He knew where he needed to go. The same trees that afforded him a certain amount of cover also deceived him as well—with a false sense of security. The gray dwarf could not hear the muffled beating of great wings in the distance, or that they were growing closer. While Justikar moved farther away from his former owner, something began to track him.

By the time the first rays of dawn colored the forest in its early light, he could see the outline of the Sunrise Mountains not far on the horizon. He was certain if he could reach them, he would be safe. Once in the rocks and tunnels that were like a second home to him, the duergar would be practically invisible. He was certain there would be no way for him to be taken. His only concern was crossing from the protective concealment of the woods across the open plain to the lower ridges of the mountains. Having spent almost his entire life underground, Justikar was loathe to admit that he suffered a horrible fear of open places. The only reason he had been able to stand his time in the open auction square was because he didn't want to show any weakness to the foul humans around him. Now, faced with the vast, barren plain between him and the rocks, he hesitated. His upper lip curled into a snarl, and he made a break for it.

Running at top speed, he told himself, it wouldn't take more than a few minutes to cross the gravel field. His heart pounded, not from the exertion, but from his fear. Oily sweat poured down his scalp into his stone black eyes and stung miserably. He wiped at his brow savagely and didn't slow his pace once. With his eyes fixed firmly on the protection that he knew the mountains provided, Justikar failed to notice the fast-moving shadow that passed along the plain off to his left.

"Deep Duerra," he panted, "let me reach your safety." He never resorted to prayer before. His people believed the best ways to honor their gods were to simply continue on with their labors. But he was desperate now, and as soon as the words left his lips, Justikar realized just how frightened he was.

The lower ridges were tantalizingly close now. With only a few hundred feet to go, safety was at hand. But when the dwarf had left the shelter of the trees, he had also left himself visible and vulnerable. So focused on the mountains ahead, Justikar did not look back to the woods or to the skies.

Several hundred feet up, a huge griffon was circling. Its keen eyes, unable to penetrate past the thick bows of the forest trees, now had a clear view of its prey. The monster let loose with a fierce screech and dived toward its victim.

Justikar heard the horrible sound and turned his head wildly from side to side, so caught up in his fear that he didn't look up until it was almost too late. But he did, and he saw the huge creature swooping down from the skies. In the gray light of pre-dawn, Justikar estimated the golden beast was almost eight feet long from head to tail and had a wingspan of almost thirty feet. It must be full grown. The dwarf couldn't seem to gather his thoughts coherently, and the only course of action he could come up with was to keep running and try to reach the cover of the boulder fall nearby.

He almost made it.

With the rocks nearly in his reach, Justikar thought he was safe. But, as he approached a jumble of stones, some taller than he was, he could feel pulses of air on his back. The great wings of the creature beat strongly as it tried to slow its decent. The force of those appendages nearly bowled the duergar to the ground. As it was, the griffon managed to rake Justikar's back with its talonlike forearms as it passed over. The dwarf hissed in pain as the razor sharp claws tore through his tunic and flesh. He arched his back in pain and partially whirled in time to see the griffon pull up before it attempted an additional attack. Justikar had reached a rough circle of rocks that afforded him only the most rudimentary of cover. But it did make it almost impossible for the griffon to continue any kind of air attack. It was going to have to face him on foot and that evened things up as far as the duergar was concerned.

Justikar watched as the creature began its landing ten feet from where he stood. The beast's upper body resembled that of an eagle with its sharp beak and feathered forearms. From the withers toward the tail, however, the griffon's body became that of a muscular, fur-covered lion with the exception of its great wings. It was the powerful rear legs that touched down first, but it held its eagle arms poised in the air. Justikar knew he had to keep clear of those slashing limbs, or he would be nothing more than a pile of ribbons in short order. Even as he thought this, his stone black eyes caught sight of a section of his tunic that still streamed from one of its claws, like some flag of defeat. Never, he thought angrily.

Without any formal plan, the duergar let loose with a bellow of rage and charged the griffon. Surprise was on his side, for the beast squawked at the foolhardy and unexpected attack. The griffon was shocked enough by the charge that it lost the first opportunity to slash at the dwarf with its forearms. The griffon touched ground completely, and Justikar saw his chance. He clasped his two hands together and swung straight for the griffon's beak.

The creature turned its head enough to deflect the brunt of the blow, but the dwarf's hammerfist strike did some damage. Justikar smiled grimly as he heard the satisfying crunch of the griffon's beak as he made partial contact. The creature, momentarily distracted, swung its head, spattering the dwarf with its blood, which now poured freely from the partial break. The dwarf knew that if birds lost blood, they could go into shock quickly and even die if the flow wasn't staunched almost straight away. He hoped the same held true for griffons, but he didn't know. He had never tried to kill one before.

While the creature was temporarily blinded, Justikar remembered his earlier find. He reached into his belt and pulled out the natural hand axe. He moved in even closer to the screeching monster and swung his makeshift weapon at the griffon's exposed neck. He felt the tool cut through feathers, but he didn't think it sliced into the flesh very deeply. The griffon exploded in a mixture of fury and pain and reared back on its powerful hind legs, wings beating furiously. Justikar feared he had missed his one chance. But he refused to give up.

As soon as the griffon stood on all four of its feet again, the dwarf launched himself at it once more. He flung his arm in a wide arc, slashing at anything he could. Unsettling the griffon with the flurry of movement near its eyes, the duergar used his feet and smashed the griffon's front left talon with all his might, hoping again that its bird half was more vulnerable than the rest of its lionlike body. The griffon screeched again and swung its bloody head down in an aggressive attack. Justikar's wide shoulders absorbed some of the force, but he still tumbled backward from the blow and landed hard on his back, knocking the wind out of him.

He could see, even though dazed, that the griffon focused its limited attention on its wounded limb. Justikar saw one last chance to make a run for the ridge one hundred feet away and the absolute cover he believed it offered him. He picked himself up and ran, pumping his arms as hard as he could. His heart pounded and every breath burned like fire down the length of his lungs, but he didn't slow down. He was almost there when he saw a shadow growing on the ground all around him, and he felt the sting of air against his shredded back. He refused to turn, though.

With a tunnel opening in the mountain wall within sight and the escape it offered tantalizingly close, Justikar's view was suddenly blocked as a huge pair of feathered wings surrounded him. They enfolded his body completely and as the golden limbs blotted out all sight, Justikar knew there was no escape.

"To business then," Naglatha told Tazi as she sat down with her, "since you've made such a wise decision."

Tazi nodded but said nothing.

"As you've already noticed," Naglatha explained, acknowledging she was aware of Tazi's gaze, "I am nearly ready to leave after traveling so long and so quickly. And I am not the only one," she added.

"Really?" Tazi asked only because she felt Naglatha

wanted her to, not because they were having any sort of an actual dialogue.

"There are many Red Wizards who are, even as we speak, making their way to the Thaymount. Do you know the area?" she asked Tazi.

"Aren't they the chain of volcanic ridges that lie in the middle of High Thay, above the Second Escarpment? I understand that some of the smoldering peaks reach heights of seventeen thousand feet or more and sooty glaciers dot the tops of these," she responded easily.

"You know of it then," Naglatha replied, pleased with Tazi's working knowledge of Thay's geography.

"I obviously didn't pay enough attention to your social mores, but I know where most of the main sites are," Tazi explained. "I thought the area was strictly off-limits and trespassers were executed immediately?"

"You are correct about the security of the region," Naglatha agreed, "but the area is accessible to certain invited Red Wizards and their guests, such as us. Right now, a nearly unprecedented event is under way." Tazi regarded her with feigned interest, sensing that Naglatha needed the audience. "Our Zulkir of Necromancy, Szass Tam, has invited nearly every tharchion and zulkir to the Citadel. These Red Wizards are the power behind Thay," she explained. It was obvious to Tazi that Naglatha was growing excited. "Do you know about the Citadel?" Naglatha questioned. Tazi shook her head from side to side.

"Well, I'll get to that in a moment. This is only the

second time I have ever been to this fortress. Zulkir Szass Tam controls it, and it is he who has called all of us to discuss the course of the country there." Naglatha paused for a moment, and Tazi could see something dark cross her features.

"Szass Tam has directed the path of Thay from one of conquest to that of trade over the years. I'm sure this council is to reiterate that plan to all of us," Naglatha said. She stood up, and Tazi watched as she paced the room. "We were once a proud country and were feared by our neighbors. We wrested control of this land through force from those who sought to subjugate us centuries ago. Now Szass Tam has us buying and selling goods like the greedy, grubby merchants one could find in any city anywhere. Even in a common one like yours," she shot at Tazi.

"I take it you're against this policy," Tazi stated the obvious.

"'Make trade instead of war,'" she laughed. "How preposterous! We are the laughing stock of Faerûn when we should be the most feared. I hate this game-playing," Naglatha said as she continued to march animatedly around the room. "We should embrace our past and the honest ways . . . killing, war, and occupation. Instead we hawk magical wares like street vendors."

"What can you do alone?" Tazi asked her.

Naglatha whirled to face Tazi. "Ah," she replied with a slow smile, "but I'm not alone. There are several of us in positions of authority who want to change history and have Thay assume its rightful position in

Faerûn. We have hesitated because Szass Tam is so very powerful. And, as Zulkir of Necromancy, many of us realize that if we should fail in our efforts, not even death would keep us from his wrath," she answered ominously, and Tazi could see the woman was, despite all her plans and bravado, afraid of the zulkir.

"How can I be of any assistance to you?" Tazi asked. For the first time since Naglatha started her speech, Tazi was genuinely curious. "If he is this powerful, I can't see what use I would be?"

Naglatha sat back down at the small table with Tazi. "What I want from you is really quite simple," she told her. "As I mentioned before, we are all making our way to the Citadel. The Citadel is a unique structure, older than Thay and was here before the first humans came to this land," she clarified. Tazi hated to admit it to herself, but Naglatha had intrigued her.

"It was carved into one of the higher peaks of the Thaymount. Because of certain drawings that have been discovered inside, our best guess is that the structure was probably constructed by ancient lizardfolk who once inhabited the land but have since vanished. We have lizardfolk that inhabit the Surmarsh now, but they are a simple lot and do not possess the skill to have carved such an amazing edifice," Naglatha told her. "The structure is forbidden to the Thayan people and outsiders do not even know of its existence.

"Many years ago, a successful group ventured into the bowels of the Citadel and discovered a near-endless series of subterranean tunnels and caverns. The area came to be known as the Paths of the Doomed and there are supposed to be horrendous creatures that inhabit those tunnels. The party that returned also brought a book back with them that rumor has it mapped the area as well as contained many, important binding spells," Naglatha added. "Szass Tam confiscated that book and has kept it ever since. I and several of my allies are aware of the book and the fact that Szass continues to add more spells to it. If I could get my hands on one or two of the most powerful magics in it, I know I could overpower the zulkir. In my years as The Black Flame I have cultivated so many agents throughout Faerûn, just waiting for this moment. Everything is in place." Naglatha paused and Tazi saw that she was nearly glowing with rapture.

"With him gone," she continued, "I would be able to sway the other powers back to the old ways, the right ways, and Thay could finally achieve its destiny." Naglatha turned to regard Tazi with an unreadable expression. "And all you have to do," she told her slave, "is steal them for me."

Tazi was somewhat daunted by the demand even as she was tempted by the challenge. Her eyes widened, and she pulled her head back imperceptibly. She chose her next words carefully, seeing how animated Naglatha had become.

"I have had a few dealings with wizards and necromancers before," Tazi explained. "I have somewhat of an idea of what they're capable of doing. What I don't understand is, given you and your powerful allies, why do you need me at all? Why not do it yourselves?"

The words had barely left her mouth when Naglatha waved her left hand, palm forward, at Tazi. The thief found herself knocked across the room by a bolt of unseen energy and slammed into the wall. Tazi slid down to the floor, momentarily stunned. Naglatha strode over to where she had landed, and Tazi could see her black eyes storming.

"It is not your place to question my decisions!" she shouted at the dazed Tazi. "Weren't you listening? The Citadel is a fortress of sorcery. There are wards and traps everywhere, but they are the kind of traps designed to catch wizards. We," she explained, pointing to herself, "stand out like stars in the night there. But you, little Tazi," she added more calmly as she dropped to her knees and leaned over her, "you will be nearly invisible." She grabbed Tazi by the chin and forced her to make eye contact.

"It will take a thief of extraordinary ability to succeed," she warned Tazi, fingers biting into her flesh, "and I know you are the one." Before Naglatha could threaten her further, there was a short rap on the door.

"Come," Naglatha ordered and released her grip on Tazi.

Tazi struggled to her feat as Milos Longreach entered his mistress's chamber. He bowed deferentially and waited for permission to speak. Naglatha walked back to him and brushed at her clothes as though her sorcerous action had sullied her garments somehow.

"What is it?" she asked, giving the bodyguard leave to speak.

"Mistress," Milos began, "we have returned with the duergar." Tazi snapped completely back to attention at the mention of Justikar.

"Is he alive, or did you simply recover the body from Karst?" Naglatha asked.

"He lives for now," Milos responded. "What is your wish?"

Before Naglatha could pronounce what Tazi was certain would be a death sentence on the dwarf, she spoke up. "Let him live," she requested and braced herself for the wizard's potentially furious response. She had to try, Tazi told herself. But Naglatha surprised her.

"Explain to me why I should," she demanded. "Perhaps I'll agree."

Rubbing her sore neck with one hand, Tazi offered, "He escaped, didn't he? That alone should show that he has some uses, not the least of which is resourcefulness."

"But he was captured," Naglatha countered.

"Yes," Tazi agreed, "but he's alive. And I am sure that was his doing, not yours or your servants. And, from what you've told me before that servant returned," she shot a discreet look at the bodyguard before continuing carefully, "a dwarf might prove even more useful. I could use him." She could see her words were having an effect on the Red Wizard.

"If you offer him his freedom," Tazi told her, "I am fairly sure that he would help."

"You think so, do you? I am less trusting than you, Tazi," Naglatha said. "I have had a few dealings with the likes of his type in the past and have my doubts."

Tazi stepped up to Naglatha and, in a low voice, warned, "I'm not trusting. Don't make that mistake with me."

Naglatha nodded and pressed her lips together in something that resembled, but was not quite, a smile. "Very well, Thazienne. Don't be wrong."

Tazi nodded. She watched Naglatha return to the table and grab her sack of gold. She turned and tossed the sack to Tazi. The thief snagged it from the air with one hand and looked questioningly at Naglatha.

"Part of our agreement," she told Tazi. "Was it worth it, Tazi? Was it worth all this?" she finally asked. Tazi, however, remained silent.

"Never mind," she eventually added. "We leave tomorrow, so rest up tonight. I hope, for your sake, there are no more disturbances. Milos," she nodded to her guard, "see her back to her room and make sure she's comfortable, and make sure Karst is suitably rewarded for his successful efforts."

Tazi left with the guard and, as the wizard's last question rang in her ears, realized she wasn't at all sure of the answer.

# CHAPTER SEVEN

*Later that night*

**M**ilos opened the door to Tazi's comfortable prison, and she recognized the heavy scent of copper in the air. Her stomach roiled, and she nearly lost the meal she had just consumed. Tazi was not queasy by nature. It was just that the last time she entered a room that smelled as this one did, she discovered the dismembered remains of an old lover. That discovery took her on a journey many miles from home and did not end happily. She swallowed hard against the rising nausea and looked about in the flickering candlelight. Sprawled face down on his cot, the dwarf lay there more dead than alive.

Tazi rushed over to his side and sat gingerly on the edge of the blood-soaked bed. His face was partially obscured by the pillow, but she could see the slow rise and fall of his back, so she knew he still breathed. He was filthy, and his clothes were torn. As far as she could tell, the most glaring injuries he suffered were the ones he sustained on his back. His tunic was shredded and stuck to his skin in a bloody puddle. Tazi carefully lifted it away from his ripped skin and, as she had no implements whatsoever, tore it open down the length of his back by hand. She hissed in distress at what she discovered.

Crisscrossing his sinewy back were ruby slashes that continued to seep blood. Grimacing in disgust at the extent of the injuries, Tazi glanced over at the older bodyguard who still stood calmly in the open doorway. Tazi knew he and Heraclos possessed scimitars, but these were not the wounds that a sharp blade would leave in a fair battle. Tazi studied the dwarf's torn flesh and realized these were the marks of some kind of savage beast.

"Mistress Naglatha's pet griffon," the guard offered in explanation as though he sensed Tazi's confusion.

Tazi had seen a griffon only once when she was growing up and knew them to be formidable beasts. Years ago, her father had been invited to enter the Hunting Gardens of the Hulorn. The Hulorn was Selgaunt's ruling merchant mayor, and he controlled an expansive set of grounds in the northeast section of the city. He kept it stocked with various exotic animals such as hippogriffs, pegasi, and sphinxes. When her father accepted the invitation, he had taken the opportunity to bring his little daughter with him. Tazi remembered the day as something special not because she saw so many amazing creatures, including a fledgling griffon going through its first molt, but because it was a day without rules and responsibilities. It had been a day where she had been just a little girl and the Old Owl had been just a daddy.

"I see," Tazi replied, returning to the present. "Well, if he is going to survive his run-in with your mistress's pet, he's going to need a healer now." The guard remained impassive to Tazi's demand. Her bargain with Naglatha had really changed very little of their living arrangements, Tazi realized, not that she had really believed otherwise.

"All right then," she tried, "if that is too much to ask, could I at least have some basic supplies?"

"What do you have in mind?" the guard finally asked.

"Another tub of clean, warm water, towels, bandages, any salves that might be handy and anything for pain that you can get your hands on."

When the guard stood motionless, Tazi snapped, "Look, Naglatha spared his life at my request. Right now, she wants me, and I suspect she'd do a fair bit to see that I at least have the illusion of happiness. If you don't get me at least some of those items, the only thing that is going to please me at the moment will be to see you try to hold your own with that griffon, and I won't hesitate to tell her that. Now go!"

Tazi could see that Milos contemplated her words very briefly before shutting the door. Maybe he even went to get me some supplies, she thought ruefully. She turned her attention back to the dwarf who needed help regardless. Careful not to move him unnecessarily, she rose slowly and went to the table where the tub of old water and linens were. The water was dirty but would do in a pinch if that was all she had to work with. She found a few linens that were still fresh, and she began to rip them into strips that she could use as makeshift bandages. While she was gathering up what supplies she could, Milos pushed open the door with his shoulder. His arms were full of gauze, salves, a fresh tunic and a few other items Tazi could not easily recognize. Heraclos marched in behind him with a small basin of steaming water. Tazi moved the small table against Justikar's cot and motioned to it.

"Just put all that here," she directed them. The bodyguards obliged silently and stacked the medical supplies carefully on the small stand. Without a word to her or a backward glance at the dwarf, the two filed out. Tazi shrugged, pleased that she at least had something for the dwarf's injuries. Then she set about cleaning him up.

Tazi took one of the clumps of gauze and dipped it into the warm water. She wrung out the excess moisture and began to very delicately clean out some of the dirt and debris from Justikar's wounds. As soon as the warm, moist cloth touched the dwarf, he moaned and stirred.

"Leave off," he murmured angrily. "Don't touch me."

He feebly tried to swat at her with one hand.

"Just hold still," Tazi tried to soothe him. "I want to clean these up a little," she explained, referring to his messy wounds. "I'll be quick about it."

"I don't need you touching me," he growled, his voice growing stronger as the water roused him some. He squirmed a little, and that caused one of his many wounds to flow more freely.

Tazi threw the bloody cloth on the floor and grabbed the dwarf by his shoulders. As she tried to pin him down, she shouted, "Keep fighting me, and you're going to bleed to death! Judging by these wounds, dying is something you seem to fight tooth and nail. You've made it this far, so don't ruin it now." The dwarf lessened his struggles, but Tazi wasn't sure it was because she demanded it, or he was just growing weaker.

"Look," she explained, "twice now you owe me your life."

"What?" he rasped.

"Naglatha would have let her manservants feed what's left of you to that griffon if I hadn't asked for your life." The duergar managed a snort, and Tazi smiled slightly. "That's right; thanks to me you get to continue to breathe, at least a little while longer. The deal she and I struck was that Naglatha's to give you your freedom in exchange for your assistance. Just like me."

"I see," Justikar whispered painfully.

"I agree," Tazi said. "I don't believe her either, but it buys us more time. As for me, I'll consider us even if you help me in this mission she's scheming. Do that," Tazi added, "and we're quit of any debt between us. Agreed?"

The duergar mumbled something unintelligible to Tazi. She knew he was angry but counted on the fact that he hated to be obliged more. She picked up a fresh bit of gauze and started on his wounds again. When he didn't squirm, Tazi smiled and suspected they had a deal.

She continued the long process of cleaning his injuries of debris. She had learned the hard way that if they weren't cleaned well, infection and scarring could set in. Her right wrist still bore the scars of a dog attack she had suffered as a child. She had been afraid to tell her father about it and had hidden the injury. It was only after it started to fester that she told anyone at all. Tazi's mother had her healed, but asked that a scar remain to remind her daughter of foolish choices.

As she dabbed at the wounds, she saw the dwarf's shoulders tense in pain, though he remained stoically silent throughout her ministrations. Tazi attempted a trick, of sorts, to take his mind off of his cuts.

"So," she asked him casually, to distract him from what she had to do, "just how did you manage to slip out of here last night?" She was about to ask the question again, uncertain if Justikar had heard her or if he was simply trying to ignore her again, when he turned his head the other way on the pillow to face her. She could see his left eye had swollen almost shut. He peered at her through a narrow slit.

"Wouldn't you like to know?" he replied, and Tazi was certain there was almost a moment of bantering between them.

"Actually, I would like to know," she answered with a touch of admiration in her voice. "After all, not only did you get past me, but past those two," she paused to hook a thumb toward the door, "as well."

"Simple enough," he hissed as Tazi worked on a particularly deep gash.

"Really?" Tazi prodded, continuing her work.

"Yes," he answered. "Those two guards aren't that sharp, and it didn't take me long to get past them. I have a 'skill' when it comes to types like them."

"You'll have to share it with me," Tazi told him. "All right, so you got past those two. Then what happened?" As she questioned him, Tazi examined him to see if any ribs had been damaged in the attack.

"I was going to make my way to the Sunrise Mountains, because they were the closest," he explained. Tazi realized he must have been in serious pain to have been so forthcoming. She rummaged around on the table to see if any of the bottles or sundries that Milos brought might be something to relieve pain. She wasn't sure of most of their contents.

"Don't bother with that garbage," Justikar said through gritted teeth. "I wouldn't trust that tainted stuff. I'll be fine without it."

"I'm sure you will, but why turn away something you might need?" Tazi countered. "Your bleeding—"

"It will stop in short order," he informed her. "My family wasn't just given the surname 'Stoneblood.' We have it. It'll start to thicken up soon enough. Though," he grudgingly admitted, "I suppose it was smart to clean those scrapes out."

When he closed his eyes for a moment, Tazi smiled. She didn't want him to catch her laughing at his admission. "So," she prompted, "you were going to make your way to the mountains. What happened next?"

"I was close," he whispered, and Tazi could hear the disappointment in his voice. He kept his eyes closed and continued, "I had cleared the forest, and I could just see the cool darkness of an inviting tunnel in the foothills ahead of me."

"And?" Tazi asked.

"And Naglatha's pet bird showed up. You can probably figure out the rest for yourself since you're cleaning up most of it."

"Tell me anyway," she said, "it takes my mind off of the mess back here."

"If I would have had any real weapon on me," Justikar defended his loss, "I could have fought that thing off. But, unarmed as I was, I suppose it could have been worse."

"Not by much, I'll wager," Tazi quipped. She finished up with his wounds and tried to make him a little more comfortable without being obvious about it

"I hurt it, but not enough. The thing caught me with its wings and tossed me around like I was a child's doll. Eventually, I simply played dead. That's when it dragged me back here," he ended. "Must've had orders to bring me back regardless of my condition as proof that it succeeded." Tazi moved the small table aside and brought a chair over near his cot. She sat down and began to idly sort through the bottles and potions the guards brought.

"It seems, given how things turned out, you were

the one who made the right choice here," he told her reluctantly.

"I tried to tell you," she replied calmly, "there was no choice for me. I stay for my family's safety."

"Mmm…" was all the dwarf said.

"Look," she told him more softly, "I don't trust Naglatha for one moment. She desperately wants a part of some book that's located deep within a place called the Citadel." Tazi saw him open his swollen eye as far as he could and regard her with a gleam. "You know the place?" she asked.

"No," he rasped and shut his eye again abruptly.

"Hmm…why do I not believe you? No matter. She'll turn on me the minute she has what she wants in her icy grip. I'm no fool," she told him. He opened his eye again and looked at her with a sharp awareness.

"But," she said and leaned even closer in a conspiratorial whisper, "if I get her what she wants, then I'll be in the better position to barter with her. You see?"

The dwarf moved his head in agreement, and Tazi could almost swear that he smiled. "You know," he said slowly and Tazi was once again reminded that his voice sounded like rocks rubbing together, "you might not be as naïve as you look."

Tazi grinned back. "You haven't seen anything yet."

Tharchion Pyras Autorian had to walk quickly in order to keep up with Zulkir Szass Tam. The young Tharchion of Thaymount was amazed at the speed the lich managed when he moved. He had to remind himself once again that his mentor, as he generously liked to think of Szass Tam, was already over two centuries old. He himself was only past thirty years, the youngest tharchion in Thay. "The beginning and the end," he told his autharchs when he referred to his relationship with the Zulkir of Necromancy.

But there were times, mostly in the dead of night, when Pyras wondered why Szass Tam had chosen him over so many of the other autharchs. Over the few years Pyras had embraced the life of politics, mostly to please his father, who rode him constantly over his minimal arcane abilities, he had seen that only the most ruthless and powerful ever moved up in rank in Thayan politics. With his unusual head of red hair that resisted both mundane and magical attempts to remove, he stood out amongst his clean-shaven companions. But that was the only reason why. Pyras again preferred to think of himself as fair-minded, though he heard more than one competitor refer to him as weak willed. And yet, he had caught the attention of the powerful lich, Szass Tam, a few years ago. Under his tutelage, Pyras had been appointed tharchion of the Thaymount over many others who had fought for the position.

I must have some abilities that have yet to show themselves to anyone but Szass Tam, he thought to himself. That must be it.

"Try and keep up," Szass Tam ordered him.

Pyras trotted alongside the lich, glad at least to be free of the horde of bodyguards that normally accompanied him. Only in the Citadel and only when he was alone with the lich was he allowed to travel without his armed shadows. By order of the Zulkir of Necromancy, Pyras had to be surrounded by a small garrison at all times, except in situations such as this one. The young tharchion took it as another sign of his importance to his mentor, that the lich kept him so well protected.

"Now," Szass Tam said, "I expect most of our guests to arrive within the next two days. Did you remember the seating arrangements that I asked you to make?" He smiled gently at Pyras. But Pyras knew that smile could hide much.

The young man hurriedly consulted a small journal he carried in his hands. As they continued to walk, he flipped through the pages until he came across a rough seating diagram. Before he had a chance to go any farther, Szass Tam plucked the book from his unresisting soft, white hands and studied it. Pyras watched his mentor as the lich thumbed through the rest of the tharchion's notes for the occasion. He saw that the lich nodded at some notations, while he frowned at others.

Pyras used the opportunity to study his mentor unobserved for a moment. He was amazed at the lich's advanced years. He knew well enough that it was the work of a spell that gave Szass Tam the appearance of a man in his forties, with long black hair graying along the temples, ruddy cheeks, droopy mustache and close-cropped beard. But Pyras seriously doubted that it was a spell that gave the lich his fire. The zulkir practically glowed whenever he was around others, he was so driven. Pyras found himself shaking his head in wonder.

"You disagree?" Szass Tam asked, breaking the young man's reverie.

"N-no," he stammered and tried to recover himself. He hoped the lich hadn't been aware of his lack of attention. If he had, the young man knew there would be a fierce penalty to pay. But, it appeared Szass Tam was so caught up in his own plans that Pyras's gaffe escaped notice.

"Good. It's a little late in the day not to see eye-to-eye on that, don't you agree?"

"Absolutely," Pyras agreed to whatever it was the lich had mentioned, glad that Szass Tam hadn't caught his mistake, and he returned the lich's broad smile.

As he and the lich passed down a hallway that was comprised of decorative stones resembling frozen seawater, there was a faint rumbling. Both Red Wizards stopped in their tracks. The rumbling grew louder until the floor shook faintly beneath their feet, and a few fine lines appeared and grew in the stonework of the surrounding walls like spider webs. Pyras squeezed his eyes shut as the rumbling continued, clutching his temples. He swayed as black spots danced in front of his hazel eyes, and he feared that he was about to faint. He reached out blindly, trying to find the wall for support. Inadvertently, he caught the lich by his forearm instead. But he was too unsteady to let go. He hung onto the zulkir until the shaking faded away.

"Are you quite through?" the lich demanded, and

there was no way for Pyras to miss the contempt in Szass Tam's voice.

As soon as the spots cleared from his vision, he sheepishly released his hold on the lich and tried desperately to compose himself.

"I'm so sorry," he offered lamely to the necromancer, "I don't know what happened."

"Perhaps you are coming down with something," Szass Tam offered as he smoothed out the wrinkles on his red robe where Pyras had clutched his arm, "or perhaps these occasional rumblings are frightening you more than you care to let on, hmm?"

"I am not sure what is wrong," he replied softly. "These headaches have been growing increasingly painful."

"Well," the lich said after some consideration, "I suppose it would be a shame if you became so incapacitated that I would be forced to look for a replacement for you amongst the other autharchs." He stroked his beard thoughtfully. "However, it wouldn't be the first time that happened. You do recall your predecessor, don't you?"

Pyras blanched as he remembered the man who had held the position of tharchion before him. He could still hear the man's screams in his dreams some nights. And, judging by the look on Szass Tam's face, Pyras suspected he wouldn't have any compunction removing him either. Fearfully, Pyras scurried along to keep up with the lich. He didn't want to give him another reason to be displeased. He tried to redirect the necromancer's attentions.

"Uh, there was something else I wanted to tell you, Zulkir," Pyras began, trying to somehow win himself back into his mentor's favor. Szass Tam returned to his brisk pace again, and Pyras had no choice but to speak to him on the run, as it were. "My network of spies," he started, trying hard to ignore what sounded like a soft chuckle from the lich, "has come to me with some disturbing news."

"And what might that be, dear Pyras?" the necromancer asked, and Pyras could see amusement dance in his black eyes.

"They have reported that more than a few of the standing armies of the other zulkirs have been getting restless lately," he explained.

"Really?" Szass Tam questioned.

"Yes," the young tharchion continued, "more so than usual, and even the regular entertainments have not been effectual in relieving their tension. Certainly, the gladiatorial games are as popular as ever with the local populace, but the members of the armies themselves are not as distracted as they once were by them."

"So what do you suggest?" Szass Tam asked his young protégé.

"I don't have anything to add to what you've already come up with," Pyras told him, trying hard not to sound breathless as he struggled to keep up with the lich. He didn't want Szass Tam to see that he had become a touch weaker lately.

"I'm so glad you approve, tharchion," said the lich.

"I only meant to say that once again your timing is

perfect," Pyras replied and secretly hated himself for the groveling tone that he had adopted. "To have all of the other zulkirs and tharchions here in the Citadel will be a perfect opportunity for you to quell their unease and refocus their energies."

The necromancer stopped short, and Pyras nearly stumbled in to him. He knew that would have been the biggest mistake of all to make. Pyras was fearful that he had, again, said the wrong thing. But he was not the object of the necromancer's scrutiny. He followed the lich's gaze and realized it was fixed on one of the many support columns in the hallway. Pyras could see that there were new cracks along the top. As he moved closer, the floor made a horrible screech. Lifting up his sandaled foot, Pyras discovered several small marble chips scattered along the floor. Probably from the column, he thought morosely. I'm sure I'll be blamed for this somehow.

But the necromancer remained silent and contemplative. He ran his strong hands along the length of the column and rapped his fist against it as though testing its integrity. Pyras almost thought the lich looked worried, but then dismissed the notion. Pyras had never seen Szass Tam anxious about anything, so he didn't even have an idea what that emotion might like look on the lich's dead features. He was certain the zulkir was just looking for where he might have slipped up again.

Pyras wasn't sure if the lich was more displeased with him lately or not. And he didn't want to admit it, but the recent volcanic activity had made him somewhat anxious. Granted, living in a series of volcanic ridges, a certain amount of tectonic activity was unavoidable. The peaks did erupt now and again—they always had. In fact, the quantity of ash falling in the northerly and eastern areas of High Thay, downwind of the Thaymount, was so copious that it rendered the area nearly uninhabitable. Nevertheless, a few determined Red Wizards struggled to raise their own towers in the desolate spots regardless. So, quakes and tremors were not unusual. But something was different this time, Pyras felt it. Added to that was his distress and puzzlement over his recent headaches. They might have been the result of the endless nights of planning the lich had put him through for this upcoming counsel. That was a possibility. He was definitely under more stress because of it, but maybe he was just a touch frightened by the quakes as well. He knew most of the other Red Wizards that inhabited High Thay and the Thaymount had expressed their concerns to one degree or another over the last few tendays. So he wasn't the only one who felt something was amiss.

And there was Szass Tam. Pyras felt he was under constant pressure to please the lich. And he wasn't mistaken there. Over the last few tendays, as Pyras sat bent over his desk making plans and taking notes, Szass Tam had been always over his shoulder. That had to have been when the headaches started. Who wouldn't suffer from them under those conditions? On the surface, though, Tam had been supportive and instructional the whole time. He even brought me carafes of wine when he thought I needed them, Pyras remembered fondly. He had never done that before. Pyras dismissed his concerns with the thought that he couldn't fail the lich.

Pyras realized that the necromancer was studying his face closely. There would be no disguising the fact this time that the young, clean-shaven tharchion had not been paying attention with the proper amount of rapt fascination to the zulkir. However, the lich's next statement caught Pyras off-guard.

"Your eyes look more yellow to me than usual. Are you feeling well?" he asked, but Pyras wasn't sure if there was concern or calculation in his black eyes.

"I am fine," Pyras replied. "I just want to make sure that everything goes the way you've planned. You've worked so diligently toward this." Once again, the wheedling, needy tone had crept back into his voice.

"I am so pleased my efforts have not gone unnoticed. You do have such a sharp eye," he snapped, and Pyras knew he had angered the lich.

"See to it everything else is as I asked," he ordered and turned to leave the damaged hall. "No need to follow. I am done with you today." And in a swirl of maroon and black, the lich was gone, more than likely to his inner chambers in the lower level.

No sooner had the necromancer departed than another quake rumbled through the edifice. Pyras lay a hand across his forehead and felt his knees turn to water. As he crumpled backward in a dead faint, his last conscious thought was one of relief that Szass Tam had not witnessed this latest embarrassment.

# CHAPTER EIGHT

*2 Kythorn, 1373 DR*

Tazi looked out across the plateau to the west. She placed her hands against the small of her back and tried to ease the ache that had settled there since she had left Pyrados, days passed. The road was not as well maintained as some of the others in Thay, and the bouncing of the carriage was wearing on her.

She and Naglatha rode in the first carriage while Justikar and the two bodyguards followed up in a modified cart that also held all of Naglatha's personal effects stacked high. The griffon, tethered to the last cart, brought up the rear. Tazi had been surprised their wooden vehicle hadn't cracked under the weight, and she sympathized with the two horses forced to pull that load. The Rashemi drivers Naglatha had hired, however, swore the vehicles and the beasts could stand the burden. Of course, they had only had to load the cargo, not pull it themselves. Tazi suspected they simply didn't want to share the hefty fee that Naglatha had offered them with anyone else. Greed was the same wherever Tazi ventured.

For days now, she had traveled alone in the Red Wizard's company. Naglatha had obviously felt secure enough in her bargain with Tazi because she had relegated her servants to ride with the duergar. She was right, Tazi had mused. With her family at stake, there was no way Tazi would have tried anything. The trip had been without incident, and the only point of discussion at all had been at the beginning of their journey as Naglatha had debated what route she wanted to take to reach the Citadel. Her manservants suggested the Eastern Way to Tyraturos and from there the High Road to Eltabbar. Milos offered up the fact that while the route was less direct, the roads were so impeccably well maintained that they would cross them quite quickly and make up time that way.

"And well they should be," she had said in response to the road's condition, "considering the fees they charge everyone at those cursed tax stations."

She had considered the matter for a while, and Tazi was somehow not surprised when Naglatha chose to disregard her bodyguard's advice. She picked the more direct, but more difficult route.

"We'll go along the Surague Escarpment and skirt Lake Thaylambar until we reach Eltabbar. From there we can use our own transportation the rest of the way to the Citadel," she informed them.

Heraclos had pointed out that the Sunrise Mountains were just to the east of that route, and that was where they had recaptured the dwarf. "He could try it again and slow us down all the more."

Tazi recalled how coldly Naglatha had regarded her at that instant. "I don't think there is much likelihood of that occurring, do you, Tazi?"

"Not a chance," Tazi had promised her, but in reality, she wasn't so sure herself.

"See, I'm certain the dwarf will be no trouble for you both," she had informed her servants. Heraclos had started to protest, but she cut them off.

"Tazi and I will be just fine. I prefer to take in the scenery with her alone," she said, stressing the last word.

And so, for the last few days, Tazi had ridden alongside Naglatha in their partially covered carriage and took in the sights of the Thayan countryside. If she hadn't been a prisoner, she would have almost enjoyed it. To her right, Tazi watched the River Thazarim flow along contentedly, knowing that it would eventually meet up with the Sea of Fallen Stars to the south and in due course with Lake Thaylambar to the north. Naglatha explained that it was the largest body of water in the country, feeding the River Thay and the River Thazarim.

A few carts passed them at that point, and Tazi could see several men outfitted with strange gear, nets, and hooks too large and bulky for conventional fishing, and towing small water craft behind them. She finally broke down and questioned Naglatha about it.

"Deep in the heart of the lake, which is as cold as a slaver's heart," she recounted, "live huge herds of dragon turtles. Men have been trying for years to cull their numbers and catch the creatures. Most," she said with a smirk, "fail miserably and not all these parties come back intact, if they come back at all. Ever since an associate of mine, Brazhal Kos, actually managed to capture one of the magnificent creatures alive, it seems that the number of these forays has at the very least doubled. Oh well," she added, "the less fools alive the better."

Tazi turned away at those hash words. She still had a difficult time understanding why life was valued so poorly here. The view to the west was of a vast plain that was covered by rich fields and orchards. To Tazi, it appeared every square foot of useable tract was farmed. Granaries were stuffed to the point of bursting, and she could see no end in sight to the fertile ground.

"Why deal in slaves," she asked Naglatha, "when you've been so successful with your produce and grains?"

"The farm goods simply paved the way and opened up the markets for the slaves. That's where the coin is, after all," she explained.

"I thought you didn't believe in the trade policy?"

"I never said that. I can certainly appreciate the benefits of trade relations," Naglatha expounded. "I simply don't want them to usurp the natural course of Thay's growth."

Tazi grew silent and admired the fertile areas of

land. But, even as she appreciated how well tended and rich the orchards and fields were, she knew they hid a horrible secret. It was the blood and sweat of slaves that made all of it possible. Living beings that didn't benefit from their efforts but more than likely died from them. Somehow, she believed, that had to taint everything the land produced. And she wondered how many of the things she had taken for granted in life had some darkness behind them.

As she looked out over the rolling fields, the sun was setting in the distance. In those last few rays of evening, the fields changed from verdant green to a dark red. The color washed over everything as far as Tazi could see. It was as though a wave of blood covered the land, and Tazi shivered. If only there was something that I could do, she thought helplessly.

For the next few days, the small caravan held a simple schedule. They camped along the river each night, and the drivers broke camp every morning at the first light of dawn. The only other chore performed with any regularity was the brief grooming Naglatha's servants offered to the griffon, Karst. She did not allow her beloved pet to go neglected.

The nights were much cooler than in Pyrados, with rain every night. The closer they got to the Second Escarpment, the colder it got as they climbed higher in elevation. Only once did Tazi see Justikar through the journey; Naglatha must have given explicit orders that they were not to see or speak to each other. But, as they were breaking camp, Tazi caught sight of the duergar. His arms were bound and, if it were at all possible, the dwarf looked angrier than ever. However, He also looked to Tazi like he was moving somewhat easier, so she believed his injuries were healing up without complications.

The group stopped only briefly in the capital city of Eltabbar. There, Naglatha released the drivers and their gear from her service as she kept a small town-house of sorts in the city and assured them she had ample supplies of her own. Tazi was pleased to see that she also left most of her various trunks behind at her residence and traveled fairly lightly from that point onward. Tazi couldn't stand all the gear and the noise they made. It reminded her of the last trip she made with her family.

They lingered in the city only long enough for Naglatha to confer with her spies. As soon as she received confirmation that the tharchion of that city, Dmitra Flass, had already departed, Naglatha hurried the group along.

As the troupe departed the canal-ridden city, Tazi could see the forbidding ridges and snow-capped peaks of the Thaymount. They looked to Tazi like rotted, frostbitten fingers reaching for the sky, and she wondered what mysteries lay buried beneath their surface. She suspected she would find out soon enough.

They traveled along the River Eltab on their way to the Citadel. Tazi and Naglatha sat side-by-side, while Milos drove the carriage, and Heraclos and the griffon brought up the rear. Justikar sat alongside Milos, in front, where he was in plain view. When they had left the capital, Naglatha had untied his bonds. Tazi had started to thank her, but Naglatha had held up a hand in warning.

"It would simply be too hard to explain why I traveled with anything less than a trusted servant in these parts," she elucidated.

Now, climbing into the Second Escarpment, Tazi saw a few fields again, though less expansive then some of the ones she saw on the plateau below.

"These are not meant to yield the quantities of produce and food as the tracts below," Naglatha answered her. "What you see now are some of the private plantations and properties of some of the tharchions and zulkirs and, to a lesser degree, some of our wealthier nobles."

"But I thought most of the government officials would have residences in their own provinces?" Tazi asked.

"True," Naglatha replied. "Think of these places as summer retreats. When the next few months hit, many will vacation up here to the cooler climates. And, it is logistically easier for the zulkirs and tharchions to keep these here instead of in their regions," she finished and pointed to a structure some miles in the distance. Tazi tried to see what it was that Naglatha was referring to. It was only after they were closer that Tazi could make it out.

Along a ridge of one plantation, there was row after row of buildings that could only be best described as barracks. And in a small, cleared field, Tazi saw fifty or so humanoid creatures running drills. She squinted to determine what manner of beasts they were and saw that Justikar's back tensed up at the sight of the creatures. As well as she could remember from her lessons, there were few creatures that dwarves in general hated beside drow and orcs. Judging by their size, Tazi speculated the creatures had to be orcs.

Their carriage came relatively close to the training ground, and Tazi could see that there were several squads of the beasts training. Dressed in shabby colors of purple and yellow with haphazardly assembled armor, the beasts had the typical stooped stature, sloping foreheads, and piglike facial features Tazi knew to be common for orcs. They even had the protruding lower jaw with heavy canine teeth and the wolfish ears. But Tazi thought that all orcs had gray skin, much like the duergar, and blood-red eyes. These soldiers, though, were mottled in appearance, with patches of maroon all over, and even from a distance, Tazi could see the orcs' eyes were bright yellow.

"What are those things?" she asked Naglatha.

"Blooded Ones," she explained. Tazi looked at her quizzically and Naglatha laughed. "We have much here in Thay you never knew existed, don't we? It's too bad we don't have more time. The things I could show you. But I digress. What you are looking at there is probably one of the finest fighting forces you will ever live to see.

"Some time ago," the Red Wizard continued, and Tazi could hear the pride in her words, "our finest minds turned their research toward the creation of an ultimate warrior. And instead of trying to create something from nothing and wasting energy and effort, they looked to see how they could improve upon creatures that already existed. So they turned to orcs, who have many desirable qualities, but had proven to be unruly and untrustworthy at crucial moments.

"They refined a process where the orc young were treated in an alchemical bath of almost poisonous blood. After they emerged from the treatment, they were stronger, more pliable, and more willing to obey commands. What you see before you is only the first steps. Now that this method has proved fruitful, other species will be experimented upon next."

"Are there barracks of these monsters all over the Thaymount?" Tazi asked and couldn't imagine that many creatures in one relatively small area.

"No," Naglatha told her. "These creations are fairly expensive. Most of the other zulkirs and tharchions only have hordes of darkenbeasts, gnolls, and other, less-unusual forces around the Thaymount. The longer Szass Tam keeps us buying and selling, though, the more bored we grow. So," she told the amazed Tazi, "we play with things in our liberal free time."

Tazi looked at the troops and tried to picture thousands of these creatures nestled like pockets of vipers around the Thaymount. The image that it painted was overwhelming. What would happen if these Red Wizards ever did try to occupy the lands of their neighbors, or Faerûn for that matter, Tazi pondered, and why don't they?

"Milos," Naglatha shouted suddenly, "pull up to that orchard ahead."

While Tazi tried to make sense of what she had seen, Milos halted the carriage next to a small grove of orange trees, well tended, with nearly overripe fruit hanging like tumors from their branches.

"Get out," she ordered everyone. "We're nearly there," she told Tazi as they dismounted in unison. "It will be our last chance to speak somewhat freely before entering the Citadel, and I would not miss that opportunity." She pointed to the dwarf and ordered her guards to watch him as well as water the griffon. Naglatha motioned to Tazi, and the two women hopped the low fence and entered the orchard.

"Won't someone get angry?" Tazi asked sarcastically as she watched Naglatha help herself to a ripe fruit. The woman laughed and leaned against the tree as she started to peel the thick skin of the orange.

"Not likely," she chuckled. "You see, these trees belong to Pyras Autorian, and I have never met a more useless—"

"Watch out!" Tazi shouted.

From behind the tree, a soldier suddenly appeared with sword drawn. But as Tazi got a better look, she realized that it was no ordinary man. Its skin had a grayish cast to it and a leathery quality that no living being possessed. While its gait wasn't shambling, it lacked the fluid movements of the living. Its equipment was rusted, its clothes tattered.

"Zombie!" she yelled and grabbed Naglatha by the arm, yanking her clear just as the undead creature slashed at where the Red Wizard had been reclining. Suddenly, four more appeared from different areas of the orchard and began silently closing in on the women.

"To me!" Naglatha cried, but no one came. Tazi turned her head toward the carriage and saw that the dwarf and the guards had their hands full as several armed zombies cut them off. The griffon, Karst, reared up against his tether at the approach of the undead.

"Use your powers and do something," Tazi yelled to the Wizard, who appeared dazed.

"These are juju zombies," she explained in a low voice full of dread. "My magic is useless against them." And she shrunk behind Tazi.

One of the undead charged Tazi with a longstaff held at chest height. When it was nearly upon her, she kicked out at its solar plexus. The zombie bent over slightly and extended its arms forward from the force of her blow but made no sound. Tazi swung up the same leg and kicked the staff from its hands straight into the air. She caught the rod in the center with her right hand and, as the creature tried to charge her again, she bent sideways at the waist and caught the zombie with a final kick to the throat. It flew back several feet and didn't rise again.

No longer weaponless, Tazi swung the staff, which she held against her right arm, in an arc to her left and back to her right to give herself a little breathing room. She carried the staff like an extension of her arm, moving toward a larger clearing in the orchard in an attempt to draw the zombies away from Naglatha, who was proving worthless in the battle. The woman simply frowned and pressed both her hands against her temples but did nothing else. Tazi twirled the staff so that it was parallel to her body and let it slip through her fingers until it touched the ground. She struck a cocky pose and hoped to draw the creatures toward her.

"Come on," she baited them.

Perhaps sensing she would be more fun than the other woman, the remaining four closed in around her silently. With an evil grin on its face, one soldier drew its sword and charged Tazi. Swinging its weapon straight down toward her head with both rotted hands, the zombie came within inches of striking her. But Tazi swung the staff up with both hands somewhat at an angle and blocked the monster's blow. Simultaneously, while the monster's arms were still high in the air, she kicked it in the midsection, and the creature fell backward.

She turned her head and shoulders in time to block another's attack as it swung a cudgel at her back. She pivoted first and blocked the blow with the staff and continued to twist the rod, so that it struck the creature in the head. The very end of her weapon caught the zombie in the jaw and, as its head turned to one side, its lower jaw broke free with a ripping sound and flew across the orchard.

Tazi turned in time to see the remaining two rush her simultaneously. She threw the staff up with her arms to block them, stopped their sword blows, and pushed them back with the staff. She turned her weapon parallel to her body again and planted it in the fertile soil with a solid thud. Certain that it was anchored, Tazi grabbed the staff and turned sideways, using her momentum and the support of the staff to vault herself off of the ground. She kicked her legs in opposite directions and caught each zombie with one of them. She continued her swing, landed on her feet, and pulled the staff free with both her hands. She swung the weapon in an arc again and surveyed the ground to see who was next.

As suddenly as the attack began, it stopped. The juju zombies that were not completely incapacitated rose to their feet and stood at attention. Tazi turned with a wondering look at Naglatha, but the Red Wizard shook her head in denial. Likewise, the servants and Justikar also looked surprised as their battle had been paused for them as well. Beside Naglatha, the air shimmered.

About the size of a full length mirror, a pool of radiance appeared, and a shape started to coalesce in the center. Tazi, breathing hard, her weapon still in hand, watched in fascinated interest as a man's face and shoulders became clearer. He appeared to be in his forties and had piercing black eyes. With just a touch of gray at the temples of his black mane, Tazi thought he was very vigorous looking and found something about him oddly attractive. Judging by the sour expression on Naglatha's face, Tazi realized the two were not unfamiliar to each other.

"Ah," began the image in the pool, "Naglatha. I am so glad you were able to get a message through to me just now." The image looked at the battered zombie soldiers and Tazi could hear a 'tsk' sound escape the man's lips. "Luckily, I was able to stop my garrison before any harm could befall you."

"I am most grateful, Zulkir," Naglatha addressed him respectfully, but Tazi could see it irked the wizard to do so.

"I am sorry for the confusion," the image continued, "but I did not expect any of my guests to be robbing my orchards." A slow smile played about his lips, and Tazi realized that this could only be Szass Tam, the man Naglatha wanted to destroy. She tried to study him as best she could.

"Well, don't you mean Pyras Autorian's orchards? These are still his lands, aren't they?" Naglatha asked, and Tazi could see the calculating gleam in her eyes.

"Yes, yes," the necromancer dismissed, "his orchards."

"Well," Naglatha told the image, "no harm's done."

"No," Szass Tam agreed. "This matter is best forgotten. Considering how close you are, I will make sure that quarters for you, your servants, and your pet are waiting." Without warning, the image faded away.

Tazi kept a cautious eye on the zombies, but they lined up and filed away in the direction from which they had appeared. She tossed the staff to the ground and walked over to Naglatha. The wizard had her eyes closed and her brow furrowed. Tazi stood before her and waited until she opened them again.

"Well?" she asked Naglatha.

"I was making sure that no one was watching us any longer," she explained. "He is no longer scrying us."

"Szass Tam?" Tazi asked

"Yes," Naglatha nodded. "You handled yourself well," she acknowledged to Tazi.

"Not a scratch," Tazi replied.

"That incident was no accident, though," Naglatha deduced. "I wonder how many others attending the council might meet with misfortune before this is all said and done."

"Right this way," the elegantly dressed servant said as she led Naglatha down an elaborately carved corridor toward the other visiting dignitaries.

"Please make sure that my servants are treated accordingly for my rank," she said as she gave Tazi a parting wink. She and Justikar stood in the hall and waited for one of the other servants to assist them. It only took a few moments for a young girl, not nearly as richly decorated as the first, to appear. She smiled easily enough, and Tazi thought she was new and her probationary job was to assist the servants of the lich's guests. Not many of them were likely to complain if their bedcovers weren't turned down, so it was not a critical assignment.

"This way," she directed them in a high voice.

She took Tazi and Justikar down a narrow but well-lit passageway. There were several doorways open along the corridor, and Tazi could see humans that must have been the trusted servants of the important and wealthy guests of Szass Tam. They looked a bit confused in the large, well-furnished rooms with nothing to do. Tazi saw one young man who simply sat on a huge bed and stared straight at the wall in front of him, totally lost. She shook her head sadly and kept walking.

At the end of the passageway, the servant pointed to a room on the left. "I hope this will be satisfactory. We did not have any other rooms left, so I am afraid you and your companion must stay together." And the girl lowered her gaze. Tazi suspected she was almost embarrassed that the two of them, being of opposite sex, had to share quarters.

"It will be fine," she told the girl.

"You are welcome to maneuver through this corridor and you have access to a few of the work spaces along the next set of passageways. But that is all," she warned them.

"And how will we know when we've reached our boundaries?" Tazi asked.

The plump girl lost her timid smile. "Oh," she said gravely, "you'll know." She bowed and left them alone.

Tazi stepped into the room and was surprised at how well it was furnished, considering it was being used to house slaves. She figured that these wizards went out of their way to outshine each other, so some of the opulence had to spill over to the servants' quarters. While the girl who had led them to their room had been dressed well enough, Tazi wagered she didn't have a chamber nearly as fine as this one. Tazi padded over to one of the large beds and sank down gratefully with a huge sigh. She looked tiredly at the dwarf and could see he was furious.

"What?" she asked him, but her heart was not in it, and she was in no mood for a verbal fencing match.

"Is this worth it?" he demanded. "Is your crimson gold worth all the misery that this adventure of yours is going to cause? Will you be satisfied only when everything crumbles around you?"

Tazi jumped to her feet and prowled around the stylish furnishings. She was tired and sore and didn't want to fight with the duergar on top of everything else. But, most importantly, his words had struck a nerve. What had started out as a simple enough undertaking had rapidly turned on her, and Tazi didn't know for sure what she had mired herself into and what the final cost was going to be. She eventually returned to the bed and sat on the end of it. She rested her elbows on her knees and laced her fingers together.

"I don't know," she answered quietly. "Maybe you can tell me."

The dwarf appeared surprised by her response, perhaps because he expected more bravado from her. He searched the room until he found a stool the right size, and he pulled it up to her, but not too close.

"Why are you doing this?" he asked again, but in a softer tone, as he sat down.

Tazi looked at the dwarf and pursed her lips for a few moments, weighing things in her mind. Finally, she started, "When I was very young, I took it upon myself to learn how to steal. Why I did it is none of your business, nor do I think you'd even care," she said. "But I did. And the easiest place for me to start was in my home."

Tazi got up and moved around again. "I lived in a big house," she explained, "with lots of rooms. There were my parents and my two brothers and more than a handful of servants, so there was a lot for me to choose from.

"Mostly, I would take little trinkets from my mother or brothers. For a while, no one suspected me. After all," she paused to glance at the dwarf with a sideways grin, "I was just a little girl. And, as we always had some help coming or going, the servants took the brunt of the blame."

"You mean your slaves took the blame," Justikar corrected her.

Tazi winced at the implied accusation. "No," she said vehemently, "we did not own those people. They could come and go as they wanted. My family simply hired them to perform household duties for us. They always had a choice."

"Were there other jobs some of them could've taken instead of cleaning up after you? Did they have a vast skill set that allowed them to pick and choose their lot in life? Do you think they all had a real choice, Thazienne Uskevren?" Justikar asked her.

His accusations did not sit easily with Tazi. "Did you want to hear my reasons or not?" she snapped, irritated that there wasn't a single window to look out of and avoid the duergar's shrewd gaze.

"Go on," he told her.

"The servants took the blame," she continued, "but

I always managed to get the various baubles back to their rightful owners eventually. All right," Tazi admitted as she sat on the bed again, "returning the things took a bit of convincing by a trusted family...friend," she tripped over the word. "He taught me more than a few lessons.

"The last thing I planned to steal belonged to my father. I had pilfered something from everyone else and considered an item of my father's to be my crowning glory. He is—was," she corrected herself self-consciously and lowered her eyes, "a very powerful man. Sometimes I used to think he was cold to me, but now, I suspect he was simply afraid to show me how he felt about me.

"He was a great collector of the beautiful and the unusual. Most of the things he treasured were fairly large pieces of artwork, and I was a bit daunted by how I might hide a painting or some such," she told the dwarf. "I snuck into his study and started to look around and see what I might be able to lift. As I prowled around the room I had only been invited into on a few occasions at that point, something glowed softly from his desk and caught my attention." Tazi became somewhat lost in her memory and did not notice how closely the duergar watched her face.

"I crept over, careful not to disturb anything, and saw this odd lump of metal no bigger than my fist. It sat, carefully nestled in a chamois cloth on his big desk, amidst stacks of papers and quills. I had never seen anything like it before. As far as I knew, it was a piece of gold, but I had never seen gold that red before." Tazi paused to tug at her lower lip as though she was contemplating the theft right then and there.

"Whatever kind of gold it was," she told Justikar, "it was perfect for my plans. I pocketed the treasure and was gone like a shot. My father was livid when he discovered the crimson gold was gone," she ducked her shoulders and smiled sheepishly. "I had never seen him so furious before. He went on and on about how hard it had been to obtain and what he was going to do with the thief when he got his hands on him. . . ." she trailed away, lost in thought.

"So," Justikar asked, "what did your father do when he found out it was you?"

"He never found out, as far as I know," she replied. "My older brother discovered I had the stuff, and he played a 'prank' on me. After it was over, my left arm was broken, and my father's gold was lost forever. I was never able to return it to him.

"That was years ago," Tazi added after a long pause. "And now my father is dead, much too soon. There were things I still wanted to tell him, but that opportunity is gone now." Tazi chewed her lower lip, unaware that her eyes were brimming with unshed tears. She jumped up and walked over to a painting and appeared to study it.

"The house was too quiet, and my mother was desolate for a while after his death. When she was unhappy, I was all right as if somehow I could mourn my father through her. But a few tendays ago, I saw her smile again. I knew it was time for her to start to put away her grief. But that's when I became somewhat lost," she said softly.

"I didn't know how to let him go, I realized. And it came to me. I could bring back the only thing I ever stole from him, the only thing I ever ruined between us as an offering. I could say good-bye finally. That was what was worth coming to this forsaken place for and still is. . . ." her voice trailed away. She rubbed at her face and turned back to the dwarf.

"Foolish, wasn't I, all things considered?" she asked, prepared for the duergar's snide remarks and ridicule.

"No," he said with a dignity she didn't imagine he would ever show her. "No."

She was nonplussed and simply stared at him for a while. In due course, she walked back over to the bed and sat down, studying him.

"All right," she said finally, "now you. Why are you here?"

"I'm a prisoner, in the wrong place at the wrong time," he replied.

"Look," Tazi shot back at him, "I'm too tired for this. I admit, I don't know much about duergar, but I do know you are a long way from home. And people don't normally stray too far away without a good reason. I'd honestly like to know, if you would be willing to tell me. We are stuck in here together."

The dwarf turned his head slightly and stared at her. Eventually Tazi became ill at ease and cast her eyes downward.

"What are you doing?" she asked and felt the heat rush to her cheeks.

"Faces are like stones," he answered enigmatically. "Their history, their character is written there plainly if one knows how to read it." He sighed deeply, as though he had come to a decision.

"Fair enough," he said after a pause, "a truth for a truth. I came here for family, too." Tazi watched him encouragingly but didn't want to interrupt him if he was willing to tell her about himself.

"My brother left our home several months ago and traveled here to Thay. You don't need to know where 'home' is, either," he shot at her in anticipation of her question, but Tazi just nodded in agreement. "He is the dreamer in the family, not me. You say you know something of dwarves. I'd wager not too much. Most humans don't bother. Did you know, for example, that up until a few years ago, our numbers were dwindling? And when I say 'our' I mean all races of dwarves."

"I didn't know that," Tazi acknowledged honestly, "but I always suspected that there were not great numbers of you."

"Great numbers," Justikar snorted. "You have no idea. And I'm not going to tell you, either. But a few years ago, the dwarven people received the Thunder Blessing, and suddenly we can't stop making whelps," he explained, and Tazi couldn't understand why he sounded disgusted. "All of the dwarves except us—except the Duergar." There was no mistaking the bitterness that edged his words.

"Once again, the gray dwarves were cheated out of what every other dwarf benefited from. That seems to be our lot in life, though we don't deserve it. I expected no less. But, as I said, my brother is a dreamer and a scholar. He wanted more. He was always searching for evidence, proof that there was more to it than just us. Adnama came across some parchments some months ago that led him to believe that there might be an offshoot of our kind located here."

"Here?" Tazi asked and pointed to the floor of their room. "Is that why you lit up when I mentioned the Citadel the night you were wounded?"

"Somewhere in the depths below the Citadel," the duergar nodded, "and here he came. I know he made it as far as some of the tunnels below, but that's when I lost track of him."

"So you're here to find him," Tazi finished, "and reunite your people."

"If there is another vein of duergar, if we were to combine numbers, we could become an unstoppable force," he informed her.

Tazi frowned. "And here I thought you just wanted your brother back and maybe what was best for your people. How are you any different from Naglatha or any of these other Red Wizards?" She shook her head and climbed all the way onto the bed. As she stretched out, she looked at him again.

"Get some rest," she told him, suddenly exhausted, "so we're ready for tomorrow. I think I understand you better now." She closed her eyes and was asleep in mere moments.

Justikar watched the woman sleep for a while. When he was sure it was a deep slumber, he moved silently to her side and deftly removed her worn sack without jostling her or it at all. He swung the leather sack in his grip twice and smiled.

"I came here for family, too," he whispered to the sleeping Tazi and slunk out of their chamber into the darkened hallway beyond.

# CHAPTER NINE

When she heard the light footsteps in the room, Tazi opened her eyes and instinctively reached for the knife she had secreted in her night table. As she fumbled around for it, and came up empty handed, Tazi remembered that she was not in her bed in Stormweather Towers, though it was as comfortable as hers, but in the depths of the Citadel. While her eyes focused on the source of the noise, she realized it was not some unknown intruder, but the duergar that had roused her. She sat bolt upright when she saw he was standing in the doorway to their room with her sack in his strong hands.

"What do you think you're doing?" she demanded and jumped from the bed to pull her bag from his unresisting fingers.

"Take a look inside," the dwarf directed her,

and Tazi saw he had a pleased expression on his face. She peered into the sack and looked back down at him incredulously.

"What have you done?" she whispered.

"While you slept, I did some exploring. Since that fat, pasty-faced girl said there were some workshops available to us, I thought it best to see for myself if that were true. There is a passable forge and bellows, so I made use of them during the night," he told her smugly.

Tazi could see that the dwarf was watching her closely. She pulled the drawstrings farther open and extracted a small, razor sharp dagger that radiated with a deep red shine from the bag. She would have described the piece as delicate if she hadn't seen the evil glint to its edge.

"That metal was a little tough to work with and I had to use almost all of it. It's not nearly as malleable as regular gold. In fact, it appeared to be even harder than steel. And there's something else about it," he added quietly, "a quality I can't put my finger on. It's not something I have ever run across before. I wouldn't mind having some of it myself."

Tazi relit one of their lamps and inspected the dagger in its ruddy glow. The blade felt like a natural extension of her hand. The weight and balance were perfect. And she wasn't able to deny that the workmanship was some of the best she had ever beheld. And Tazi was a woman who had seen and could afford the finest. When she gazed at the dwarf again, she could see he enjoyed her pleasure in his skill.

"But, Justikar," she asked in a curious voice, "why

did you do it? I know it's a good idea to have a weapon, but why did you do it to my gold?"

"I thought about what you told me last night," he explained to her seriously, "and I think this will make a more fitting offering to the spirit of your father."

"How is that?" she wondered.

"Because this," he nodded to the dagger she held expertly in her white hand, "is what you have become, Thazienne Uskevren. If you think long and honestly, you will know I am right about that. And to make peace with your sire, you will have to make peace with yourself."

Tazi frowned at his words and had little to say. She busied herself with wondering where she could secret the blade, but all the while the dwarf's words echoed in her ears. Had she become something sharp and deadly like the dagger? A woman who appeared to be one thing and yet was really something else? Weren't the dwarf's sentiments similar to the words Steorf had voiced when he gave Tazi her necklace saying the chain was deceiving, like her?

"You see more than I give you credit for," she informed the duergar.

"You just don't know me," he replied.

"I think I might like to," Tazi told him with a smile.

"No," he warned her seriously, "no, you wouldn't."

Tazi shrugged her shoulders and slipped the dagger into her right boot for the time being. Given all the wizards that were housed in the Citadel, she decided there were probably enough magical items present that the dagger might go unnoticed. If it did, she would have a fine weapon that would come in handy. And if it was discovered, she would at least know it had been confiscated and not search for it fruitlessly later on.

"What else did you find while I was snoring away? Surely you didn't spend your entire time making one, little blade?" The dwarf gave her a dirty look at her last statement until he saw her crooked grin and realized she was teasing.

"Why don't you come with me, and I'll show you?" he invited.

Tazi grabbed a glass from her table and rinsed the morning taste from her mouth and ran her fingers through her tangled, shoulder-length hair. The dwarf moved over to a dressing table against the wall while she was busy and rummaged around the bottles and brushes. When he found what he wanted, he grabbed it and came back to where Tazi sat.

"Is this what you need?" he asked and held out an item to Tazi.

She turned and saw he was holding a hand mirror for her. She was about to snap at him until she saw his sly smile. She wasn't the only one who liked to slip in a joke.

"Show me," Tazi told him, ready to go.

Together, they snuck out into the hall. The rest of the chamber doors were shut, and Tazi wondered if the other servants were taking advantage of the events and resting in or if they had already gone to assist their respective masters.

"Do you think they've gone?" she whispered cautiously to the duergar.

"You'll see," was all Justikar offered.

Tazi studied the walls. There were many designs carved into them. She still marveled at the fact that they were now deep underground. Whoever had constructed the structure, be it the lizardfolk Naglatha mentioned or some other equally fantastic beings, Tazi was overwhelmed at their abilities. Stones and other decorative tiles and mosaics covered the hallway, and the tunnel had been cut with such precision and squared angles, it looked like a corridor one would find in any well-built house or mansion. There wasn't the slightest hint that it was bored through solid rock except for the absence of windows.

Tazi followed Justikar like a shadow. When they reached the end of the servants' quarters, the dwarf turned to the left, though the corridor continued in two directions. The very next chamber they came to was the metal shop.

Tazi followed Justikar in and shut the door behind them. Truthfully, Tazi was glad they didn't go any farther down the passageway as she was unwilling to test the girl's warnings regarding their boundaries just yet.

She moved about the room, and Tazi could still feel the heat from Justikar's recent fires. Without any windows, though, Tazi was puzzled why the place didn't smell more of burning metal. She looked questioningly at the dwarf, and Justikar pointed to a few, well hidden openings. A unique venting system in the chamber allowed the excess heat and smoke to escape without filling the room with its noxious odor.

"I had the same thought as you," Justikar explained to Tazi, "before I started working in here. When I found those," he pointed to the series of openings, "it got me thinking."

"If there are hollows up above," Tazi replied, following the dwarf's logic, "then there might be hollows elsewhere."

Justikar nodded and walked over to a far wall, motioning for Tazi to follow. She studied the spot where the dwarf was standing and ran her fingers lightly over the façade of brickwork. She felt two spots that were somewhat suspect but, try as she could, she couldn't release any of the stones or trip any mechanism.

The dwarf half-pushed her aside and deftly pushed a brick face at a certain angle. A slice of the block slid a few inches to one side. With that pin free, the entire brick twisted ninety degrees. Justikar released his hold on the stone and took a step back. With a slow grinding, a section of the wall shifted back and slid to the right, exposing a pitch black maw.

"You were close," he told her. "You just lacked the right touch."

"Nicely done," Tazi complimented the duergar and chose not to take his words as an insult though they irked her. She'd been breaking into things for years now and felt she would have found it, given more time. Pride and her temper, she realized, had no place here if they were going to work together.

"It's nothing to someone who spends their life

around such things," he said as he dismissed her compliment.

He partially bowed from the waist and motioned to the black entrance. "After you," he told her.

"You first," Tazi replied. "After all, this is second nature for you."

Justikar shrugged and moved easily into the hidden passageway. Tazi followed right behind him, understanding that she needed his skills in the shadowy walkway. She was amazed at his ability to move through the darkness. It made sense to her that he could, being a person at home in the Underdark, but it was still impressive to experience. She tentatively touched his shoulder for guidance and either he didn't feel it, or he wasn't bothered by her hand because he didn't shrug it off. Even with his lead, she barked her shin against a minor obstacle and swallowed the yelp she wanted to make.

Tazi wasn't certain, but she thought the passageway doubled back, but without any visual frame of reference, she couldn't be certain. They walked slowly, and Tazi's eyes began to adjust to the gloom. There was a faint light coming up ahead. She thought she could make out thin, slivers of illumination, and they slowed their pace even more. A few feet in front, bars of pale light crisscrossed the floor in alternating patterns. When they got to the first one on the right, the duergar crouched down near a small portal located only a few inches above the floor. Tazi did likewise and peered in.

As she had thought, they had doubled backed and

were in the servants' quarters once again, only on the inside, as it were. Tazi realized that every small portal was a diminutive window into a different chamber. The one they were spying in was furnished similarly to theirs. Tazi could see two women seated near their dressing table, rifling through the various sundries that were littered about the table like children in a toy shop.

"Try this one," the blonde-haired woman said to her companion. She held out a blue, crystal perfume bottle and, before the other girl could reply, spritzed her with the contents. The blond then took in a long breath and sighed appreciatively.

"I'm sure that Zulkir Lauzoril will find you irresistible, smelling like that," she giggled.

"I'm sure he would, if he ever took his mind off of finding a way to best the lich long enough to notice me," she replied in a low voice. Both women looked around after that and sobered up some.

"Still," the fragrant girl added, "I wouldn't mind if the zulkir turned his green eyes toward me once in a while. And that blond hair..." she sighed.

While the two servants discussed various paramours and dalliances from their past, Tazi and Justikar crawled to another portal.

"I still can't believe Zulkir Mythrell'aa fell out of favor with Szass Tam," a black-haired youth said in sotto voice to the two other young men that sat around the table in their room.

A brunette nodded, "Yes, and I understand that she'd love to see him fall. I think she's considering throwing in with Aznar Thrul." Tazi noted how knowledgeable he was trying to sound and deduced he was probably a new purchase trying to prove his worth to his peers.

"That's not what I heard," the third interjected. "I heard it on the best authority that she's going to side with Lauzoril. And everyone knows he and Aznar Thrul hate each other like fire and water."

The first youth slapped the third on his arm and corrected him. "How can you say that? Didn't you see how well they got along at the Spring Festival? You've got it wrong."

"Do you think we need to help with the morning meal?" the brunette interrupted their banter, and he seemed suddenly concerned with the time.

Tazi took that as a cue for them to keep moving, too. She and Justikar peeked in a few more of the windows, but the conversations were almost identical to the others they had already overheard, and they learned nothing useful from them. She signaled to the dwarf to follow her, and they made their way carefully back to the metal shop. As they exited the passageway, Justikar flipped the brick back into place, and the panel sealed shut, without a trace that they had been there.

"I'm surprised this country even functions at all," she told the dwarf disgustedly.

"When I passed through there the first time," the dwarf agreed, "the talk was much the same. It seems like they all want to make an alliance, but don't trust one or the other of their neighbors enough to forge a strong one."

"It makes no sense," Tazi said shaking her head. "Though," she added thoughtfully, "I think I can see now why they haven't been more successful in their attempts at conquest. Their hierarchy is so fractured because of their personalities, it can't function effectively. It's almost like they do need just one, strong leader."

"What would happen if they did have just one?" the duergar asked.

Tazi shuddered. "I don't care to dwell on that thought too long. Let's get back," she told him, "before we're needed to polish Naglatha's toes or some other mundane chore." Justikar snorted, and they walked back to their chamber.

When Tazi opened the door to their room, she was momentarily surprised to see Naglatha seated at the dressing table. The Red Wizard was combing her thick hair languorously, one long stroke at a time. She glanced at Tazi through the reflection of the mirror, and Tazi saw how black her eyes were.

"Where have you two been?" she asked them angrily, continuing to regard Tazi and the dwarf by means of the mirror as if they weren't worthy of more direct contact.

"You want me to steal for you, don't you? Well, I need to know the layout of the place. How else am I going to find that out without some reconnoitering? That's what we were doing," she told Naglatha, seizing the beast by the horns. She cast a sideways glance at the dwarf. He gave the wizard a curt nod of agreement.

"Hmm," Naglatha murmured and appeared somewhat mollified by Tazi's quick answer. "Be careful, though. We've come too far now to tip our hand prematurely."

Tazi shifted uncomfortably at Naglatha's use of the word "we." She didn't like to think that the Red Wizard believed they were anything other than unwilling partners, each with a different desire and goal.

At that moment, Naglatha managed to tear herself away from the mirror to actually look Tazi in the eye. It was not lost on her that the wizard didn't give the bearded dwarf a second glance. "I have to admit, I appreciate your initiative." Naglatha gave Tazi a measured smile.

"You saw an opportunity to get a feel for the place and gather information. So you took it. Those are the kind of qualities I look for in a useful spy, you know," she told Tazi and swiveled back and forth on the padded stool slowly.

"In fact, those are the kinds of skills I like to cultivate in potential associates. You never know," she said slyly, "you might have a future in this sort of thing. I was only a little younger than you when I started," she added, casting an appraising eye on Tazi. "If you carry this off like I expect you will, you should think carefully about your next step." Then those same obsidian eyes froze over.

"Step out of here again without my express directive, however, and you won't be taking another step ever again. Do I make myself clear to you both?" she asked and took in the dwarf as well with her threatening glare.

"Understood," Tazi agreed.

The dwarf grunted.

"Good," Naglatha replied and rose gracefully to her feet. "Tonight, the two of you will accompany me to the evening meal."

"As what?" the dwarf demanded.

Naglatha continued to look only at Tazi as if she couldn't be bothered to lower her gaze for Justikar. "Because it suits me for people to think Milos and Heraclos are other than they are, you will act as my personal bodyguard for the duration of our stay.

"I expect that you will act accordingly. I was going to have you change your attire to match mine more closely," she told them, "but I think I will leave you as you are, presuming, of course, you both clean up."

"Of course, right away," Tazi replied sarcastically, though Naglatha did not seem to notice.

"You two will more than likely cause a bit of talk, and I rather like the idea of being the center of attention for the evening." She brushed past them, only pausing by the door.

"And sometimes," she added thoughtfully, "the best place to hide a secret is out in the open."

After Naglatha left, Tazi turned to the dwarf and said, "This should be interesting."

On the way to dinner, Tazi once again had the opportunity to marvel at the construction of the Citadel. She marched down a corridor a few hundred feet long that was devoid of any decoration except for the imposing figures of armor displayed in niches every ten feet on either side of her. Some of the plate mail and designs Tazi was familiar with, but others were completely unrecognizable to her and bordered on the fantastic. Suits stood anywhere from three to ten feet tall, and some of the weapons were so exotic, with blades curving and twisting in every direction, Tazi wondered where on Toril they would have come from. The duergar was even more enamored than she was, and she could tell he was just as eager as she to touch some of the metalwork. A sharp word from Naglatha stopped them both, though.

"Don't," she ordered. So they walked by, and Tazi knew the dwarf would have given much to study the pieces longer.

The passageway emptied into another, large chamber. Tazi found herself in a huge banquet hall that far surpassed any she had visited in Selgaunt, and she had been to more than a few in her time. The entire room, with its soaring ceilings, was lit by torchlight and candles. There was even a very large, elaborate chandelier suspended twenty feet above the table. Tazi didn't envy the slave who had to maintain those candles up so high. Tazi wondered why they didn't use spells and thought perhaps, in a country where sorcery was so very commonplace, that would have simply been too gauche.

In the center of the room was a long banquet table, with a glossy, lacquered finish. It was set with the finest place settings and silver cutlery Tazi had ever seen. Several vases of flowers and greenery dotted the table as if to make up for the fact that there was no view in the entire chamber. But, Tazi thought, their perfume seemed oddly out of place. They were almost sickly sweet, and she wondered if the smell was meant to disguise something else. Thick-cut crystal goblets winked in the firelight, creating a warm, friendly scene. Tazi recognized that the table was staged thusly for effect only.

As she and Justikar flanked Naglatha, it was only when the wizard turned to them with a frown did Tazi realize she was put out. When Tazi surveyed the room and saw no one else had entered, she speculated she knew why the woman was mad. She had made a point of being late so as to be "fashionable," as she put it, and now to Naglatha's obvious disappointment, most everyone else had decided to be fashionable as well.

"Where are they?" Naglatha whispered, displeasure evident in her tone.

Tazi wasn't sure what to tell her, but then she heard the sound of voices coming from a different passageway nearby.

"I think they're here now," she said quietly.

"Well," Naglatha told her, "if I can't be last then I may as well be the first. Follow me." And she led the way into the chamber.

Tazi and Justikar trailed behind as Naglatha strode into the chamber and selected a seat in the middle of the table, opposite what was obviously a seat of honor and could only have been meant for the Zulkir of Necromancy. Tazi was uncertain if, as a bodyguard, she was supposed to pull out Naglatha's chair, but the wizard saved Tazi from the potential gaffe by seating herself.

"You may sit to my right," she informed the duergar and she added to Tazi, "and you may sit on my left."

"Shouldn't we remain standing?" Tazi asked.

"It isn't unheard of to have one's bodyguards close at hand at these events," she explained quietly.

The other zulkirs and tharchions slowly filed in and made their seating selections seemingly at random. But Tazi knew there was far more going on below the surface. The process, she thought to herself, was a strange dance of positioning, and she wondered if they really thought they were fooling anyone with the act. She also noticed that many had one or two servants with them and, as Naglatha had said, they had one or both join them at the table.

"The woman to your left is Zulkir Zaphyll," Naglatha whispered to Tazi and nodded toward a bald woman with steel blue eyes.

"She looks like she's even younger than you," Tazi commented, not realizing the unintended insult to Naglatha's vanity.

"Well," Naglatha replied in a huff, "do you see that gaudy amulet she's fiddling with? Tear that from her scrawny neck, and she'd look her true age: a doddering seventy or so."

"She hides it well," Tazi replied.

"The tall zulkir sitting beside her is Lallara Mediocros. They are the best of friends these days and allied with Szass Tam. If I can turn either one of them," Naglatha explained, "the other will surely turn as well.

"The men over toward the far right end of the table are also loosely allied. The older man with the gray hair is Zulkir Nevron. He and I have had some interesting conversations," Naglatha told Tazi, and Tazi briefly wondered if the two had been close. "He has an extensive collection of demon spells. And the blond man next to him is—"

"He is Zulkir Lauzoril," Tazi finished for her, recalling the female servants' earlier comments about the handsome man.

The black-eyed wizard gave Tazi a beaming smile. "You have been listening," she said with obvious admiration. Tazi simply tipped her head in the acknowledgement of her skills.

Naglatha pointed out a few others to Tazi, and the thief made a few mental notes for herself. Then a black-haired, brown-eyed woman that Naglatha addressed as Thessaloni drew the wizard into a conversation about some of the ships in her navy, so Tazi continued to simply watch and listen to those around her.

"I've increased the number of darkenbeasts in my stables to nearly one thousand," bragged a bald man who Tazi did not know. Like most in attendance, he had various tattoos across his smooth pate. But Tazi was familiar with the monstrous creatures he was referring to.

Part bat, part prehistoric bird, Tazi had fought such a creature not long before her father died. Tazi shuddered inwardly at the thought that the man possessed so many of the creatures, and she fervently wished he was exaggerating for appearances sake.

"For myself," the vigorous woman to his left replied, "I prefer the Blooded Ones. Much easier to control."

"But, Azhir," he responded, "how can you afford them? They're terribly overpriced. Or have you and Szass Tam come to a new arrangement?"

Before the woman could respond, the room began to shake slightly. Everyone grew silent. The plates and goblets rattled, and the chandelier above swayed from side to side. The tremor did not last long, but Tazi could see concern on more than one zulkir's face. Tazi had felt a few minor quakes since they had entered the Thaymount region, but she had written them off as natural occurrences. Judging by the expressions of the Red Wizards all around her, she reconsidered her earlier appraisal.

It took a few moments for the conversations to resume after the tremor tapered off, and when they did, they were more muted. The banter that had been more verbal fencing than anything else stopped.

Tazi looked at the two spaces that were directly opposite Naglatha. They remained empty, and Tazi assumed the one in the middle was meant for Szass Tam. She didn't know who they other one was for, but supposed it must be someone closely linked to the necromancer. Tazi noticed more than one wizard glance at the vacant seats and whisper to their dinner companion.

A sudden hush fell over the room like a pall, and all eyes turned toward the main passageway of the banquet hall. A tall, handsome man with black hair and a matching beard walked determinedly into the chamber, rightfully commanding everyone's attention. He alone did not wear the red insignia cloak of a Red Wizard. All of the others had dressed in varying degrees of opulence and ornamentation, but they had all worn the cloak that denoted their station. Not this man. He set himself apart.

As he pulled out the center chair and seated himself with unconscious regality, he looked steadily at Tazi for a long moment. She met his black gaze without blinking and felt a charismatic pull. His cheeks had a hint of color that was lacking on so many of the sallow faces she had seen in Thay. It gave him the appearance of ruddy, good health. She had to remind herself that this was a lich, and what she was seeing was surely the work of some illusory spell. Even still, she felt drawn to him, mostly because he cast an aura of self-possession and certainty that Tazi had envied in other people all her life. Her passion was to feel that comfortable in her own skin, and it was a quality she constantly fought for.

"Naglatha," his deep voice broke the silence, "I must compliment you."

"And why is that, Szass Tam?" she asked demurely.

"Out of everyone in attendance tonight," he explained, "you have, by far, brought the most interesting decorations to the table." His gaze flickered over the duergar as well, Tazi noticed, and he seemed to recognize the dwarf.

"I thought you'd be pleased," she replied, and Tazi

could see Naglatha glow with the necromancer's attentions. Tazi herself bridled with anger at the idea of being classified as decorative.

Turning his attention to take in the whole room, the lich began, "I am so very pleased that all of you were able to find the time to come here. I am truly surprised that you could, given the relatively short notice and your full schedules," he added, and Tazi knew that no one in the room would have dared to miss it.

A few of the wizards made pointed glances to the vacant chair to Tam's right. The lich noted where their eyes lingered.

"Unfortunately, Tharchion Pyras Autorian is unable to attend tonight's festivities. He has had a fresh spate of maladies and most recently has been suffering from terrible headaches," Szass Tam explained to the gathered wizards, forced to address their looks. A very low murmur could be heard.

"I suspect that like you," he continued easily, "many of the recent events have been weighing on him and have taken their toll. He is still rather young and hasn't your stamina or vast experience with such issues. But, he has assured me he will be able to attend tomorrow's council."

"And what is it exactly," Zulkir Lauzoril asked, "that we are to discuss tomorrow?" He cocked an eyebrow at the lich, and Tazi could see Szass Tam did not like to be interrupted. She sensed Lauzoril knew that particular fact quite well.

"I do not want to speak too much of it tonight, since dear Pyras is absent. But I feel it is important that we discuss some of the more pressing issues of late."

"Such as the increased volcanic activity in the area?" demanded one of the wizards.

"That would be one of the more important points, Tharchion Dimon," the necromancer agreed, "as well as the state of our current economy and the success of the Enclaves as well as our continued support of them."

At this point, he stopped and slowly looked at each of his guests. "I want to make sure we are all in agreement over these things." Tazi couldn't miss the coldness that crept into the lich's voice, and for a moment, he didn't look like the scholarly gentleman he had first appeared to be, but something much more sinister. She didn't flinch when his gaze included her again, and there was another strange moment between them.

"And now, I will let you enjoy your evening meal. Please, eat your fill and have a good rest before tomorrow's busy schedule."

With that, the necromancer rose to his feet and gave a slight bow with his head to the gathered assembly and exited down a different corridor. Tazi found herself almost wishing he hadn't left quite so soon.

Not a minute after the lich left, everyone began to speak to one another again.

"Interesting that Pyras was not able to attend, eh Aznar?" Tazi heard Lauzoril ask the bald, black-eyed man near him.

"Makes one wonder if Pyras has been demoted," Aznar replied. "Demoted permanently, that is."

More than one zulkir or tharchion commented on the absence of the man with the same speculations. While they discussed their various opinions on the Enclaves of Thay, a bevy of servants skittered in and out, carrying trays laden with all types of food and drink. They moved silently from one person to the next, letting the guest choose items from the various platters at their leisure.

"Now, I assume that Zulkir Druxus Rhym was not allowed to help in the kitchens. Am I correct in that assumption?" demanded a woman with hollowed cheeks in apparent good humor.

"That's a good point, Mythrell'aa," chuckled Naglatha. "Didn't you kill an entire dinner party a few years ago by changing their desert pastries into poisonous snakes?"

There were several polite laughs at the banter, but Tazi saw that most everyone had not yet touched the food on their plates. The bald, black-eyed wizard that Naglatha had addressed looked her straight in the eyes and said, with all seriousness, "It was scorpions, not snakes." And he picked up a knife and fork and began to eat.

A few others began to eat as well, but some of the guests got up to have more discreet conversations with others. Naglatha stood as well.

She placed her hand lightly on Tazi's shoulder and whispered, "I need this time to talk to a few of my colleagues. Feel free to have something to eat as well."

Tazi watched as Naglatha slipped over to where Nevron and Lauzoril were seated. She placed her hand, as she had with Tazi, delicately on the older man's shoulder and immediately became engrossed in a serious discussion.

Tazi observed the various groupings around her. More than one had become heated. The words "Thay" and "trade" and "army" were tossed around a bit. Whenever anyone got too impassioned, one or more of their immediate companions would remind them where they were, and that wizard would then compose him or herself. Tazi was so engrossed in the wizards' discussions, she was barley aware when another servant came over to her and the duergar and placed plates piled high with delicacies in front of them.

She did see Justikar sniff at his food and take a small bite of some of the meats on his plate. He scowled foully, and Tazi shook her head. She suspected that nothing except metalworking could ever bring a smile to his grim features. She turned to say something to him, but he fixed her with such an unpleasant look, she turned back to eavesdrop on the conversation to her left.

"I still think gnolls are the next to try experimenting with," she heard one wizard tell another and proceeded to expound on the creatures' virtues as soldiers. She absently picked at the food on her plate and brought a forkful of cheese to her lips, barely noticing what she was doing. The next moment, she felt a powerful blow to her stomach and realized the duergar had punched her directly in the stomach.

Tazi bent over her plate slightly and had no choice but to cough up the food she had just eaten. She wiped at her mouth and threw her napkin into her plate. Livid, she whipped her head around toward Justikar and opened her mouth to demand an explanation, but a strange event stopped her in her tracks.

*Poison,* she heard the dwarf speak inside her head.

*What?* she thought.

*I said,* the dwarf thought angrily, *there was poison in the food.*

*How?* demanded Tazi.

*You obviously didn't notice,* the dwarf explained, *but we had a different server from everyone else. Didn't you see that all the others and their servants got to choose what they wanted while we were brought plates already full of food?*

*But—*

*My kind has a tolerance for the stuff,* he told her gruffly, *so even though I had some, I'll be fine. You probably would not have been so lucky. Obviously,* he added, *a colleague of Naglatha is less impressed with us than that lich was.*

*What I'm trying to ask,* Tazi said, *is how can you be doing this? How can you be inside my thoughts?*

*Oh,* Justikar replied, *that. Centuries ago, my kind was ruthlessly enslaved by illithids. We developed a limited, mental ability over time because of it.*

*This might come in handy,* she told him after a moment.

*I think it already has,* he shot back at her.

Tazi smiled ruefully and nodded slightly in wordless agreement.

*One thing,* she added. *Next time you suspect poison or something like it, why don't you just tell me instead.* She rubbed her stomach lightly. The dwarf, however, didn't say another word.

# CHAPTER TEN

*Later that Night*

Tazi and Justikar sat in their room, without speaking. Just as the dwarf had said, the poison in their food made him somewhat ill. He had wretched into a chamber pot violently upon their return. Tazi moistened a cloth and offered it to him after he had emptied his stomach contents into the container. But he had pushed the offer aside and dragged his sleeve across his mouth.

"At least this rag has some uses," he grumbled, referring to the gaudy tunic Naglatha's men had provided him with after the griffon attack. "Are you going to vomit, too?" he asked, and Tazi thought he might actually be concerned for her.

"No, I'm fine," she thanked him.

"Good. I'm not doing her bidding alone," he replied.

So much for concern, Tazi mused.

And they sat in silence, waiting for the black-haired wizard to make an appearance. In fact, they sat for several hours waiting for Naglatha's return. Neither spoke, and Tazi used the time to mull over what she had seen during the evening's events while she sat in the windowsill of a trompe l'oeil, one leg dangling over the side and the other propped up against the window frame. She glanced over several times to the dwarf, but he simply sat hunched over on the small stool, his hands planted firmly on his thighs, a dour expression on his face. She wasn't sure if he was angry or perhaps contemplating the fate of his brother.

He's probably more eager to go than I am, Tazi thought. At least I am fairly confident my family is safe right now. He knows nothing about his brother, other than he lost contact with him.

She started to ask him about his sibling when Naglatha quietly opened their door.

"Good," she said without preamble, walking over to stand between where they were seated, "you're both here."

"As if we had a choice?" Tazi quipped.

"You didn't," Naglatha replied easily, "but that didn't stop you before, now did it?"

Scrutinizing their "host's" face, Tazi could see a rosy stain across Naglatha's cheeks. Tazi wondered if the wizard had imbibed too much of the wine at dinner, or if the flush was from the excitement of her anticipated success.

"What now?" the duergar demanded, and Tazi felt

sure it was impatience to find his brother that was weighing on him. She believed he wanted to proceed more than anyone else in the room at that moment.

"Now is when you go get me those spells, little man," and her tone turned deadly. She regarded the dwarf coldly.

"It's time, then?" Tazi asked her in an attempt to turn her attention away from Justikar. If she was drunk, then chances were her actions would be even more unpredictable than they had been previously, and Tazi knew Justikar was only alive because she had asked it. Naglatha hated the duergar, and Tazi was unsure if that hatred was for him alone, or if her dislike spilled over to anything dwarven. She didn't want to find out.

Naglatha turned back to Tazi and said, "Yes, it will have to be tonight. Tomorrow, Szass Tam will hold his council," she said, "and after he beats it into us all again that we must continue to make trade our highest priority, he will find a way to politely evict us one by one." She sighed deeply. "I don't think this chance will come again," she added, "not for a very long while."

"Then" Tazi asked, "where do we start? You've mentioned his book of spells several times, but you haven't given us an exact location."

"That's because I can't," she replied simply.

"Helpful," the dwarf spat.

"Do you have an idea where to start?' Tazi asked, redirecting the wizard from the duergar.

"There is a chamber I know of just beyond the banquet hall that descends into the lower depths of the Citadel," she told Tazi. "Follow it down. Supposedly you will find rooms of fabulous jewels and metals below. Not far past them will be the chamber that contains one of Szass Tam's vast collections of spells. There," she breathed deeply, "you should see his prize book. Take it, or take as many of the spells that you can. But bring them to me."

"Not much to go on," Tazi replied. "And I'm certain there will be guards on so valuable an item. Not asking for too much, are you?" she inquired, unable to contain her sarcasm any longer.

Naglatha walked up to where she sat so nonchalantly and gripped Tazi hard under her chin. "I never said it was going to be easy," she hissed. "If this was meant to be a simple task, anyone would do." She released her biting grip on Tazi's flesh with a jerk and smiled again.

"I suggest that if you—" she paused and fleetingly looked at the dwarf as well and corrected herself— "if both of you want your freedom, bring me what I want. If you can't do that, then I recommend you die trying. It's that simple." She strode over the door and tossed a look back at the two. "But I have great faith in you, Thazienne. I know you like I know myself, and I am certain you will do well."

Before she left, Tazi pushed herself off of the windowsill and called out, "Any weapons for us?"

"My dear Tazi," she replied, "it is not as though you're venturing out unarmed." Tazi kept her face blank, but she feared Naglatha knew of her golden dagger. "You've got him, after all." She smiled broadly and pointed to the dwarf. "You chose him, you know. Hopefully you won't regret the decision." And she left.

Tazi looked at the closed door and shook her head. She turned to Justikar and nodded. "Let's do it."

It was simple enough for them to slip through the few passageways they were already familiar with and make their way to the corridor leading up to the banquet hall. Once more, they found themselves slinking down the array of exotic armor. Tazi slowed and reached out to touch a thin rapier that rested in the gauntlet of a statue of armor.

"Take it," the dwarf whispered. "You know you'll need it."

"Someone might notice," Tazi replied.

The dwarf ran a hand appreciatively over a large war axe, before pulling it free from its stand.

"Tonight, they're all going to be too busy plotting who to kill next to notice these missing items."

Tazi shrugged and reached for the rapier. "And I suppose if they do find that they're gone, they'll only watch their own backs." She noticed the thin, chainmail gauntlets and after a brief hesitation, she took those, too. They slipped over her own leather gloves like a second skin, and she marveled at how light and flexible they were. She could see the duergar was equally impressed with his new weapon. He yanked a leather strap off of another piece of armor and strapped the axe to his back. For the first time since they had met, Tazi saw that Justikar look comfortable.

Tazi took a page from the dwarf's book and stole

a scabbard for her weapon as well. With the rapier fastened to her side, Tazi suddenly realized she had missed the familiar weight there. She found that even she breathed easier now with the unusual steel next to her hip. She walked no less quietly, but straighter than she had since her auction. For a fleeting moment, she entertained the notion of trying to escape.

It will take Naglatha at least the night to notice I'm missing, she calculated. I could be in Eltabbar by morning and perhaps get some kind of word out to my family before the black-haired witch could do anything.

But even as she considered it, Tazi tossed the idea aside. Naglatha could have some magical means here to send out a message or even gain access to a gate to take her or those two fat slaves of hers to Selgaunt. And she twisted her head to look at Justikar.

He so desperately wants to find his kin, she considered a little sadly. I know how important blood is, and I'd like to help him, too.

She shook her head to free her mind and caught up to Justikar, who peered into the banquet hall from the entryway.

"All clear," he whispered. She wondered for a moment why he didn't use his thoughts more to communicate, but she figured it was probably a taxing feat and one that he saved for extreme emergencies. Or he might have been trying to reach his brother; she wasn't sure which, but she didn't know and he hadn't told her. That exact situation reminded her once more that she and the duergar had only the most tenuous of alliances. She still wondered if he would be there to cover her if her back was truly against the wall.

They moved past the deserted table, now bare of its finery, and found the corridor opposite it, precisely where Naglatha said it would be. Surprisingly, there was no trap on the door, and Tazi suspected there might be some magical ward on it. But her quick investigation revealed none, and the dwarf agreed with her. Tazi was surprised, given how powerful Szass Tam was supposed to be. Not for the first time, she debated if the absence of magic here meant he had his energies focused elsewhere. There was a faint light farther down, and the uneven flicker made Tazi think there were some torches at least partially illuminating the passageway. She knew she wouldn't need the dwarf's darkvision, at least for the moment, so she drew her new sword. Tazi shifted it in her grip once and noticed the balance was very good for a weapon not made specifically for her. It wasn't as finely crafted as the dagger, but she knew the steel, if it was indeed made from steel, would be more than accurate. She took the lead.

The passageway started out as many of the others had within the Citadel, finely carved and resembling a typical hallway, albeit one that steadily sloped downward. But as they passed farther into the depths, the passageway slowly lost its finished look. The decorated and covered walls became sparser until finally only the bare rock was visible. Even the stone lost its smoothness, and as the passageway curved to the right, the walls had returned to their natural, unfinished state. Tazi nodded to the dwarf that they were on the right course. She saw how closely he regarded their surroundings, scanning from one side to the other.

Tazi was tensed, straining to hear anything that sounded amiss, realizing she couldn't be sure of her surroundings. As they descended, she expected to come across some sort of guardians and was surprised they hadn't seen any. When the tunnel took a sharp turn to the right again, she turned back to ask Justikar a question. But the dwarf had stopped to study something in the rock wall that had caught his attention.

"What is it?" she asked him.

"That zulkir that everyone fears must come down here a lot," he replied.

"Why do you say that?"

The duergar grabbed Tazi's free hand and guided it over to the wall. He pulled her gauntlet off and laid her bare fingers on the surface.

"Do you feel those?" he asked.

Under her fingertips, Tazi could feel cold, hard lumps no bigger than her thumb. But in the fading light of the nearest torch some feet behind her, she could barely see the white twinkle that had so fascinated Justikar.

"Some people call them 'lich weepings,' but most know them as Kings' Tears," he explained. "There's a fortune in this wall alone," he finished, and Tazi could hear a touch of avarice in his voice.

"Maybe another time," she told him and replaced

her glove and gauntlet. "I think I need you to take the lead now. The torches have all but run out," she told him. "There's a slight, greenish glow ahead, but it's very faint. I think I'd trust your vision better." She wiped her forearm across her brow, suddenly very aware of the growing heat.

Justikar padded past her and looked at the walls that cast the emerald glow. He shook his head at what he found.

"Ormu," he told Tazi.

She had run across the moss before, but never in such large quantities. But, while there was still a healthy portion that lived, much of it had dried to a crisp brown and died.

"This looks like it has been burned," she told the dwarf.

He nodded in agreement. "And recently, too. I think there must be something graver to the tremors those Red Wizards kept harping on." He moved in front of Tazi, and together they continued down the narrow pass.

Steam hissed out from several fissures in the rocks, and Tazi became increasingly aware of the danger all around them. She blinked hard as her sweat stung her eyes and didn't see the nearby threat. She was nearly scalded by a geyser of boiling water, but the duergar yanked her out of the way right before it blew.

"How did you know?" she asked him, breathing hard.

"You have to listen for it. I can't explain it better than that."

"I'm glad you're here," she admitted gratefully.

"I'm not," he groused, and Tazi smiled at him. At least he's consistent, she laughed to herself.

They were continuously on guard but came across no signs of anything living. In a relatively low tunnel, wide enough for them to walk abreast, Tazi spotted a small pile of what looked like white sticks. But she recognized them for what they were: bones. She raised her weapon higher, though she knew they were not fresh remains. Tazi reached down for one of them, but the dwarf knocked her hand away. She was about to snap at him when the realization dawned on her that they might be the bones of his brother. Her face softened some.

Justikar bent down and gingerly lifted one bone close to his eyes. He turned it around thoroughly and sniffed it. His nose crinkled up, and he threw the skeletal remains to the ground.

"Stinks," he told her. "Trog bones." She nodded and knew he was both relieved and frustrated that they were not his brother's.

"Judging by those teeth marks," she added, "something feasted on these creatures not too long ago. But where are they?"

"Maybe the heat has something to do with it," Justikar replied. "Drove them away or something."

"Maybe," Tazi responded, less certain.

They walked farther and came to a split in the tunnel. "Any ideas?" Tazi asked the dwarf.

Unexpectedly, he pulled at the shoulder of his tunic and ripped his right sleeve off, tucking the torn cloth in his belt. Tazi could see that a series of black marks covered his arm. He held it up and consulted the designs. "We go left," he told her.

"What kind of map is that?" she asked.

"My brother's," he replied curtly. "Just before he left, he had this map tattooed onto his arm, figuring it was the best place to keep it."

"So did you," Tazi pointed out the obvious. "I thought you said it was your brother who was the dreamer."

"He is," Justikar answered her seriously. "I'm the one who has to clean things up."

"I'm sorry," she apologized, not exactly sure why she should suddenly feel so sad for him.

He shrugged, and they went farther into the depths, certain that Szass Tam's cache of arcane knowledge would be along the same route his brother had taken, the only viable path through the depths below. Perhaps because they had come across no obvious threat as yet, Tazi and Justikar became sloppy. Perhaps the growing heat and steam obscured their vision and other senses. For whatever reason, neither of them realized just what they were literally walking into.

"Justikar," Tazi began.

The duergar turned back toward Tazi just as a tremor shook the tunnel. Before he could respond to her, though, the walls appeared to suddenly collapse around him and immediately obscured the dwarf from her sight. Tazi herself was knocked flat.

"Justikar!" she cried. As she struggled to regain her balance and blink the dust from her eyes, she couldn't comprehend how a portion of the passageway had closed over him so quickly. There appeared to be only a few stones between them, but Tazi couldn't make out any large boulders that could have trapped him so completely.

"Tazi!" she heard him cry in a muffled voice. She crawled over on her knees toward him. When she reached the large pile where she had heard his voice emanate from, she tried to move the debris away to free him. But even as she searched with her hands, she couldn't get a good purchase on any of it. She pulled off her gauntlets, and Tazi was startled to feel something that was not quite rock under her hands. The lump shifted at her touch, and Tazi heard the duergar scream in pain.

"Hold on," she called to him and drew her rapier. Acting on a hunch, Tazi slashed at the mass and was not really surprised when a strange, viscous fluid oozed from the gash she had inflicted. She did not expect, however, to hear Justikar cry out as though he had been cut, too.

She raised her arm back and prepared to slash at what must've been a monster, but never got the chance. A tentacle, thicker than her own forearm, encircled her waist with lightning speed. Before Tazi could counter the attack, she was lifted bodily and felt herself slammed into the tunnel wall. Dazed, she could see that the lump that covered the duergar had begun to ripple slowly, and she suspected that the creature, whatever it must be, was beginning to digest him.

"Hold on," she called out again. Though the tentacle had encircled her waist, and it held fast, her arms were still free. Tazi had not released her hold on her rapier even when the creature had smashed her into the passageway. She managed to raise her weapon, point down, with both her hands high into the air. With a deep grunt, she slammed the weapon down and stabbed the tentacle close to where it joined the main body. The blow was so strong that the rapier actually impaled the tentacle to the tunnel floor. Tazi was able to pull away the wounded appendage from her waist and free herself from its limp grasp. She scrambled over to where she thought Justikar was still trapped. She called out his name but received no response, and she began to dread that she might be too late.

As she turned back to retrieve her rapier, Tazi saw a portion of the war axe the dwarf had stolen from the halls above suddenly pierce its way through the center of the creature's body. Tazi grabbed a flap of flesh and began to pull. She groaned with the strain as she pulled. The dwarf popped his head out, and Tazi could see that he looked mostly none the worse for wear. Between the two of them, they managed to tear a wide enough opening for Justikar to extricate himself. He tumbled to the passage floor in a messy heap, and they both lay panting quietly for a few moments.

The ruined mess of a creature simply lay there, and Justikar shoved at it with his foot. All of a sudden, though Tazi would've thought it was impossible, the creature disappeared down the passageway as though something larger had yanked it from the opposite side. Tazi sprang to her feet and grabbed her rapier, but Justikar waved for her to settle down.

"Rock worm," was all he said by way of an explanation.

"What?" Tazi asked.

The dwarf brushed at himself and sighed. "The thing's known as a rock worm. I should've noticed it, but I guess I was distracted. They simply expand and adhere to the sides of tunnels and wait for prey to stumble in."

"Like we did," Tazi interrupted.

"Hmph," Justikar grunted. "They lure their prey in and crush them in their stomachs. They've got two tentacles, one on each end," he explained.

"So that thing yanked itself away from us by using its other tentacle," Tazi surmised.

"So rather than wait around and see if it's got a mate," the dwarf added, "we should probably keep moving."

Tazi nodded, and the two of them maneuvered along their knees through a very low side tunnel. Suddenly, Justikar ripped the sleeve he had tucked into his belt into two wide bands.

"Here," he said to Tazi and passed one of them back to her. "Use it to cover your nose and mouth. The smell is going to get worse from here."

"Worse than how we smell now?" she joked. The dwarf snorted.

When the tunnel widened into a larger vault, Tazi was aghast. She didn't need the dwarf to point out the features to her. They had moved from the cook pit right into the fire. The room was aglow with a flickering red light. And she hastily donned the makeshift mask before the smell of sulfur overwhelmed her and seared her lungs. The entire chamber was filled with pools of bubbling magma, each one nearly as wide as Tazi was tall.

"I think this is why we haven't seen much besides that worm," she told the dwarf, pointing to the boiling earth. "What could live down here?"

"Remember those bones," he reminded her. "Something does live down here," he added. "Something does."

"Over there, see that opening?" Tazi asked him after scanning the vault.

He nodded, and she said, "Looks like it's more intentional than just a random fissure, don't you think?"

"Good eyes," he complimented her. "Now let's see if we can get there without burning." And the dwarf, completely recovered from the creature's attack, hopped like a rabbit along the narrow bits of rock that separated the pools. Tazi sheathed her sword and held her arms out for balance. She could feel the heat against their undersides and knew they would burn if she stayed down here too long. Sweat poured down her back and the crease of her chest under her leather vest. Her hair was lank with sweat and hung in stands plastered to her scalp and neck.

She watched as Justikar jumped the last few feet over to the relative safety of the opening Tazi had spotted. The ground crumbled a little and she watched, horror struck, as Justikar pin wheeled his arms frantically to regain his footing. To make matters worse, a quake rocked the chamber at that exact moment. Tazi had to dodge a splash of lava that nearly engulfed her foot and couldn't help the duergar in time. Justikar righted himself, though, and Tazi joined him soon enough on the ledge.

"Let's get this thing," Tazi shouted over the noise of the quake, "and get out of here."

Sure enough, Tazi was right. The opening was not a natural occurrence, but had been hewn from the cave wall. She drew her sword again, and Justikar pulled his axe free, holding it high in front of him with both hands. He nodded to Tazi, and they moved into the room in unison. The place was lit only by the flickering of the lava pools from the other chamber. The glow revealed something had been in there recently before them. Tazi could see that torches were knocked askew, and a small dais had been overturned. There were papers thrown about everywhere, and there was an overwhelming stench, even stronger than the sulfur. She shook her head in bewilderment, not anticipating the chamber to look as it did.

"Did someone beat us to it?" Justikar asked.

"I don't think so," Tazi replied. "It looks too random, like someone or something just ransacked the place because it was here. And the smell," she paused and reached for something to steady herself, "is overwhelming even with this rag on."

"I don't understand, though," the duergar said. "Naglatha made this out to be so much of a challenge, and other than a few pitfalls, this has been too easy."

"You're right," Tazi agreed. "If she had truly known how simple this was, she wouldn't have risked bringing someone else into her confidence." Tazi paused and looked around. "I think whatever is happening down here is more serious than any of those Red Wizards suspects. I think what's happening down here might be killing everything in its path."

Before she could say more, the ground started to rumble again, only stronger than the last tremor. Tazi was tossed onto a bookcase that had tipped over, while the duergar braced himself in the entryway until the quake subsided.

Tazi struggled to her feet and said, "Grab as many of the parchments and scrolls as you can, and let's get out of here before we get trapped down here."

Together they raced around, stuffing papers and scrolls into their belts. Many of the pages had been ruined, and Tazi wondered again what had done this and where had they gone. She sorted through some papers when another quake struck.

"Move!" the dwarf yelled at her.

"But I think there's more under the bookcase. If you give me a hand, we can—"

"There's no time. Trust me."

Tazi looked at him and nodded once. She staggered over to the entryway, while the ground moved and shifted under her. It was like trying to run while drunk, she thought to herself. She left the chamber with the duergar immediately in front of her. No sooner had they fled the chamber when a rending sound issued from the ceiling, and several large chunks of rocks tumbled down and sealed off the room with a deafening crash.

"Let's go back!" Tazi yelled, but the dwarf ignored her. He stormed past the now-sealed room to another passageway farther to the left. Tazi was confused by his actions as they had what they had come for, and the tunnel the dwarf was nearing looked like it continued farther underground. She raced over to him, dodging bits of the ceiling that continued to tumble free. When she finally caught up to him a short distance into the tunnel, a blast of heat stopped them both in their tracks. The dwarf moved slowly around the bend in the passageway and froze, his body as rigid as stone itself. Tazi peered around the corner and was forced to throw her hand in front of her eyes as a shield from the heat. Even still, she could not look away and was mesmerized by the sight in front of her.

The tunnel had probably continued down much farther at one time, but there was no way it was possible to pass any longer. The path had been transected by what could only be described as a river—a river composed entirely of molten earth. It ran with surprising speed, bubbling and gurgling like some cheerful meadow stream. Colors of gold and crimson and near-white blended together hypnotically, twisting and turning, reshaping everything in its path. It was an unstoppable force.

When Tazi was finally able to tear her eyes away

from the amazing sight, she saw the dwarf continued to stare past the fiery death to what was no longer visible. His shoulders sagged as if in defeat, and Tazi cursed herself for not remembering that he was only here to find his brother and there was no chance of that now. In fact, she realized that their entire time down there, he must have been straining and hoping to find some sign of his kin, living or dead, to know his fate. She placed a hand on his shoulder and shared a moment of silence with him.

"We have to go back now," she finally said.

"I'll never know, will I?" he eventually asked.

"Let's go," was all she could say, and they turned away from the red river.

Tazi swung open the door to their chamber and saw Naglatha reclining comfortably on her bed. Unlike Tazi, who was slick with sweat and smelled of sulfur, Naglatha appeared fresh and rested. Tazi noted she had lost the flush to her cheeks and suspected that the Red Wizard had sobered up since they were gone. Tazi was too tired to even be startled when the door shut unexpectedly behind her. She and the duergar turned to see Heraclos and Milos now barring the exit.

"I wondered when you boys would show up." she quipped.

Naglatha swung her legs onto the ground and regarded Tazi and the dwarf for a moment before she demanded, "Well?"

Tazi ignored the threatening presence of her Thayan Knights and grabbed the scrolls Justikar collected and her own stash and thrust them at Naglatha, too tired and too trapped to bargain with her.

"Choke on them," she said tiredly.

Naglatha took the tattered sheaf of parchment without saying a word. She turned to the dressing table and, clutching the precious spells against her breast with one hand, she swept the bottles and gewgaws onto the floor with the other. She spread the papers out and started to scan each and everyone one, her fingers racing over them. However, paper after paper was tossed ignominiously to the floor. Then she stopped and held one up. The woman's hands trembled as though palsied.

"This is it," she whispered, and the color returned to her cheeks like twin flames.

Tazi looked at Justikar and stepped forward. The bodyguards were watching them closely.

"We're done now," she told Naglatha, uncertain if the woman even heard her words, as enraptured as she was with her prize. "We've kept our end of the bargain, and we are quit of you."

Tazi turned back to Justikar and added, "Let's get out of this cursed place." The duergar nodded, and they walked to the door. Heraclos and Milos, however, remained as impassive and immoveable as stone.

Tazi whipped around. "We struck a bargain, and we've met our part."

The Red Wizard tore her obsidian eyes from the

parchment to meet Tazi's sea-green ones. "And you have succeeded beyond my wildest hopes. A bargain is a bargain," she admitted, and Tazi had a fleeting expectation that Naglatha might actually release them. "But," Naglatha continued, "I would not think of denying you the glory of watching what is about to transpire next. It is only fitting that you witness first hand what your actions have wrought."

Tazi reached for her sword with lightning speed, and she saw from the corner of her eye that Justikar had started to unsheathe his war axe, too. But before either of them could proceed any farther, Naglatha pointed at her and the dwarf with two of her fingers, and Tazi felt her body stiffen. She was suddenly unable to move even her smallest finger, and it was as though she had been turned to stone. From the corner of her eye, Tazi saw that Justikar appeared to be affected in a similar fashion. She remained frozen while Naglatha padded over to them on jeweled sandals.

"Now it is time to write history," she whispered gleefully to her captives. She marched past them, and her Thayan Knights opened the door for her. She looked around at the backs of Tazi and Justikar and added, "Don't keep me waiting."

Tazi suddenly felt her legs move of their own accord, and she turned like some clockwork toy to trail woodenly after the Red Wizard. The duergar marched stiffly alongside her. Though Tazi couldn't turn her head, she heard the heavy steps of the bodyguards bringing up the rear.

They advanced past the corridor that led to the

banquet chamber and continued in a direction Tazi had not ventured to before. She struggled against Naglatha's enchantment but, try as she might, she could not wrest back control of her body. She had no choice but to trail obediently, if stiffly, behind the Red Wizard as though she were a faithful hound. The dwarf was in the same predicament, and when he occasionally appeared in her peripheral vision, she could see his brow knotted in effort as he tried to unsuccessfully fight his way free of her control as well.

Turning a corner, Tazi felt herself grow chilly, and gooseflesh appeared on her exposed arms. Somewhere, there was a draft of air that had passed over her sweat-covered skin, cooling her. But Tazi could not see the source of the draft, only the back of Naglatha's head and a pair of smooth, double doors a few feet ahead of them.

*Must be the council room*, she thought.

*Of course*, the dwarf replied.

*Justikar?* she wondered.

*Who else ?* he replied. *Now what do we do?*

*I think we watch hell break loose,* Tazi answered.

*Comforting.*

Naglatha flung open the doors and strode into the room. Tazi could see that she was reveling in the sensation she was causing amongst the other wizards who had already gathered there. Though she could not turn her head, Tazi did have a fairly good view of the table, and the wizards already seated at it. After a quick inventory, Tazi realized that almost everyone from the night before was in attendance. And there was also someone unknown to Tazi with the others. He looked fairly young, but Tazi now knew that could have been a simple illusion of vanity. Out of everyone in the room, he was the only one with a shock of red hair. He sat slumped in his chair, with his head resting wearily in his hands. And he was the only one who didn't look up when Naglatha burst into the chamber.

He doesn't look well, she thought vaguely. He must be the tharchion who didn't attend last night. He must be Pyras Autorian.

The only person missing now, as far as Tazi could see, was Szass Tam. Naglatha, however, didn't feel compelled to wait for his appearance.

"Always one for an entrance, eh Naglatha?" chuckled the handsome Lauzoril. "Last night you were first, and today you are almost the last."

Naglatha smiled and stood in front of the gathered assembly. She placed her hands on the table and leaned forward, taking them all in with a glance. "I have within my means the ability to remove Szass Tam from his seat of power permanently," she stated simply. A few of the zulkirs and tharchions laughed quietly, but Tazi could see one or two prick up their ears and regard Naglatha with a shrewd gleam in their eyes.

"Better not let the Zulkir of Necromancy hear you speak like that," warned Pyras weakly, "even in jest." He then lowered his head back into his hands, squeezing his eyes shut tight.

"It is no jest, my dear, weak-willed Pyras," she replied, "and I am not afraid of him like you and so many of the others are." Naglatha nodded to her

Knights. Heraclos and Milos moved to separate ends of the table, their robes parting enough to reveal their impressive scimitars. Tazi and Justikar had no choice but to move along with them, still under her influence.

"Enough is enough," shouted Azhir Kren rising to her feet. Tazi could tell the tharchioness kept a watchful eye on their position as she challenged Naglatha. "What nonsense are you speaking of?"

Naglatha did not back down. "I know you hate Rashemen, former general. Well, I say you have reason to hate them. We should take that country and any other that stands in our way!"

"And how to you propose garnering support for that?" she asked, but even from where Tazi stood riveted, she could see the other woman was intrigued as well. Naglatha had struck a nerve with more than just one of the guests within the walls of the Citadel.

"With this," Naglatha told them proudly, and she removed the stolen parchment from the concealment of her long robe. "With this one spell, all our dreams can come true. Thay can take its rightful place as the true power of Faerûn. And we will claim that right through blood," she informed them, "not through petty commerce. People will say our names in hushed whispers and fear us as they should, not think of us as common merchants. We shall be terror itself."

Tazi could see some of the other wizards were starting to get agitated. But none of the others in attendance had brought any slaves with them for this gathering, and they were well aware that Naglatha's servants were all armed, even though they didn't know two were unwilling.

"And what will that do?" asked the black-eyed Zulkir Aznar Thrul.

"Watch as I call forth all the atrocities that live beneath the Citadel and the Thaymount. With these beasts under my control, I will finally rid this land of that undead lich once and for all. His end will be permanent with no hope of resurrection. And with him gone, we shall guide Thay into the future."

Naglatha held the parchment in one hand and gestured for silence with the other. Slowly, she began to read the ancient spell. Tazi heard uncertainty in her voice as she tripped over some of the words written in an ancient hand. But as she progressed through the spell, her confidence grew. A mild tremor shook the building, and the other wizards looked to the floor and each other in some confusion. The Zulkir Mythrell'aa, small as she was, was even thrown to the floor by its force.

Suddenly, from the other side of the room, a cracked voice cried out in anger.

"Stop!"

And Tazi found she could turn her head ever so slightly. She believed that Naglatha was so focused on her spell that she must have had difficulty maintaining her other enchantments, or she had simply lost interest in them. She turned her head farther, saw that the duergar had some mobility as well, and beheld a fearsome sight beyond him.

From a corridor opposite the one Tazi had used,

Szass Tam appeared. But it was not the visage that had charmed Tazi the night before. The lich was so enraged by Naglatha's impudence that he had entered the chamber wearing his true form. Gone were the healthy features of silky black hair and beard, the full cheeks and the coal eyes. Only his luxurious robes remained unchanged, though they now hung off of a skeletal frame and were frayed at the edges. He floated into the room, with his robes fluttering behind him like some winged beast of prey, and Tazi could see his eyes were burning points of red light in his skull, skin stretched paper thin across it. He held out one bony arm toward Naglatha and screamed again, but she ignored his skeletal claw and finished her heinous chant before the lich could stop her. As the last words left her lips, she raised her head to meet the lich's frightening stare and smiled in absolute triumph, the ground trembling beneath her feet.

From somewhere deep within the bowels of the Citadel, howls and screams slowly rose in volume until the cacophony momentarily drowned out all other sound within the chamber. Tazi pressed her hands against her ears.

But the noise did relent and fade until the only sound in the room was a deep, rumbling laughter. Tazi looked to Naglatha, but it was not her. As Tazi realized the Red Wizard's hold over her was almost gone, she twisted at her torso to see where the sound came from. As soon as she turned to the table, Tazi could see that all the wizards faced Pyras, who was now rising to his feet.

Gone was his sickly pallor and demeanor. He continued to laugh deeply, and a smile formed on his full, fleshy lips. No one seemed more surprised by the turn of events than Naglatha herself. As he straightened himself, Tazi rubbed at her eyes, temporarily disorientated by the vestiges of Naglatha's spells, because she thought he appeared to be growing as he stood. But then Tazi realized that was exactly the case.

Pyras knocked back his cushioned chair and spread his arms forth. The muscles bulged and inflated along his arms, and at the same times, claws stabbed through the tharchion's former fingernails. With a tearing sound, his robes gave way as he reached a height of almost fifteen feet. Tazi could see his skin darken from its former pale flesh color to red and black. And his skin appeared to harden and split into a series of plates that more closely resembled armor than flesh. He dropped his head forward and screamed. Tazi watched, horror-struck and fascinated at the same time, as the skin on his face seemed to melt and run forward to accommodate the muzzle that sprouted out from the center of his skull. He threw back his head, and Tazi could hear flesh splitting and tearing. Great horns speared their way through his scalp and twisted above him, and a pair of giant, insectlike wings opened up from his back.

As the creature regarded the others in the room with his red-slitted yellow eyes, he flexed those monstrous wings behind him. Tazi saw some of the other wizards scramble backward, and one or two actually fled. Naglatha, however, was transfixed with wonder—but also surprise—as though this was not her doing.

Tazi turned to the lich and she saw something akin to recognition on his skeletal visage.

"Eltab!" he hissed.

# CHAPTER ELEVEN

The towering fiend laughed again and pulled back his lips in what Tazi supposed was a smile, though it looked more like a monstrous grimace.

"Yesss…" the demon hissed at Szass Tam. "It is me once again."

Tazi turned to the lich and could see surprise play across his skeletal features, which was difficult to do.

"Did you think I was truly gone?" the tanar'ri lord mocked him.

"My spell of Twin Burning—" Szass Tam began.

"It was incomplete, old man. You failed." And the creature flexed his great wings again, spanning the length of the table, reveling in his physical freedom.

Tazi, now completely free of Naglatha's

power, drew her sword. She heard the dwarf snort. He was actually laughing at her and the sorry picture she presented. But he had freed his war axe as well. They stood ready though no one in the hall moved an inch. Somewhere deep in the corridors below, the screaming started up again, and the ground began to shake once more. Yet everyone was mesmerized by the tableau in front of them.

"You sought to bind me, that is true," the demon admitted. "But you made a crucial error in your ritual. You tried to close the gate on me, but you were sloppy, and left it open just a crack. And that was all I needed." He laughed again.

"Oh, it took time. But that was something I had. You understand that, don't you, dead man?" he looked at the lich, but Szass Tam remained silent. "I was weak after you tore me free from my prison under Eltabbar, and that was the only reason you were able to paralyze me with your Death Moon Orb and bind me to your Throne. But you weren't strong enough to make it last, though you thought you had.

"As I sat there, I reached out with my powers, knowing there existed a way to escape. Granted, I couldn't go far, but I didn't need to, did I? I found what I needed easily enough under your roof."

Tazi looked from the lich to the tanar'ri lord and wondered why neither struck the other. Or why no other wizard, including Naglatha, made a move to flee or fight. However, Tazi found she was just as spellbound as the others by the demon-king and wondered if that was somehow his doing.

"You kept your young puppet here, always under your wing, under your watchful eye," he explained in his ancient voice, referring to Pyras. "You needed him because of his weakness. So did I."

"Where is he?" demanded the lich, and Tazi doubted the necromancer truly cared about the fate of his minion. The tanar'ri lord only smiled more.

"Over the years of my entrapment, I sent my energies over to him. Slowly, oh so slowly, so no one would know. And you helped me grow strong, Szass Tam. You kept this vessel," he paused to tap his chest with a heavy claw, "so safe and so protected from harm. Even you must appreciate the irony in all of that. And all this time I have been waiting and watching and planning," the demon-king finished and the ground rumbled again.

"Now I am free," he cried amidst the howls from below and jumped onto the table in a low crouch. "And I shall have my revenge against you all," he warned them and swung an accusing claw at the gathered Red Wizards. "Just like your predecessors who called me forth on that windswept hill so long ago, here you all gather again—awaiting my return."

Tazi was briefly distracted from Eltab's monologue when she saw Naglatha sway and nearly fall. The woman looked truly frightened and calm at the same moment, like someone caught up in a dream or a nightmare.

"I was the instrument of Thay's birth, and I shall be the instrument of its death. From deep within the bowels of the Thaymount, my numbers have grown and are now released. With them at my side and with the power from the core of Thay itself under my control, I shall decimate this land and bury its people. From its very heart, I will strike you all down."

With that, the tanar'ri lord sprang from the table and took flight. His massive wings struck the chandelier suspended above the ceiling and ripped it free of its moorings. The massive circle of wood and metal fell with a crash, splitting the table down its length. Zulkirs Zaphyll and Lallara barely escaped being crushed by it though Zaphyll caught part of her robes under the broken remains of the chandelier. As she tore herself free, her amulet must have been wrenched off in the process, for Tazi watched as the young woman turned to a withered crone before her very eyes. She screamed and covered her face with her shriveled hands. Lallara wore a look of disgust and horror at her friend's transformation, but she pulled the old woman's arm around her shoulder and helped her hobble from the room nonetheless. They did not return.

Tazi turned back and saw the demon-king circle the room once, and she held her sword at the ready though she didn't believe it would do much good. She also noted that the dwarf stood at the ready as well, and she smiled grimly at him. The drafts of wind from Eltab's beating wings knocked several torches free, and they fell like rain. Tazi dodged to her left to avoid one that dropped with a thud to the stone floor. But others were not so lucky.

Tharchion Dmitra Flass, a woman that Naglatha

had referred to as the First Princess of Thay, was too busy staring at the circling tanar'ri to notice the torch that fell near her. She was laden with jewelry and ostentatiously clothed with robe upon robe layered on her person. Because of that, she didn't immediately realize the torch had ignited one of her garments. When she did, she let loose with a high, piercing scream and began to run frantically around the chamber, unintentionally feeding the flames. Tazi tore her green eyes away from the beast at the sound of the woman's painful cries and saw no one moved to help her.

"Dark and empty!" Tazi spat and sheathed her sword. She turned and ripped a tapestry that had so far escaped the flames free from the wall and threw it over the tharchion when she passed by. Tazi covered her completely with the heavy fabric, smothering most of the flames with the cloth and her body as they rolled about on the cold, stone floor. She batted the length of the woman's body and rolled her over many times, despite the Red Wizard's feeble cries of protest. When Tazi was sure she had doused the flames, she pulled the tapestry far enough open to see Dmitra Flass's burned face. Tazi winced at what she saw.

Dmitra had been heavily adorned with earrings and necklaces, both draped around her neck and around her forehead like a series of crowns. The warmth from the flames had heated those metal objects until they were white hot. They had burned through the woman's flesh to varying degrees, some only leaving a few red lines and blisters, others charring her flesh an angry red and more ominous gray.

Now she bore tattoos of a different sort, Tazi mused. A touch on her shoulder brought Tazi back to the reality of the chamber. Tharchion Azhir Kren was crouched over them. "Let me," she told Tazi, and she bent over the injured Red Wizard. Azhir was the only one who had offered to help, and Tazi was impressed amidst the destruction that someone else actually gave a damn.

"Hush," she soothed the burned Dmitra and scooped her up easily in her arms.

"Is—is it bad?" Tazi heard the woman croak out between coughs.

"I've seen much worse on the battlefield," Azhir crooned to her. "We'll get it taken care of, and your husband will never even notice." And she carried her from the smoke-filled room.

Tazi picked herself up in time to see Eltab make one last pass around the chamber and shoot through the entryway with his wings tucked close against his body like the swallows that nested around Stormweather Towers did when they dived.

In an instant, he was gone.

Chaos reigned in the now-destroyed council room. Tapestries were burning from every wall and what furniture remained was also aflame. A heavy black smoke began to fill the chamber and Tazi noticed, between coughs, that the room did not have the ingenious ventilation system that the metal shop did.

Of course, the council chamber was not supposed to be on fire.

Tazi turned and saw Red Wizards running about

and a memory flashed in her mind's eye. She remembered a boat that caught fire once in Selgaunt Bay years past. She had watched from the dock as every last vermin had scuttled from their hiding holes to escape the smoke and flames. They had squealed and clawed each other in a frantic dash to throw themselves into the frigid waters, only to drown. She couldn't help but think of that image now in the flaming chamber.

The quakes came closer together and grew in intensity. To her left, she saw Heraclos and Milos, both relatively unscathed, each grab Naglatha by an arm. With them as human shields, Tazi saw her former owner scurry across the chamber without a backward glance for the destruction she had helped loose on the land.

Wizards ran in every direction, most desperately searching for an escape from the acrid stench of smoke and seared flesh, dodging the chunks of ceiling that rained down on them all. Tazi searched for Justikar. When she finally spotted the duergar, he didn't see her. He appeared to be unharmed and was crouched low near the doorway where the demon-king had fled. Tazi was about to call out to him and realized it was not her place to stop him. He had failed to find his brother, and with Naglatha gone, she saw no reason for him to stay behind. She silently wished him good fortune. But the gray dwarf held his position and swung his axe in his hands a few times as though weighing something heavily. Finally, he swung it and cracked a part of the doorway with the force of the blow.

"Damn!" she heard him swear and watched as he then turned back into the room. She smiled in spite of herself.

Tazi saw that most of the wizards fled the chamber with a few, notable exceptions. The lich, Szass Tam, stood as still as a statue while the room crumbled about him. Though he remained in his skeletal form, Tazi was once more struck by a sense of dignity as she watched him float a few feet above the ground, unaffected by the tremors. To her left, Lauzoril, Aznar Thrul and Nevron remained behind, somewhat singed but not too worse for wear. And Tazi saw that Azhir Kren, no longer burdened with the injured Dmitra, trotted back into the chamber to take inventory of the situation.

Tazi realized that at least these few cared enough about Thay, whatever their reasons, not to flee the scene of the crime.

The word "crime" echoed in her head. Tazi was at least partially, if not wholly, to blame for what had transpired in the room and for whatever horrors had been let loose. She shook her head and coughed into her arm. Realizing that they were all standing around like sheep that had no shepherd, Tazi spoke out.

"We need to get outside," she shouted to Szass Tam, knowing that the others would at least follow his direction. "There must be a window or something nearby because I can feel the draft against my skin. Where is it?" she choked out.

Szass Tam turned to her and fixed her with his burning gaze. For a moment, Tazi felt fear well up inside, threatening to consume her. But she knew now was not the time to succumb to such feelings. She bit back down on that fear and held her ground. The lich almost smiled at her.

"This way," he told her and pointed to a corridor nestled under the burning tatters of a tapestry.

Tazi nodded to Justikar who stood to her right. She pushed past the others and ran through the nearly black room to the burning tapestry. Without breaking her stride, she jumped through the flaming fabric, with her arms protectively in front of her face. The duergar trailed behind her, followed by the remaining Red Wizards.

The corridor opened up onto a large, stone balcony, and from it, Tazi could see that they were several thousand feet up in one of the peaks of the Thaymount. Straight below her was a dizzying drop.

Dusk was at hand—the sun only fiery ball at the horizon's edge, tinting the sooty glaciers red. Tazi was somewhat disorientated because with the artificial light within the Citadel, she had lost track of real time. She gripped the rock banister as another tremor nearly tumbled her to her knees.

Then the first of the explosions began. Tazi turned to the volcanic mountains in awe. She watched as one after another of the peaks of the Thaymount began to erupt, spewing fire and rock across the range like an unholy storm.

She stood there, a hail of ash falling around her like the first snowfall of winter. By that time, the others had caught up to her, and they were frozen in their tracks at the armageddon unfolding before them. Tazi hardly noticed when the lich glided up next to her, but she couldn't miss his frozen voice.

"And are you well pleased, lady?" he demanded of her.

"What?" she asked and turned to look up at his threadbare skull. There was no feeling of fear this time.

"Naglatha did not do this alone," he explained. "I know she had your help. Are you pleased with all you've done?" he asked again.

"I had no choice," Tazi replied and hated that she had to defend herself to the necromancer. "I had my reasons."

The lich nodded benevolently. "I hope so, woman, for look what you have wrought on my land. Consequences," he added, "there are consequences to every action. Now see yours."

Tazi refused to meet his accusing glare and turned back to view the destruction. As another eruption shook the balcony, the mountains started to disgorge molten flows of lava, red and gold. From several of the peaks, the burning magma began its inexorable path down the slopes like a deadly tide. She could see that there was nothing to stop its flow save for the villages and towns in its lethal path. And that was not the end of it.

Tazi watched as, first from one tunnel and the next, unspeakable horrors began to pour out of every crevice in the Thaymount. Like a row of ants leaving their mound, the line of creatures seemed unending.

Demons of all shapes and sizes crawled out of the ancient tunnels. Twisted versions of darkenbeasts took to the skies and even albino creatures that had never seen the light of day cautiously clambered out. Their numbers seemed immeasurable. High up on the balcony, there was a sense of unreality as though they were removed from the danger, but another quake reminded the spectators that they were every bit as vulnerable as the unknowing masses below on the Escarpment.

"There must be thousands upon thousands," Tazi breathed.

"Perhaps we can make it down below and warn the others to flee while they can," offered Aznar Thrul, who was sweating profusely, though not from the overwhelming heat.

"You mean flee so you can escape," Lauzoril corrected him harshly. "Always thinking of yourself, aren't you?"

So much for alliances, Tazi thought as the two traded insults.

"There might be a way to stop the demon," Nevron offered. "There might be a way to bind him again." Tazi recalled that he was the wizard Naglatha had said had an interest in demon spells. She turned to regard him more closely.

"Leave off," Azhir shouted at him, the image of unbridled fury. "Magic got us into this, but it will take an army to stop those monstrosities. Don't you agree, Szass Tam?" she asked the lich, searching for support. The necromancer, however, remained impassive.

The Red Wizards launched into a tirade amongst themselves as to who had the better plan, seemingly oblivious to the rain of fire. Tazi listened for a moment then exploded at their bickering.

"Shut up!" she screamed. With ash falling around her and lava bombs streaking the sky behind her, she commanded their attention like a raging angel.

"Even in the midst of this—" she gestured with one gauntlet-covered hand to the hell behind her— "you cannot work together? Your land will die if you do nothing!

"Ignore everything else and see the obvious. Perhaps binding the demon might stop the waiting disaster, but no one knows. What we can see is death pouring down the mountainside. That needs to be stopped. And we have the means to do it."

"What do you have in mind?" Szass Tam asked her.

"On my way up, I saw the vast armies that dot the sides of the Thaymount. You yourselves bragged at dinner how many thousands of creatures you posses," she told the small assembly. "There must be more housed within these walls. We'll use them, one and all, against the demon spawn and as shields themselves, if we have to. They will stop the lava flows," she finished.

The Red Wizards regarded her with stunned amazement. Szass Tam tilted his head and scrutinized her closely, contemplating her words. Even the duergar appeared taken aback by her suggestion.

"It won't work," Aznar Thrul stated flatly and shook his head.

"Why not?" Tazi shouted to be heard over the continued rumbling as another peak vomited out more lava.

"It might," interrupted Azhir Kren. "It just might."

"They'll never do it," Nevron disagreed.

"He's right," Lauzoril said. "Those beasts will never follow just one leader. Never."

"It has to be tried," Tazi argued. "What other choice is there?"

"There is another," Szass Tam offered. Before he was able to say more, a shower of molten rocks sprayed the balcony. The group sought shelter as best they could, using the support stones of the balcony for cover. Most escaped the threat, but one was not so fortunate. Azhir Kren screamed in agony as her shoulders and arms were struck by the red-hot projectiles. Lauzoril caught her before she tumbled off the balcony, unconscious from the pain.

"Inside," Szass Tam commanded the others.

"Back into the flames?" the dwarf demanded.

"There is another corridor," he replied.

Tazi and Justikar led the way again as Szass Tam and the others trailed behind, dragging Azhir Kren with them.

"To the left," she heard the lich say, and Tazi blindly felt her way through the smoke-filled hall until she found the route he meant.

As soon as she started down the passageway, her vision began to clear. She realized that they were dropping deeper into the Citadel, and they were quickly down below the level of the smoke from the council room blaze. The corridor began to twist downward in a spiral, and steps formed under Tazi's feet. She had no idea how far they continued down. Everyone had grown silent, and the only sound was the rumble of the mountains and the howls that grew in strength. Eventually, Tazi saw a glimmer of light ahead.

With the duergar at her heels, she led the way into another chamber and stopped in her tracks. Before her, the room opened onto a platform. Beneath that platform, it opened further into a cavernous mass too large for Tazi to see the end of. With glow lights scattered across the walls, Tazi beheld an unholy sight. Stacked up from side to side, shoulder to shoulder, stood thousands upon thousands of troops. But it was an army the likes of which she had never seen before.

Tazi heard the others behind her let out a collective gasp—all except for Szass Tam. Tazi looked from him back to the forces lined up like clay figures, but at the ready. She could see that they wore armor and clothes in varying degrees of decay, and even from where she stood, she could see their skin had a grayish cast to it. Their rusty weapons glinted in the sorcerous light.

"I think you are familiar with them," Tam said to her.

Even with the Citadel crumbling around their ears, one of the other Red Wizards found something to complain about.

"Szass Tam," Aznar Thrul shouted, "you never said you had this many housed here. This goes against any agreement we might have—"

"Enough!" Tazi whirled around and shouted to the bald wizard. "Now is not the time!" He looked at her with his hateful, black eyes but held his tongue. She turned her attention back to the lich.

"Up there," she motioned with her sword, "you said there was another way. Let's hear it now."

"I think you were on the right tack with the obvious use of the armies. But for us to be successful, we must work together, lady."

Tazi shivered despite the heat when she heard the necromancer link himself to her.

"Explain," she said and hated herself for not seeing another choice.

"Lead the forces as you said, and I will work with Nevron to find a spell to bind Eltab," he explained to her. "I bound him once; I can do it again. With him under our power, the rest of the demons will obey. It is Thay's only chance." And, for the first time, Tazi heard true emotion in the lich's voice. She believed he might find a way.

"Will they follow me?" she asked and looked past him at the hateful troops of juju zombies. Though their bodies were dead, Tazi could see an evil light in their eyes. They shifted in place but made no sounds. Tazi almost wished they would groan just so she would know where they were when she turned her back on them.

"Do you take this on, lady? The choice is, as always, yours to make," the lich said and glided in front of her. Tazi saw the dwarf raise his axe questioningly.

Tazi looked from the lich to the dwarf and finally

to the troops. Another quake shook the building, and she could hear inhuman growls from deep below them. She knew the hell that was loose was her doing, and Tazi shut her eyes solemnly. There was no other choice to be made.

"Yes," she replied and looked the lich straight in the eye. "I will."

"Good," he answered and seized her by her left shoulder. Tazi felt energy course through her like lightning, and she was joined to the lich. She screamed in pain and shut her eyes tight; all the while, the lich's bony fingers burned into her skin. Her head lolled back, and Tazi felt a strange power course its way through her veins. When he finally released her, Tazi stumbled a bit backward and blinked hard. Her shoulder ached where the necromancer had touched her, and when she was able to focus her vision, she saw a strange mark located there, no bigger than a gold piece where the lich's fingers had been. The burn resembled two hands, one skeletal and one human, gripping each other. She looked at him in wonder.

"They will answer to you now, Thazienne Uskevren," he told her, and Tazi was startled to hear Szass Tam address her by her given name. She briefly wondered what else he now knew about her and what, if anything, she might know about him after their intimate exchange. Save that for another time, she told herself.

Tazi surveyed the number of zombies and remembered the scene from above. "More," she told Szass Tam. "We need more than this."

"Come," he told her and Tazi saw he now smiled at her. He floated back along the platform to another passageway and motioned for the others to follow.

"How many tunnels honeycomb this place?" growled the duergar questioningly.

"More than you could discover in several lifetimes," the necromancer answered. "And even if you had the time, you would never find what you seek."

Tazi was certain that Szass Tam now knew about Justikar's brother through her.

*I'm sorry,* she thought to the dwarf but got no response.

Farther down they went, all the while the screams and calls grew louder. A violent shudder gripped the building, and Tazi slammed into the wall and tumbled down some of the stairs, the dwarf right after her. Lauzoril struggled with the unconscious Azhir in his arms, and Nevron and Aznar clung to each other. Only Szass Tam remained upright since he floated above the mêlée.

The corridor spiraled farther down, and Tazi braced her hands against the narrow walls to keep herself from tumbling again as the quakes continued with hardly a break between them. Tazi seriously wondered if the structure was going to be able to take much more abuse before it collapsed and buried them all. However, a few twists and turns later, they found themselves in another chamber. Not nearly as large as the one that housed the zombie forces, it was still of an impressive size. Tazi swallowed hard when she saw that it sheltered flocks of darkenbeasts. The creatures squawked and pushed against each other, snapping at one another's eyes. Standing as tall as the dwarf, the monsters had wingspans nearly twice that. Their bodies mostly resembled a bat's form, though a reptilian head perched atop their curved necks. Their skin was stretched tight across their skeletal frames, and Tazi could see their bones glowing through. Some were green while others were an odd shade of purple. They had razor sharp claws, and they scratched at the stone floor incessantly. Created by fell magic, the creatures could only survive as they were in the darkness. If sunlight struck them, they turned back into their original, untainted form, be it field mouse or rabbit, and died.

"And how can I control them?" Tazi asked and was afraid that she and Szass Tam might have to bond again.

"These creatures are a bit simpler to manage. They respond best to mental rather than verbal orders. Pictures in their minds work best. I think you would be best served if you used your pet in this case," he told her.

"My pet?" Tazi asked.

The lich nodded toward the duergar. Tazi realized that the necromancer was aware of Justikar's mental abilities. Whether he knew that from his brief communion with her, or if he could simply sense the duergar's telepathic abilities, she wasn't sure. And it didn't matter. Tazi turned to Justikar and sat on her haunches before him. Another tremor shook the structure, and the darkenbeasts screeched and cawed at each other even more frantically.

"I can't ask this of you, but I will. Would you do this, Justikar?" Tazi asked the dwarf. "Would you lead these creatures into a battle we will probably lose for no other reason than to save people you don't even know?"

"With odds like that, how could I refuse, human?" he sniped.

"I mean it," she said, all joking aside. "Will you?"

The duergar regarded her with his river rock eyes. "I never joke," he replied. Tazi gripped him on the shoulders but restrained herself from embracing him any further.

"Out of my way," he said gruffly and brushed her hands aside. He stepped past her and the lich and faced the hordes of darkenbeasts solemnly. Tazi's skin crawled as she recollected what it was like to face the monsters in battle. She had no idea what the dwarf felt at that moment.

Tazi watched as he sheathed his axe and raised his hands out toward the screaming creatures as though he were pronouncing a benediction. His eyes widened, and Tazi could almost feel the tug of his mind. She saw that some of the creatures shrieked in apparent protest. Some flapped their wings in anger, while others just ignored the duergar. She could hear Justikar mutter foul oaths under his breath. It seemed to no avail, though, and Tazi thought he had failed. But, after what seemed to be an eternity, the crowd of birdlike things began to quiet down and calm themselves. Amazed, Tazi saw them fold their wings against their thin bodies and focus their small, black eyes at Justikar. Sweat rolled off of the dwarf, and he slowly lowered his hands. Tazi caught a glimpse of them trembling.

"I think we understand each other," he announced to the silent group, after collecting himself.

Tazi faced the lich again. "What else have you got hidden here?" she demanded.

"There is one more place to go. Follow me," he told her.

"Stay here," Tazi said to the dwarf. "I can see a gate down there. Does that lead to the mountainside?" she asked Szass Tam. He nodded and Tazi turned back to the dwarf. "Wait with them until the last rays of the sun have faded," she instructed him.

"Then what?" Justikar asked her tiredly.

"Then kill everything in your path."

"I can do that," he replied with an evil grin.

Tazi followed Szass Tam and the others to one last set of barracks within the Citadel. The room resembled a laboratory more than anything else, with shelves of jars and potions and a large vat off to one side. Large, armored humanoids milled about inside. Their stooped posture and pig faces marked them as orcs. And these, like the ones Tazi saw with Naglatha on their journey to the Thaymount, had mottled skin the color of dried blood.

The tremors had set the beasts on edge, and they were quarreling with themselves. Unlike the zombies, though, their armor was in the best of condition, and Tazi could also see a wall that held an array of fine weapons behind them. The orcs grunted and paced about, itching for something to crush, their yellow eyes flashing.

"These were to be a gift for Azhir Kren," the lich explained. "She has been anxious for some time to invade Rashemen, and I would not allow it. I thought if she had a set of new troops to train, it might keep her occupied for a while.

"They've been imprinted to recognize her," he continued and glanced at Lauzoril's unconscious burden. "Sadly, I fear she is in no condition to lead them now."

"What can we do so that they will follow me?" Tazi asked. "Unless, of course, one of you would like that honor on the field of battle?" The other Red Wizards remained silent. Bits of the ceiling tumbled down, emphasizing how little time they had left.

"What can you do to make them follow me?" Tazi asked Szass Tam, knowing it would have to be her.

"That is the tricky part. Aside from Azhir Kren, the only other they would follow would be a leader of their own kind."

"What?" Tazi said.

"They will only recognize another Blooded One. You must become one of them if you are to lead them."

"How can I?"

"In the corner there," Szass Tam pointed to the large vat Tazi had seen when they first entered the room, "is where we create the Blooded Ones. The young are dipped in a vat of alchemical blood and when they emerge—"

"They're stronger and more powerful and easier to control," Tazi finished for him.

"Correct," replied the lich.

"But I thought the process only worked on the young?"

"Correct again, Thazienne. In the past, it has proven potentially fatal on adults," he finished. "I do not know what else it might do to you, or how long the effects might last, if you even survive the process. But it is a risk you will have to take."

"My choice?" she questioned him.

"Always," he replied easily. "It is always your choice. Remember that."

Tazi faced the gathered wizards. Then she looked back, swallowing hard. "What do I have to do?"

"Climb into the vat and submerge yourself completely in the blood. When you rise, if you live, you should be able to marshal the orc forces."

"If..." she pointed out.

Tazi walked over to the wooden vat that was nearly ten feet high and swayed as another tremor rolled past. She climbed the small set of steps along the side of the container and peered over the rim. She saw the maroon liquid roll and slosh with the quake, thick and syrupy, and she briefly wondered where it came from. She banished the question immediately from her mind.

Doesn't matter now, she told herself.

Tazi felt her gorge rise and burn the back of her throat. The smell of hot copper filled her nostrils as well as a burning whiff of acid. She swallowed hard and looked over her shoulder at Szass Tam. He floated gently above the ground, his robes barely brushing the stones set in the floor, and regarded her with his cold stare. Tazi turned back to the vat and climbed the rest of the way up.

She balanced on the tiny platform for a moment, and the room grew deathly silent. Then she crossed her arms over her chest and stepped forward to plummet straight down into the pool of blood.

Tazi cut through the liquid like a knife. The moment she hit the fluid, Tazi felt every part of her catch fire. Hot and cold sensations ran along her body, from the ends of her hair to her toes. She felt nauseous and light-headed at the same time. She wanted to scream but knew if she opened her mouth she'd be drinking the tainted blood. Images stabbed through her brain—foreign and familiar at the same time, and she felt a rage burn into her. Lights flashed behind her eyelids, and she twitched spasmodically.

When she could stand no more, Tazi burst up from the blood like some blighted phoenix, and she sucked in great drafts of air. When her breathing had calmed a measure, she grabbed for the platform and pulled herself up. She hooked a leg along the side of the tub and used that and her arms to haul herself back onto the platform. She kneeled there for a moment, feeling her heart pound so loudly she was certain the organ might rupture from the strain. Her leathers were soaked in blood, her skin no longer recognizable.

She rose slowly to her feet and spread her arms wide, her hands curling into fists. Anger boiled up within her. Blood dripped from her arms and her hair was plastered to her face and neck in thick strips. Tazi was a study in crimson. She let her head fall back and bellowed out an animal cry of fury and pain. From the barracks, the orcs stopped their quarreling and gradually lowered their arms. They heard Tazi's call and responded to her in kind. First one orc then another joined until all of them roared back as one. Zulkir Nevron clamped his hands over his ears against the horrendous cry.

Tazi straightened her head and opened her eyes. Blood tracked down her face like a trail of ruby tears. She met Szass Tam's amazed stare and said evenly, "I'm ready."

# CHAPTER TWELVE

Tazi was lost in a red haze. She pushed past the astonished wizards and entered the barracks of the orcs. They continued to howl and snarl but parted before her. Some smashed chairs and others beat their swords and spears against the floor. Tazi spun around until she found what she was searching for: a gate like the one in the darkenbeasts' pen, which opened to the mountainside. She pulled at the handle fruitlessly, foot braced against the wall.

"Open it," she bellowed to the lich.

Szass Tam made a single pass of his skeletal hand, and the gate's lock sprung free. Tazi threw open the doors, and the raging orcs streamed past her into the growing darkness. She cast one backward glance at the necromancer and charged after her troops.

The barracks opened up onto a gentle, downward-sloping stone field. Tazi felt the ground crumble beneath her boots. The heat from the mountains had turned much of the upper layers of rock to brittle pumice. To the east, the lava had made some progress down the peaks, and the demons continued to flow out of the crevices of the Thaymount. Off in the distance, Tazi saw the darkenbeasts swirling around Justikar and beyond them, the zombie troops began their march out.

A strange caw made Tazi turn her head and draw her sword. Not twenty feet away, a stable of riding animals was ablaze. The same intense heat that had cracked the ground beneath her had ignited the wooden slats of their pen. Tazi ran over to them and kicked out at the fence. Wood splintered everywhere, and the frightened mix of animals, eyes rolling wildly in their heads, burst out. Black unicorns and more ordinary horses galloped past her, as well as stranger creatures. One of the last ones to run past Tazi was Naglatha's own griffon: Karst.

She must have tethered it here, Tazi thought, and forgot about it in her hasty departure.

Tazi caught the beast by the neck, and it reared but couldn't break her fierce grip. Tazi swung her leg around the creature's lionlike body and hung onto to its mane with its mixture of feathers and fur. The griffon stood back on its powerful legs and thrashed about with its front claws in an attempt to buck Tazi from its back.

"No!" she screamed defiantly and held on tight.

Tazi had only seen a griffon once before in her life, though it was too young to be ridden. But, as a pampered child from a wealthy family, she had ridden her fair share of horses. And, as soon as she was old enough, Tazi had joined her brothers when there were mounts to be broken and displayed an aptitude for the task that surpassed her brothers, much to their chagrin. She hoped that breaking a griffon would be much the same.

Tazi wasn't disappointed. After a few minutes, the griffon settled down and seemed resigned to its rider. She kicked at its sides and clucked her tongue like she would've at a horse. The creature turned its large eagle head back toward her and glared with its golden eyes. And it took off in a grand, loping run.

Before the griffon had gone thirty feet, it sprang into the air with a great flapping of its wings. Tazi felt a moment of exhilaration as they soared into the air, the horror forgotten for one fleeting second. She pulled on its feathers like reins and turned the griffon, so they banked back around toward the barracks. Tazi leaned over to one side and shouted to the orcs.

"To me!" and she didn't even realize she had switched from Common to Orcish, though the language was previously unknown to her. The orc troops stormed after her as Tazi headed over to Justikar.

With the wind rushing past her face, Tazi hoped her burning cheeks would cool. But the air was dry and hot and did nothing to soothe her. She could see the duergar cursing and shrieking at the sky, assembling his fell forces. Most, as far as she could tell, responded to him to one degree or another. As she glided in closer, Tazi saw that there appeared to be no end in sight to the line of monsters that spewed from the Thaymount, though they seemed to be mostly concentrated around one of the central peaks.

Creatures the likes of which Tazi had never seen, even in nightmares, crawled down the steep slopes. There were darkenbeasts by the thousands streaming from their caves. Unlike the others, these creatures had burning red eyes, and their bones glowed red as well—not the green and purple she had seen before. Otherwise, there was little else that set them apart from the creatures under their own control. Lamias slithered from their dens by the dozens. But these sluglike creatures were fat and bloated like corpses left too long in the sun. Mostly gray, they had long, stringy hair and shiny bodies. By the red radiance of the lava and the eruptions, Tazi realized they left a slime trail behind them, and her gut instinct told her that trail would be poisonous.

She tugged along the griffons left flank, and they banked that way, slowly gliding down to the dwarf. But in the other direction, Tazi observed a different group of Eltab's forces. Climbing with great expertise against the slopes were monsters as tall as an average human. At first glance, Tazi thought they were the lizardfolk indigenous to the Surmarsh that Naglatha had mentioned. However, like the Thaymount lamias, the lizards were albinos. And Tazi recalled that the other lizardfolk were supposed to be simpletons at best. From her perch, Tazi could see several of the ones in the lead clearly give orders to those bringing up the rear. She watched as they fanned out and moved down the cliffs like they were a part of them, descending on all their limbs or walking upright, changing between modes when necessary.

The griffon lighted down next to Justikar, and he pulled his stolen war axe free, ready to ward the creature off.

"No," Tazi called to him and jumped off her mount to stand protectively in front of it. The griffon flapped its wings and squawked at the dwarf.

"Remember me, do you?" he asked. "Well, I remember you and what I owe you."

"No," Tazi warned him again and shoved him back, striking him in anger for the first time.

Justikar stumbled from her touch and turned back to her in surprise. "Who did you slaughter?" he asked, and looked her up and down.

"No one yet," she replied bleakly, "but that's all about to change." She grabbed him by the shoulder and continued.

"You see there," she said and pointed to the range of peaks east of them. "As far as I can tell, most of the demons are escaping from those points." She released her hold on the duergar and squatted down, drawing a map in the fresh soot at their feet. "If we can get our forces to form a semi-circle from here—" she motioned with her finger to the drawing of the gorge between the peaks— "to here—" she then drew a line to the location where she had seen, from her aerial pass, a dormant field of ashfall— "we might be able to cut them off."

"And what about the lava?" he added.

Tazi looked up to meet his grim stare. "One thing at a time."

She rose up. "I'll take the foot soldiers and lead them into position. Can you handle those in the air?"

"Do I have a choice?" he grumbled.

Tazi heard the echoes of Szass Tam's words when she answered, "You always have a choice."

Without waiting for a reply, Tazi mounted the griffon and kicked it hard with her heels. The winged animal leaped into the sky almost joyously, and Tazi felt that it was only happy when in flight. Or perhaps it just felt safer there, away from the trembling ground. Considering the black and red clouds of darkenbeasts that were forming along the gloomy horizon like a storm, Tazi was certain the beast would soon revise its notions of safety in the sky.

She pulled on its feathers, and they swooped down low over the battalions of zombies. Though dead, they wore an eager look on their faces as though anticipating the coming bloodshed. Tazi was uncertain how to order them. She reached over and gingerly rested her right hand along the fell mark on her left shoulder. She closed her eyes and imagined the undead lining themselves up as she had envisioned it. She kept the images clear and simple. When she opened her eyes again and circled back around, she could see that they had begun to take up her formation.

Tazi soared down close to the ground where the troop of Blooded Ones had gathered just downhill from the zombies. They were hardly winded from their run, and Tazi could see several of them were gnashing their heavy canines and sniffing the air hungrily. Watching them, she could feel the blood start to throb in her own head. She drew her sword and pointed toward the ashfall in the distance.

"We meet up with the soldiers to the west and form a line to the ashfall along the eastern slope," she called easily in Orcish. "We form that line and let nothing cross it alive. Do you hear me?" she screamed at them. The troop howled in agreement, beating their swords and cudgels against their shields. Tazi took to the air and assumed a position circling her growing wall of soldiers.

She could see Justikar holding an arm up toward the mass of darkenbeasts that were swirling around in frenzied flight, awaiting her signal. From one side to the other, the legions of undead and the Blooded Ones joined forces, forming a solid barricade, an unholy alliance. Farther north, Tazi could see more and more of Eltab's demons surge out of the Thaymount. Another eruption shook the region as Tazi turned her head from one side to the other to take one, last inventory.

"Now!" she screamed long and loud. Justikar released his hold on the darkenbeasts, and they swarmed forward. The Blooded Ones broke out into a full run, while the undead marched relentlessly onward. Tazi kicked at her winged mount and dived straight into the demon hordes, sword flashing.

Szass Tam and Nevron re-entered the council chamber. Lauzoril had taken the unconscious Azhir Kren to a more secure location, with Aznar Thrul trailing close behind.

The gray-haired Nevron had called after them, tauntingly, "Do you really think there is a safe haven in this place as long as the demon-king is free?"

Lauzoril had ignored them and wearily carried Azhir away. Aznar Thrul shouted back over his shoulder to them as he departed, "This is all your doing, with your secret scribblings, so you should be the ones to take care of it."

Several of the lich's human servants had come into the chamber not long after the Red Wizards and Tazi had abandoned it. They had tried vainly to salvage what they could from the room and douse the many fires that still blazed. The lich's zombie servants had pointedly stayed away, as he suspected they would, because of their inherent fear of those very flames. He briefly wondered how Thazienne was going to manage to get his troops to fight with the burning earth all around them, but dismissed those queries as her concerns to deal with. The lich had other matters that occupied his attention.

The room was in shambles. Two women batted at the tapestries that still smoldered with heavy blankets that they had scrounged up from one of the many linen closets. Another was mindlessly collecting up the bits of shattered dinnerware and glasses, simply needing to do something. An elderly man slapped several parchments with a broom. Some of the papers curled up at the edges and wafted around like injured butterflies, and he alternated between swatting them and trying to catch them. He had already collected a small pile and stacked it against the wall nearest him. That was where Szass Tam went first.

"Nevron, go around to the far side of the table where Naglatha had been standing before this disaster took place," he ordered the other zulkir. "I'll start in on these."

As the lich approached the old man, he could see the fear in his faded eyes. Szass Tam ruled with a fierce hand and had little tolerance for failure. Many of his slaves bore subtle and not-so-subtle reminders of their master's standards. And it was clear that the old man assumed the catastrophe did not bode well for any of those who served the necromancer. Szass Tam appreciated his quivering, obsequious behavior but had no time for it at the moment.

"You did well. Please continue," he murmured to the slave and floated past him to the remains of his stolen scrolls. He snatched up the fragments and didn't even notice that the man wept tears of relief as he passed.

With the pieces of his spell scrolls in his skeletal grip, the lich searched for a place to try and piece together the fractured puzzle. He saw that a smaller serving table was relatively unscathed though overturned.

"Right that for me," he told the two women who had extinguished the last of the flaming furnishings.

They scurried over, coughing heavily, and flipped the table upright.

"You may go," he dismissed them without an upward glance. He began to lay all the vestiges of parchment on the smooth surface of the table. Scanning the remnants quickly with his sharp eyes and tracing a bony finger across them, Szass Tam tried to cobble together a binding spell.

Barely looking up, he called over to Nevron, "What luck have you had?" The gray-haired zulkir was on his knees, tearing away at a portion of the smashed council table. He tossed bits of the wood madly behind him, and Szass Tam was hard pressed not to laugh in spite of the circumstances. The Zulkir of Conjuration looked for all the world like a dog frantically digging up a bone.

"I think there's a scroll, or at least a good portion of one, under the table leg—if I can just reach…" his voice faded with the strain.

"Got it," he croaked triumphantly, and when he popped back out from under the wreckage, his hair was askew and a smudge of soot crossed his forehead. But Szass Tam saw that he had a mostly intact parchment in his fist.

"Bring it here," the lich ordered. "Let's see what we have left."

Nevron walked over quickly, though he too continued to cough from the lingering smoke. Out of the whole room, only Szass Tam was unaffected by it, since he did not need to breathe. The zulkir placed the mostly intact scroll with the other pieces Szass Tam had collected on the table. Together, they read over the documents as best they could. An occasional quake rocked the chamber, but the two men were silent for some time. Finally, Nevron breathed in sharply and turned his head toward the lich with a look of horror and awe.

"I can't believe you found this," he said quietly and pointed to one of the burned fragments. "How?" he croaked.

"That is not for you to know," the necromancer replied.

"My whole life has been in pursuit of these runes," he said mostly to himself. "And now, to find them here, broken and incomplete..."

"Perhaps you can now understand why one lifetime is not nearly enough," Szass Tam told him evenly.

"No matter for now," Nevron dismissed the discussion. "Without the other pieces, I don't see how we can bind Eltab. We might be able to stop the lesser minions, but the tanar'ri lord may be beyond our reach."

Szass Tam was silent for what seemed like an eternity. He scanned the puzzle pieces again as though he might have missed the keystone, but it was not there to be found. He balled up his bony hands and pounded the table with a cry of fury. Then he smoothed his robes with those same hands and regarded the other man solemnly.

"I fear you may be right," he admitted calmly, "but we must try, nonetheless."

And he and the Zulkir of Conjuration began to chant.

Tazi flew toward another flock of Eltab's darken-beasts, carving through them with her sword as she had the others. The griffon swooped into the herd like a hunting raptor and sliced at the flapping bat creatures with its razor-sharp talons. Tazi gripped her mount with her thighs to maintain her seat on its back and hung onto its mane with her left hand. She twisted around to spear a darkenbeast that tried to find purchase on the griffon's haunches. She dispatched the creature though it left a track of bloody welts along the griffon's rear left flank. It screeched in pain.

When Tazi turned forward, she ducked low and hugged the griffon's neck as another darkenbeast swooped toward her face, missing her by mere inches. More started to surround the griffon, smelling the blood, and it reared back, flapping its wings furiously as the smaller darkenbeasts cut off all escape routes. One after another dived at Tazi and her mount, and she swiveled from her right to her left to slash at the monsters. But their numbers kept increasing. As they slashed down one, another two took its place. The griffon cawed in panic as several of the flying creatures began to target its vulnerable wings.

Like a black, rotting infestation, one after another of the darkenbeasts attached themselves to the griffon's wings. Using their sharp claws, the demon-king's minions ripped the winged beast's limbs to shreds. Golden feathers coated in blood swirled about, and Tazi could hear the animal's suffering, but she was helpless to alleviate it. The sheer numbers of the darkenbeasts weighed the griffon down and Tazi could see they were losing altitude.

A creature slipped past Tazi's defenses and punctured the griffon's right eye with its talon. Blood squirted out, and Tazi's mount plummeted beak first toward the ground, spiraling in tighter and tighter circles. The creatures that were clamped to its wings held fast, and as the ground came screaming up toward them, Tazi leaped from the griffon's back at the last possible moment.

She fell hard, taking the brunt of the fall on her shoulder as she tucked up into a ball and rolled forward to land in a crouch, weapon still held high. The griffon was not so fortunate, smashing headlong onto the hard soil. As it lay in a heap near a rock pile, Tazi could see it was done for. Its beak was partially broken and blood gushed out of the wound. The ruined eye dangled from its bloody socket to stare blindly ahead. Its wings were practically denuded of feathers, and multiple talon rakes crisscrossed its haunches.

Despite these wounds, the griffon was still alive, and a few darkenbeasts continued to peck and tear at its flesh.

"Off of him, hellspawn," Tazi shrieked.

She grabbed one of the creatures by the nape of its neck and cleanly ran it through. Some of the other darkenbeasts then shifted their attention from the dying griffon to Tazi. One hovered above her head, clawing at her face and tearing out handfuls of her black locks, while she stabbed another through its heart.

Dropping her sword, Tazi reached up and caught the one that was tangled in her hair, her chainmail gauntlets protecting her hands somewhat from the darkenbeast's talons. She flung the screeching monster to the ground and crushed its throat under her boot. With most of the beasts gone for the moment or dead, Tazi picked up her weapon and strode over to the griffon.

She reached out a hesitant hand and stroked the beast's bloody neck. It opened its one good eye and looked at her imploringly.

Tazi raised her sword and said, "I'm sorry for this." But before she could end the griffon's misery, a great war axe slashed down and practically beheaded the winged creature in one stroke. Tazi whirled to see Justikar breathing hard and leaning on his bloody axe with both hands like it was a walking stick.

"Now we're even," he spat at the dead beast.

"Justikar!" Tazi shouted, though she wasn't sure if it was anger or relief at seeing him that made her cry out so.

"It had to be done," he replied.

"But you didn't have to enjoy it."

"Yes, I did."

Tazi sighed and rested against the dead griffon, trying to catch her breath. She wiped at her forehead, thinking that it was sweat that dripped down her face and neck, but her hand came away wet with her own blood. She blinked at her gory fingers.

"Trying to look like me?" Justikar asked her with a smirk, and when she glanced at him blankly, he pointed at his bald pate.

"Darkenbeasts," she answered simply, and the dwarf gave her a curt nod. "Where are yours?" she asked.

"Gone," he replied.

"They're all gone?' she said in amazement.

"They've been slaughtered," he nodded bitterly, "but not before they took out most of Eltab's flock. There's the odd clutch scattered around, though. I can still 'hear' them. And they still listen."

Without another word, Tazi turned away from the duergar and clambered up the large rock pile that was just behind the griffon's body to get a better view. In the red blaze of the fires and the lava that continued its inevitable course down the mountains, she could see mayhem and destruction everywhere. Along the western ridge, bodies were stacked like cord wood. Tazi could make out some of the colors of Szass Tam's troops, now truly dead. Strewn in between, she saw the occasional lizard claw or bloated lamia tail poking through the carnage. On the eastern slopes, Tazi watched as her orcs slashed viciously at the albino lizards. The reptile men had acquired weapons from the fallen zombie legions and were quite proficient at using them. But Tazi's heart sank when she saw that demons still emptied out of the central peak.

She turned back toward the Citadel and closed her eyes. She summoned the last of the undead soldiers Szass Tam had left at her disposal. They marched out and began to assume the positions of their fallen brethren. Wearily, she opened her eyes again.

"They keep coming," she told the dwarf. "Szass Tam must have failed in his bid to stop them."

"You think he stuck it out?" the duergar asked. "I'm sure he and those other sour-faced wizards fled as soon as we stepped out onto the battlefield."

"No," Tazi disagreed with him. "Somehow, and I can't tell you why, I think he stayed. For his own, warped reasons he cares about this land more than we do."

"Than *you* do," he corrected her.

"It doesn't matter now, if we can't stop them," she said. She looked to the peak that erupted again and realized that it was the only one still active. It was also where the demons continued to emerge from.

"All that's left is to stop that demon," Tazi added, "and I think I know where I can find him. Justikar, you have to lead the rest of the forces in my place."

"It makes no difference," he argued. "As many as we throw at them, they match."

"No," she shook her head, "forget that. What you have to do is fortify the barricade now. It's the only chance the people of Thay have. Stack up the dead if you have to, but make a wall to stop the lava flow. I don't care if you have to kill every last one of them to do it. Understand?" she shouted at him.

Justikar smiled broadly at her. "Now you're finally speaking a language I can understand."

Tazi shot him a grin in return and broke into a run toward the central peak. She didn't look back at the dwarf. She had to trust him now; there wasn't a choice any longer. And still Szass Tam's words about choices and consequences rang in her head.

With the last eruption, a series of lava bombs were released. One came whistling down like a meteor in the night sky and nearly hit Tazi. When it struck the ground, the explosion blew her off her feet. She landed hard and was dazed for a minute. As she lay on her back staring at the red-gray night sky heavy with smoke, an albino lizard came upon her, spear in hand.

It thrust its weapon at her, and Tazi rolled to one side, narrowly missing being skewered by the monster. Its spear stuck in the ground, and she rolled back over it, using her body to snap the pole out of the lizard's claw and knock the shaft to the ground. As she rolled underneath the unarmed lizard, she stabbed up with her sword and killed it. Tazi got to her feet and took up the spearhead in her other hand.

She jumped over bodies and ran in a crisscross pattern, dodging flaming missiles and debris. Tazi sprinted as though she wore blinders like a horse. She refused to see or stop for any of the slaughter around her. Orcs raged beside her, overwhelmed in their own berserker fury, smashing the lizards and demons with incredible strength. Tazi was lost to her own red haze. She sliced anything that crossed her path and was as unstoppable as the lava flow, slowly working her way up the steep incline of the central slope along the only narrow path that was not presently engulfed in lava. At times, she had to sheathe her sword and use her free hand and the spear to hoist herself up through the rocks and boulders, walking a fine tightrope. She was covered in sweat from the intense heat as she finally neared the core of the volcanic peaks.

Close to the top, she spotted a lamia that had completely encircled a fallen zombie, locked together in a twisted, lovers' embrace. She ignored them and tried to get past. The lamia, however, struck out with its tail and slashed Tazi's right leg, while it continued to constrict the corpse of the soldier. The venomous stinger cut through her leathers, and Tazi hissed in pain. She grabbed the spear with both her hands and drove it into the monster with a grunt of rage. The weapon not only impaled the lamia, but the zombie as well and pinned them both to the ground. The two squirmed there, caught like a strange multi-limbed bug on a dissecting table. She climbed on.

Tazi had to scale the last twenty feet of the nearly vertical face of the volcano. She struggled for handholds and could already feel her leg growing numb from the lamia's sting. She fleetingly thought of her climbing boots, abandoned somewhere back in Pyrados a thousand years ago. She wiped at her eyes to clear the sweat from them and rested her head against her outstretched arms for a brief pause. When she turned her head back, she could see the forces of Szass Tam lined up across the field of battle like a hasty dyke before the floodwaters. She continued up the last few feet thinking that she might be Thay's last chance.

She pulled herself over the rim of the volcano and slid into it a few feet on her stomach, scratching her arms and face. Tazi scrambled to her feet as best she could with her game leg and looked directly into the face of hell. The volcano was framed by heavy clouds of smoke, glowing a dirty red from the fires. The heat was almost too much to bear and near the center of the fiery furnace, Eltab stood with his arms raised, great wings spread wide. In the heart of the tempest, he was speaking a strange language. To Tazi, it seemed older than time itself. But, judging from the way that the center of the volcano bubbled and boiled in time with his chants, Tazi believed he was trying to conjure up even more lava.

"Stop!" she shouted down to the tanar'ri lord, her voice almost lost in the maelstrom. But the demon-king heard her, and he slowly turned around.

His skin glistened like fresh blood, and his eyes were twin suns, blazing brightly. Tazi thought he had even grown taller, if such a thing was possible. His horns were longer and more gnarled, twisted high above his head. His huge wings flexed and twitched in excitement. Eltab gnashed his jaws and saliva hung like icicles from his huge canines.

"Ah," he rumbled at Tazi, "it is my savior."

"What?" Tazi demanded.

"I owe all of this," and he spread his arms even wider, "to you. I saw through that weakling's eyes that you were the one who brought the spells to the dark-haired woman. You gave her the key to my prison, and I am eternally grateful."

Tazi swayed as her leg started to fail her. She drew her sword and held it low at her side. "I'm here to put an end to this," she said gravely.

The demon looked at her through slitted eyes. "I should strike you dead," he told her, "but I see something in you, something familiar." He slowly strode up the slope of the volcano and stopped ten feet from where she stood. Since Tazi was closer to the rim of the crater, she was evenly sized with the tanar'ri lord. He passed his hand in the direction of her leg, and suddenly Tazi felt strength pour back into the limb.

"That is a small measure of my gratitude, woman. There is so much more than that in store for you if you want it," he promised her with the voice of a serpent.

"I don't want your gifts," she spat back at him.

"Are you so sure?" he asked her slyly. "I see you proudly bear the gifts from others such as myself." He gestured to Tam's mark, and the crystal of Shar's she still wore about her neck. Steorf was right about the chain's strength, she thought absently.

"All I want is your head," she said in a low voice.

"Try and take it then."

Tazi charged at the beast as he waved his hand at her again. This time, however, there was no healing gift. Showers of fire streaked from his fingertips. Tazi realized there was no cover for her to use, and she raised her sword instinctively as a shield. To both their surprise, the eldritch weapon Tazi had stolen from Szass Tam's armory absorbed most of the demon fire, though a spray of it skipped past the blade. She hissed in pain as her shoulder was scalded directly where the necromancer had left his sign, but she hardly felt it as she watched her sword glowing with Eltab's absorbed bolts. The glow diminished, and the blade was intact. She charged him again.

Eltab backed up, and he and Tazi began to circle around the rim of the volcano. Tazi was very aware that she could not move too close to the bubbling core for longer than a few moments because of the excruciating heat. The tanar'ri lord closed his eyes and flung out his right arm. He roared in pain as an extension of his bones burst through the webbing between his claws and grew to a length of four feet. He fashioned a sword of sorts from his own body, bits of marrow and tendon dangling from it, slick with his blood. Suitably armed, he advanced on Tazi.

They crossed swords, and Tazi knew immediately that she was outmatched in size and strength. When she blocked one of his thrusts, she felt the vibration of the force through her entire arm and shoulder. She realized that if she was going to stop him, she was going to have to find a way to outwit him. Tazi knew her life was forfeit regardless. With a cry of anger, she lunged forward and stabbed at him at every turn. The demon-king matched her stroke for stroke.

Keeping one eye on the bubbling core to her right, Tazi thought it was churning even more, and she realized she hadn't felt a tremor for several minutes.

It's building up, she thought to herself. The demon sliced her across the forearm, and the wound burned as if it had been doused in acid. As Eltab started to press the advantage, Tazi vaguely wondered why he only relied on his physical strength and didn't use more of his sorcerous powers against her. She didn't think Tam's sword could protect her from much more of it. And as she backpedaled toward the core, Tazi started to wonder if she had been mistaken from the start. Had Eltab been strengthening the forces within the volcano, or had he been feeding off of them instead?

She dodged a gurgle of lava at her feet and managed to get behind the tanar'ri lord, away from the core.

"Do you wish to fight," he mocked her, "or do you prefer to dance?"

"I prefer for you to die," she replied, realizing how foolish she sounded.

As she engaged him again, Tazi saw that on the opposite side of the crater, several of the Blooded Ones were scrambling up. Eltab had not yet seen them. Tazi was caught unaware, though, and as a bit of the superheated rock crumbled under her, she tumbled down. Eltab leaned over, and for a bizarre moment Tazi was sure he was going to help her to her feet. Instead, he scooped up a small handful of lava and threw the molten stuff at her. She vainly tried to raise her sword against the assault with little success. The weapon stopped some of it, but most of the deadly slag caught Tazi along her right side and leg.

"What I give," the tanar'ri lord told her as he pointed to her now re-injured limb, "I take away."

Tazi lay still. In spite of everything, she held her

sword more out of instinct than conscious thought. The lava flowed down the blade and though it emanated its eerie light, the sword could not absorb the heat a second time. The metal burned down as well, and Tazi dropped the blade before it could scald her. As the flaming sword fell to the ground, the initial, numbing shock Tazi suffered wore off. She howled in agonizing pain and writhed along the crater rim. Eltab raised his bone-sword for the killing stroke.

From across the crater, the Blooded Ones responded to their leader's anguish in kind. The handful that had reached the rim screamed back in a berserker rage. The demon-king turned in surprise at the new intruders. The orcs, though caught up in a frenzy, didn't attempt to run the gauntlet through the lava. They kicked and smashed at the boulders and loose rock along the volcano's edge and threw their haphazard missiles and spears at the demon-king.

While he blocked the assault, Tazi realized she had lost. Tears of rage and pain streaked her filthy face. The right side of her body was all but useless, and she could smell her burnt flesh over the sulfurous belching of the mountaintop. She watched helplessly as the tanar'ri lord raised his hands in the air, and a wave of lava rose up to shield him from the orcs' strike.

Tazi decided she wanted to die on her feet. She pushed against the ground with her left hand and struggled to rise. A glint in her right boot caught her eye.

Still nestled safely in her secret sheath, the crimson gold dagger winked in the firelight. It was all she had left, and Tazi bitterly realized that she and the bewitching treasure had somehow unleashed the chain of events that wrought the havoc all around her.

As Eltab turned to face her a final time, framed by the wall of fire behind him, Tazi reacted. She grabbed the perfectly crafted dagger and threw it underhand to strike the demon-king.

"This can go to hell," she croaked, "and so can you." With uncanny accuracy, the crimson gold caught Eltab straight through the heart. He looked down at the sorcerous metal shaft that protruded from his chest in shock and disbelief.

"I missed once," Tazi rasped in explanation, "and let a great evil escape. I don't miss anymore."

He dropped his bone-sword and wailed, all the while clawing ineffectually at the dagger. The demon-king literally began to peel into two beings. His whole body was engulfed in a cool, blue flame that started on one side of his body and raced to outline his whole form. Eltab's head snapped back, and he balled his claws into useless fists, unable to dislodge the dagger.

His howls pierced the night, but his hellish rage did not stop the smaller, human form that tumbled from the tanar'ri lord's glowing one. Tazi watched, awestruck, as a red-haired human fell forward, the crimson dagger still embedded in his chest. And the tanar'ri lord, no longer anchored to his human host, toppled backward into the bubbling heart of the volcano, his screams cut off as soon as he hit the molten bath.

Tazi blinked hard and lost her balance. She fell toward the lava, too weak from her wounds to be able to stop herself. As her knees buckled, Tazi felt herself jerked back by a strong arm around her waist. She twisted her head. Justikar's stern face peered back into hers—an almost worried expression in his eyes.

"That makes two," he shouted at her. "Now we're even!"

Tazi couldn't speak. She glanced back at the heart of the volcano, half-expecting to see the tanar'ri lord rise up from the lava, but the world exploded around them. A giant quake shook the peak so violently that the far end of the crater rim crumbled in on itself. The duergar managed to find purchase within a nook along the rim and hung on to it and Tazi.

The remaining Blooded Ones, however, were not as lucky. They tumbled into the core, followed along by the rush of boulders and rocks from the volcano rim. The earthen debris sealed off the heart of the volcano and stopped the last of the lava flow.

Tazi felt the dwarf move stones and rubble off of her. He held her in his sinewy arms, and Tazi could see from where they were that the remaining demon spawn of Eltab's were retreating back into the depths of the Thaymount.

"With him gone," she whispered and didn't even realize she spoke aloud, "Szass Tam's spells must be able to take hold."

The dwarf simply held her without saying a word. Tazi's head lolled to one side, and she could see somewhat down the mountainside. The lava had been stopped. But mired within the now-cooling flow were thousands upon thousands of bodies. Everywhere Tazi turned, all she saw was a sea of red. Finally, her wounds were too much. As oblivion called for her, Tazi welcomed the cold darkness.

# Epilogue

*10th Kythorn 1373 DR*

Tazi was lost in the shadows. There was no longer any pain. The severe burning of her flesh had eased and cold night was everywhere. She realized she had never known such peace before this moment, alone in the dark. The rage that had boiled inside her had also faded to only a whisper. And somewhere in the blackness, a voice sighed. She could almost understand the words.

"Tazi." She finally did hear her name and somehow managed to swim up from the icy depths to consciousness.

"Hmmm..." she sighed and stretched her body slowly, reveling in the feeling of comfort. Her eyelids fluttered open and, at first, she didn't know where she was. Tazi could make out that she was in a darkened room, lying in a large bed, covered by a heavy, satin coverlet.

Her head rested atop several down pillows. She was confused but not frightened. Her mind raced as she tried to remember what had happened. She placed a smooth, white hand against her forehead and rubbed her temples with her thumb and fingers.

Her face felt cool and uninjured. What happened to the burns? She raked her hands through her hair, and not only were there no longer any wounds on her scalp, her hair was thick again, and it was as long as it had been before her father died.

She threw the coverlet from the bed and saw that she wore a sleeveless nightgown of amethyst silk with a plunging neckline. But what was startling was that she could very easily see, through the near-transparent material, that she was whole again. There were no longer any burns or wounds anywhere along the length of her body. Nor did she feel the fever in her mind that had raged there since she had immersed herself in the alchemical blood. It seemed her bond to the Blooded Ones had been severed by their death in the volcano. Tazi was stunned. A soft cough startled her, and she looked about the room for the source. A shadow separated itself from the wall and moved toward the bed.

"Justikar," Tazi said and didn't hide the pleasure in her voice. She could see he had cleaned up. The soot and grime from the past few days had been scrubbed away, and he no longer wore the foolish, jade-colored shirt that Naglatha had forced him to wear. He wore new trousers and a tunic made of home-spun cloth, both in shades of the earth.

They suited him, she thought. What hair he had was combed and he had re-plaited his beard. He also, Tazi noted, carried a bundle wrapped in a ruby-red velvet cloak.

"Don't get all worked up," he said, raising his free hand in warning. "I knew you'd get it wrong and think I had stayed here for the last few days in some sort of vigil by your bedside like a lovelorn suitor."

"Last few days?" Tazi asked and a frown crossed her delicate features. Her memories were fuzzy, frayed around the edges, and she was startled at her lost time.

"Well," the duergar added with the slightest hint of gentleness in his voice, "I expect you'd be a bit muddled after what you went through. When I carried you back to the Citadel after I was certain the crater was truly sealed off, I figured you were dead, as burned as you were."

Tazi nodded and remembered her final confrontation with the demon-king. Burned severely along her right side, more than half her flesh had been charred beyond healing. She had closed her eyes after she knew Eltab was gone and had been ready for death.

"I should be dead," she murmured.

The dwarf nodded. "And you probably would be if it hadn't been for the necromancer."

"What do you mean?" Tazi asked as she sat back against the pillows—though in her heart, she already knew the answer.

"Oh, don't worry," he told her gruffly, "you're not one

of his undead. But I wouldn't be too sure he wouldn't have raised you for his own if you had died.

"When I approached the Citadel, he must have been watching from one of his perches. He swooped down right away, and I swear there was genuine sorrow on his face when he saw what a pitiful sight you were. He took you from my arms and brought you to a chamber lower down that had somehow survived the quakes intact."

"And?" she prodded him, but somewhere in the recess of her mind, Tazi saw images and flashes of herself on a cold slab as the skeletal lich worked and conjured over her. She felt, more than she saw, that the lich had cooled the rage that burned within her as well as her ravaged flesh. Tazi squeezed her eyes shut and shook her head a little, wondering what it had taken for a necromancer to heal a living being.

"You all right?" Justikar asked and reached out to her.

"Fine," she lied. "Go on."

"It took longer than he thought, because you were so far gone," the duergar explained. "And because the burns destroyed so much of your tissue, he said there wasn't much to work with. But I'll give that skeleton his due, because he didn't give up on you. I sure had," he added sincerely.

"That's why you brought me back instead of leaving me on the battlefield," she pointed out to the sour dwarf. He squirmed uncomfortably, and Tazi saved him from added embarrassment by immediately asking, "What's that tucked under your arm?"

"You're not the only one to receive a gift from the lich," he said simply. Justikar laid the swaddled bundle onto the bed with great care. He pulled back the material to reveal several ivory bones.

"My brother Adnama. Or, rather, what's left of him. After Tam was certain you were going to live, he had a slave bring the bundle to me. He said that it was a reward for my service to the Thayan people. Instead of raising him up as some dead thing to serve in his significantly smaller army, I could take his remains." The duergar became silent.

Tazi knew how much Justikar had wanted to find his brother and the hell he had put himself through for the quest. Now, to know he was truly dead had to be bittersweet. She gently laid her hand on the gray one that rested on the bones. Their eyes met briefly and something silent passed between them.

The dwarf then shrugged off her hand like it wasn't there, wrapped his precious cargo back up, and stored the package in a leather sack he had near the chair. She looked over and saw that he also had a walking stick and his stolen war axe stacked near the doorway.

"Now what will you do?" she asked him.

Justikar paused from his packing and looked at her for a moment before replying, "Follow in his footsteps, I suppose. I don't really have a choice now that he's gone. We're a dying race, and as I was so recently reminded," he paused with a wink to her, "there is definitely safety and power in numbers. I'll keep searching for our kind. They've got to be down there somewhere."

Tazi pulled up her knees and wrapped her unblemished arms around them. She watched as he made a final check of his gear and slung the pack and the war axe onto his strong back. He walked over to the door to collect his walking stick, and Tazi thought that he was simply going to walk out without another word. But he surprised her and turned to look at her a final time.

"Just so there is no misunderstanding between us," he told her, "should we meet up again, make no mistake. We are not friends. And if our paths do cross again," he warned her, "I can guarantee you that the circumstances will not be pleasant."

Tazi swung her legs off the bed. "And these were pleasant?" she quipped. She placed her feet on the ground and slowly rose, testing her legs experimentally. She realized she needn't have bothered because they were unscathed.

She padded across the thick carpeting to the drawn curtains on the far side of the room. Hesitantly, she grabbed the heavy drapes and wrapped her fingers in their velvet softness. She steeled herself and drew them back to let sunlight stream into the dark room.

In the bright morning light, Tazi had an unrestricted view of the slopes of the Thaymount. Steam still slowly rose from the lava flow that had obviously cooled considerably. It was no longer an angry red, but a dull charcoal gray, and it stretched as far as Tazi could see.

Embedded in the sea of molten slag were bits and

pieces that initially looked for the entire world like driftwood and flotsam tossed about on the frozen waves. But Tazi knew what they were. Thousands and thousands of arms and legs and claws and wings. They were all that remained of both armies, now indistinguishable in the face of the awesome force of nature.

"I know they were fell creatures, the dark creations of twisted minds," she said, unable to tear her eyes from the terrible sight, "but it was a high price. They saved the people of Thay, but it cost so much." And she closed her eyes.

"Their numbers will be restored soon enough," Szass Tam replied in a deep, rich voice.

Startled, Tazi turned around and saw that the dwarf had slipped away. In his place, the necromancer stood. And he had restored himself to his previous form. Gone was the skeletally thin frame and wispy tufts of hair. Instead, he appeared to her as he had the first day they had met. His hair was thick and black again. His black eyes gleamed out from his full face. He was dressed in his thick robes of crimson and black, and he smiled at Tazi.

She realized that she was backlit by the sun, and her nightgown left nothing to the imagination. She started to raise her hands to cover herself, but then she stopped. Tazi knew that the necromancer had seen her inside and out and there were precious little secrets between them now. She held her position and met his gaze.

"I have you to thank for this," she offered and looked down at her own body. She noticed that she still bore his mark on her left shoulder, though it had faded to almost a smudge.

He tipped his head in acknowledgement. "I prefer you this way," he smiled, "at least, for now. Oh, I believe this is yours as well." From a fold in his robe, the necromancer produced Tazi's crimson dagger. She accepted it and marveled at the lich's confidence that he freely handed her a weapon capable of stopping a demon.

"I thank you for this." Not to be outdone, Tazi also added, "You didn't need to go to all that trouble just for me." She motioned to his appearance. "I see you for what you are, you know."

Smiling more broadly, Szass Tam replied, "Why, Thazienne, I was about to say the same of you. We are well met, I think."

She turned from his critical stare and looked out the window again. The sight continued to pull at her heart. "It was a heavy price. I hope the Thayans realize what was sacrificed for their sake."

"They shall never know, Thazienne," he informed her.

"What?" Tazi asked, turning from the window.

Szass Tam walked over to a small table that held a tiny plate of fruits and a steaming pot and cup and seated himself. He motioned for Tazi to join him. She sat down and placed the dagger carefully on the table, keeping it in plain view.

"You see," he explained reasonably and began to pour her a cup of tea, "it would not do for the people to know what transpired here in the Thaymount. We cannot have them see the Red Wizards as fallible."

"So you lie to them," she replied. She carefully accepted the full cup, suddenly leery of scalding herself.

"For their own good," he added pleasantly. "They need to have familiarity, constancy. The mind looks for consistent patterns and does not want to discover the out-of-the-ordinary. It is healthier for them to go about their daily lives without interruption."

Sipping her tea, Tazi added, "You mean, it's easier for you if they go about their business, none the wiser. You would do well to remember familiarity breeds contempt. Be careful, or you'll be hoist in your own petard one day."

The lich laughed, rich and throaty. "Thazienne," he told her, "you are a delight. Truly, a remarkable woman. Like a gemstone, there are many sides to you."

It was her turn to tip her head to the necromancer. As she carefully selected a slice of fruit and realized that she was famished, Tazi casually asked, "And how is Pyras Autorian?"

Szass Tam smiled and replied, "He is doing very well under my ministrations. I believe that when I am done, no one will ever notice a difference."

Tazi grew thoughtful at what the lich said and what he didn't say. From his answer, she wasn't sure if he had healed the young tharchion as he had managed to heal her, or if he had used his skills at necromancy to raise him from the dead. She did recall, after all, that her crimson dagger had pierced him through the heart. If the act had been enough to drive the tanar'ri lord him from his body, what had it done to his actual flesh? She found she did not want to know the answer to that particular question.

She nibbled on a section of an orange and innocently inquired, "And Naglatha? Whatever became of her?"

Szass Tam's black eyes grew stormy at the mention of the renegade Red Wizard. "Your former mistress managed to escape somehow during the excitement. But she cannot hide from me forever. I will collect my due from her, trust me on that.

"Though," he added almost as an afterthought, and Tazi could hear grudging admiration in his voice, "a woman that resourceful and cunning can be a valuable asset."

Tazi dabbed at her lips with a linen cloth and said, "Where can I change into something a bit more appropriate?"

"I find what you are wearing to be very pleasing," he said slowly, and Tazi could feel the heat rise in her cheeks in spite of herself. "However, if you feel you must, you will find your clothing laid out on the settee behind that screen there." He raised his hand to point to a delicately carved screen of ivory and obsidian.

"Excuse me," she told the necromancer, and he rose as she stood.

Tazi moved behind the screen and saw her familiar leathers. They had been meticulously repaired and smelled freshly oiled. There was not the slightest whiff of smoke to them. She let the silk shift fall to a puddle at her feet and slipped on her own clothing, still not used to the feel of her long hair brushing against her bare arms after so many years. As she strapped the new sword that Szass Tam had left for her at her waist, she once again found herself impressed with his absolute confidence and surety that he could outfit a potential threat so well.

She stepped out from behind the screen and saw that the lich stood looking out the large windows. Tazi walked over to him and said, "I thank you for everything, but I must leave now."

Szass Tam looked her over from head to toe. This time Tazi did not blush. "Would you consider staying for a while, Thazienne? There is still much I would like to talk to you about. After all," he remarked in an offhand way, "we have shared much over the last few days. I have seen things in you I find intriguing. And I see things in you," he added and reached out to capture a curl of her midnight-black hair, "that I see in myself. I would appreciate the opportunity to know you better."

Tazi involuntarily took a step back. She felt uneasy that the necromancer would say they shared any qualities at all. She broke away from his touch to walk over to the small breakfast table. There, she busied herself by collecting her dagger of crimson gold, sheathing it in her boot.

"Thank you for the offer, but I have to return home. There are some ghosts that I must lay to rest."

The lich watched her carefully. "It is inconvenient at times when the dead do not stay buried. But don't try to fool yourself, Thazienne. No one forces you to do anything ever. The choices, as well as the consequences, are always yours and yours alone.

"Perhaps," he added, "you might return another time. I can wait. For time is something I have in abundance."

Tazi stood tall and answered, "As long as slavery is present in this land, Zulkir, I doubt very much that I will return."

The lich looked disappointed to Tazi. "Then that is the true tragedy here today," he remarked sadly. "For I will most likely never see you again. As long as I exist, slavery will always be a way of life here in Thay. And I can promise you, I will be here for a very long time." And he gave her a grave look.

Tazi ran her hands over her person one last time to make sure she had all her belongings and strode over to the door. At the portal she turned and looked at the necromancer, who was, in turn, watching her.

"Perhaps I will find my way back here one day," she told him darkly. "And I will put a stop to your slavery once and for all."

Szass Tam rose to the challenge. With a gentle smile on his lips, he replied, "My dear Thazienne, you are just one woman, albeit a remarkable one, and one person cannot bring about change."

"Zulkir, turn around and take another look out that window," she directed him with deadly seriousness. "Take a long look at what just one person can do."

The lich turned to the window and observed the carnage and death before him. He wasn't displeased by what he saw. Instead, he was once again impressed by the will and the strength of the woman behind him. He vaguely entertained the notion that he might have finally found a match for himself, someone worthy of sharing eternity with.

He turned back toward Tazi. "While you may have—" he stopped short when he saw the room was empty. She had managed to slip away without his notice. A slow smile played on his full lips.

"Ah, Thazienne," he whispered to himself, "perhaps our paths will cross again sooner than you think."

Tazi left the Citadel and stepped out onto the cool lava flow. From where she stood on the Thaymount, she could see the Second Escarpment stretch out before her. To the east, she was able to make out the peaks of the Sunrise Mountains. Beyond them, she knew the Purple Plains and the Endless Wastes lay. And somewhere beyond sight was Sembia and her family home.

Tazi stood on the windswept hill, and her hair swirled around her like a living thing. She thought of the necromancer's words again about choices and consequences. She thought about Justikar and how he felt he had to assume his brother's place, though his sibling's dream had not been his. He did it for family and obligation.

She pulled the crimson gold dagger from her boot and balanced it, point down, on her finger. She remembered how the dwarf had told her the dagger would make a more fitting gift for her father as a symbol of what she had become than the raw metal alone. But did she really need to give him anything other than herself?

"Isn't the person I have become," she whispered to the wind, "the truest gift I can make to you, Father?"

On that bleak mount, Tazi realized she could do whatever she wanted. And she understood, as she saw the death around her, with that freedom there came the greatest of responsibilities. Tazi recognized that she did not need to return to Selgaunt, nor did she need to explore the mysteries of Faerûn. It was her *choice*. She laughed and sheathed her dagger. She made up her mind and started down the path.

In a land renowned throughout the Realms for its heinous slavery, Thazienne Uskevren realized she was finally free.

# The Avatar Series

### New editions of the event that changed all Faerûn…and the gods that ruled it.

## *SHADOWDALE*
**Book 1 • Scott Ciencin**

The gods have been banished to the surface of Faerûn,
and magic runs mad throughout the land.

## *TANTRAS*
**Book 2 • Scott Ciencin**

Bane and his ally Myrkul, god of Death, set in motion a plot to seize
Midnight and the Tablets of Fate for themselves.

### The New York Times *best-seller!*

## *WATERDEEP*
**Book 3 • Troy Denning**

Midnight and her companions must complete their quest by traveling
to Waterdeep. But Cyric and Myrkul are hot on their trail.

## *PRINCE OF LIES*
**Book 4 • James Lowder**

Cyric, now god of Strife, wants revenge on Mystra, goddess of Magic.

## *CRUCIBLE: THE TRIAL OF CYRIC THE MAD*
**Book 5 • Troy Denning**

The other gods have witnessed Cyric's madness
and are determined to overthrow him.

**FORGOTTEN REALMS**

# The richness of Sembia yields stories within its bounds…and beyond.

### LORD OF STORMWEATHER
*Sembia*
*Dave Gross*

Thamalon Uskevren II thinks he has a long time before he'll inherit
Stormweather Towers and the responsibility such inheritance brings.
When not only his father, but also his mother and mysterious servant
Erevis Cale disappear, Tamlin will have to grow up fast. To save his family,
he'll have to make peace with his brother and sister and face a truth about
himself that he imagined only in his wildest dreams.

### TWILIGHT FALLING
*The Erevis Cale Trilogy, Book I*
*Paul S. Kemp*

Erevis Cale has come to a fork in the road where he feels the pull
of the god Mask and the weight of a life in the shadows. To find his
own path, he must leave the city of Selgaunt. To save the world,
he must sacrifice his own soul.